BROKEN

A DJINN WARS NOVEL

CHRISTINE POPE

Dark Valentine Press

BROKEN

ISBN: 978-0692589748
Copyright © 2015 by Christine Pope
Published by Dark Valentine Press

Cover design by Lou Harper

To learn more about this author, go to
www.christinepope.com.

BROKEN

PROLOGUE

Santa Fe, New Mexico
One year after the Dying

THE VOICE CAME TO HIM IN THE DARKNESS, JUST as it had for the past few weeks. He'd kept a careful count of every day, every agonizing twenty-four-hour span, drawing each one in a line of blood so he could never forget. Some people might have wanted to forget, but he held his captor's wrongs close, kept them always in the forefront of his mind so that one day he'd be able to repay each of those wasted days in the blood of his enemies. They hadn't wanted him to know how long he'd been held—the stinking djinn had taken away his watch, his belt, anything he might have found useful. Maybe that hadn't been their idea at all, but a suggestion from one of the human turncoats they were shacked up with, since the selection of confiscated items seemed to indicate a familiarity with human technology.

At any rate, his meals came at regular intervals, and he was allowed to go outside to get fresh air every once in a while, and those data points provided enough information that he had never lost count of the weary days. The last time his guard had taken him out to the sheltered street that backed up to the U.S. Marshals' building, the breeze had felt brisker, the air cooler, and so he knew the year was winding down toward autumn, exactly in line with his calculations.

Even so, he couldn't exactly recall when the voice had started speaking to him. Not right away; he knew that much. He'd spent many nights in dead silence, alone with his thoughts, trying to figure out what he could have done differently, which traps he could have avoided so he wouldn't end up here.

The most obvious solution would have been to kill that troublemaking bitch, Jessica Monroe. If it hadn't been for her scheming—aided and abetted by the djinn here in Santa Fe—Margolis would still have Miles Odekirk working for him, and Julia Innes would still be safely under his thumb.

Julia. It had been so long since he'd been with a woman that the thought of any female flesh might have been enough to get him to stiffen...but she'd been the best. She hadn't fought, but he still could sense the defiance in her cold silence as he pounded into her, taking her body for his own. The almost palpable waves of her hatred had been the ultimate turn-on.

You can have her back, the voice said.

When he first heard the voice, Margolis thought he was going crazy from the isolation. But he didn't feel crazy...and besides, the voice said such reasonable things to him, things that made sense. Surely if he was crazy, he wouldn't have manufactured such a logical companion for his solitude.

I can? Margolis thought back at the voice. Even from the beginning, he'd realized he needed to refrain from speaking out loud. There was no chance of his escaping from this cell, not in this high-security vault under the U.S. Marshals' building in Santa Fe, but that hadn't kept the town's inhabitants from keeping a guard on him night and day, just a few steps away from the door to the cramped chamber that now made up his world. Sometimes that guard was djinn, sometimes a well-armed human. Either way, he wasn't getting out any time soon.

Yes, the voice replied. *Julia Innes will be delivered to you—along with anything else you desire—as long as you do exactly what I say.*

Margolis didn't like taking orders—he'd been the one to give orders after the Dying took away all other established authority—but he figured obedience was a small price to pay for being free of this jail cell and having Julia once again. He inhaled deeply, recalling the sweet scent of her long, silky hair, the warm perfume of her flesh.

Then he sat upright on his cot, blood seeming to thrum through his veins as he contemplated the prospect of freedom. A return to power, and Julia his. That was enough to give a man hope.

Tell me what I have to do.

CHAPTER ONE

JULIA INNES PUSHED AWAY THE MOUND OF PAPER-
work on her desk and stood, then went to the window of
her office, which overlooked Los Alamos' main street. It
was a bright early fall day, the sky blue, a few puffy white
clouds scudding by. The slender aspen trees in the planters spaced along the sidewalk were just beginning to turn
gold.

Looking at the trees and their reminder of the turn
of the seasons, she realized that the Dying had struck
exactly one year ago. September twenty-sixth. The world
had been upended, and the few survivors of that hideous
plague were still trying to put the pieces back together.
Whether they'd been entirely successful or not, she
wasn't sure.

Oh, they'd definitely made progress. The residents of Los Alamos had been thrilled to have her in charge. Or maybe they'd just been so glad to have Margolis gone that they didn't care who else led them. And bringing Miles Odekirk, their resident genius, back with her to this stronghold of the Immune had also helped. After all, it was Miles's devices that had ensured their ongoing protection from the rampaging djinn, those otherworldly beings who had been so systematic about purging the world of the few humans the Dying had spared.

Only not all of the djinn sought vengeance and death. Some of them were friends, allies....

She wanted to shut her mind down before it finished that thought, but too late.

Lovers.

Not for her, of course. And she really didn't want to think about that. She *shouldn't* be thinking about that. Hadn't she already spent the last six months doing whatever she could to drive *him* out of her mind?

Zahrias al-Harith, leader of the djinn and Chosen community that had first resided in Taos, and then had moved down to Santa Fe at the orders of the djinn elders, whose word seemed to be law...except when it wasn't. Julia still hadn't quite figured out the dynamics of djinn society, and she supposed it didn't really matter. After all, she wasn't Chosen. She'd never have to deal with any of the elders directly.

But Zahrias was a different matter. She knew how foolish it was to allow him to occupy her thoughts. He'd never given her the slightest encouragement, had never said one word to her that wasn't neutral and polite and purely business. Never given her even one glance—

No, that wasn't true. If he truly had been all business all the time, then she would have had much more success in finding a way to push him from her mind. But there had been a look or two, quiet, smoldering, glances that she couldn't make herself forget. It was those glances that prevented her from allowing herself to put him out of her mind, or at least make herself think of him only as the leader of the community in Santa Fe and nothing more.

Because they still had contact from time to time. True, she'd had no reason to speak to Zahrias directly, but Miles had installed a ham radio in Julia's office so she could communicate with Jessica Monroe at the house she shared with her djinn lover Jace. The radio also came in handy for the times when Julia needed to speak to Lauren, Zahrias' assistant. Not that Lauren was going to be assisting him for much longer; she was due any day now, the child she was having with her own djinn partner about to make his or her entrance into the world.

At any rate, Julia was in contact with the Santa Fe group enough to know how they fared—not that there was all that much to report. The world had been quiet for the past six months. Maybe there were still survivors being hunted in other regions, other continents, but she had no way of knowing for sure; the radio remained silent, except for the limited bands the Santa Fe and the Los Alamos communities shared. Sometimes the echo of that emptiness would come to her in the depths of the night, when she couldn't sleep. What if the small band of survivors here in Los Alamos were truly the only people left alive in the world who weren't Chosen or djinn?

The thought chilled her. Unfortunately, Julia knew there wasn't a damn thing she could do about it. If it weren't for Miles Odekirk, she and everyone else in Los Alamos would also be dead. But his devices hummed away, keeping all djinn from encroaching on the little mountain town. He and his girlfriend Lindsay had built enough of the innocuous-looking boxes that the community was well-protected. There were even enough extra that foraging parties could take a device with them when they went down into Española, looking for supplies.

Girlfriend. Julia wasn't sure she even wanted to explore the irony of that situation. Even Miles Odekirk, the weedy, antisocial physicist, had somehow managed to get partnered up, while she was still alone. One of her duties was keeping track of the supplies in Los Alamos, and who got what in exchange for the work vouchers they used instead of money. It hadn't exactly escaped her attention that Lindsay Adarian, Miles's girlfriend, had been acquiring a new box of condoms once a month without fail. Julia couldn't help wondering how they had time to use up so many, considering they seemed to spend most of their time in the lab.

Her phone rang then, and she moved quickly so she could pick it up. Even as she did so, she couldn't help marveling at this supposed commonplace, that here in this post-apocalyptic world, they still had phones—well, in this building, at least—and electricity and running water.

When she spoke, she made sure she sounded brisk and cool. No way would she ever allow anyone to know that she'd been staring out the window and brooding over her current lovelorn state. "Julia here."

The caller was Natalie Ortega, the woman who oversaw the town's radio dispatch system. "Hi, Julia. You said you wanted to know when Sue Nichols went into labor. Brian just called me to let me know they were headed for the medical center."

"Thanks, Natalie. And Ellen's been contacted?"

"She's already at the medical center."

"Great. Thanks for the update."

"Absolutely." Natalie hung up then, and Julia slowly replaced her phone's handset in the cradle.

Sue and Brian's child would be the first baby born in Los Alamos after the Dying. Julia knew that people had been quietly pairing up for some time, but no one else had seemed too interested in repopulating the earth; Lindsay and Miles were definitely not the only ones going through boxes of condoms with some regularity. So far Sue's pregnancy had been completely uneventful, and Ellen O'Donnell, the nurse practitioner who was among the Los Alamos survivors, had said she didn't anticipate any problems. She'd delivered quite a few babies, and besides, they had the facilities at the town's medical center to ensure that everything went well. This baby would be born in a clean, modern hospital. No worries at all.

But Julia couldn't help worrying. If anyone had asked, she would have shrugged and said that she was the appointed leader of the town, so it was her job to worry. But her concern had deeper roots than that. True, everyone here was immune to the djinn-caused plague that had wiped out so much of the world's population. However, what if the baby wasn't immune? What if it got sick the moment it emerged into the world?

Borrowing trouble? Maybe. Even so, Julia felt as if she couldn't stay here in her office and wait patiently for the news, good or bad. She knew Sue's labor could take hours, and there wasn't much point in going to the medical facility right away. On the other hand, she also knew she wouldn't be able to concentrate if she didn't go.

She gathered up her purse and headed out, passing the empty reception desk. With a twinge, she remembered how Jessica Monroe had once sat there, answering the phone, doing the busywork generated by Captain Margolis' obsessive need for control. But Julia didn't want anyone manning that desk now. Yes, she had people who worked for her, but she answered her own damn phone, and her assistants had their own offices where they could perform their tasks at their own pace and without being disturbed.

Anyway, Richard Margolis was the last person she wanted to be thinking about right now. She'd been more or less successful in shoving him to the more remote corners of her mind. He was only an unpleasant episode in her past, something not worth dwelling on. The djinn in Santa Fe had him safely locked up. He couldn't hurt her or anyone else ever again.

The breeze caught at her hair as soon as she headed out into the parking lot, swirling the long, dark gold strands around her. Occasionally she'd thought about cutting it—having her hair so long really wasn't all that practical—but she hadn't yet been able to bring herself to bite that particular bullet.

It was just far enough from the municipal center to the medical facility that she drove rather than walked. There were a couple of cars in the parking lot—Ellen's Subaru, and a big old Blazer that Sue and Brian shared. The couple were among the first of the Los Alamos survivors to pair up; neither of them had been married when the Dying hit, Sue divorced and Brian a bachelor, and so they didn't have the loss of a significant other to overcome before they felt themselves ready to move on.

Julia also spotted Shawn Gutierrez's red Chevy pickup, and frowned. Why would he be here?

Former fireman, she reminded herself. He was the only other person in the community with any kind of medical training. It wasn't too surprising that Ellen would want him here.

His presence would make things awkward, though. For the past few months, he'd been subtly attempting to see if Julia had any kind of interest in getting together with him, even though she hadn't been exactly encouraging.

And that was completely stupid of her, because Shawn was not only extremely good-looking, but a very nice guy to boot. She should have jumped at the chance to erase the last bits of her attraction to Zahrias. Instead, she'd spend two months politely but consistently shutting him down.

She allowed herself the faintest of sighs as she pushed open the front door to the medical center and went inside. Only a few of the overhead fluorescent lights were on, just enough to see her way to the stairs so she could head up to the obstetrics ward on the second floor. Yes, they had electricity here in Los Alamos, but

Miles had drilled into everyone the need for conservation. They relied mostly on solar and wind, and had backup generators for the days when those resources failed them. That meant only turning on the lights they really needed.

The obstetrics ward, on the other hand, was completely lit up, and looked bright and cheerful, with its warm oak-laminate floors and softly painted walls. Julia heard voices coming down the hallway to the left, so she went in that direction and then paused outside the door.

Sue was already in bed, gripping Brian's hand and panting furiously. Ellen had apparently just finished checking her blood pressure, since she was in the process of taking off the heavy black cuff when Julia peeked in. On the other side of the room, Shawn Gutierrez looked on, although he didn't seem to be actively involved at the moment.

His eyes met hers, and she made herself gaze steadily back at him and lift her eyebrows. He nodded in reply to her unspoken question, then murmured something to Ellen before stepping out in the hallway to join her.

"How is she?" she murmured.

"Fine," he replied. "Vitals are good. Contractions are coming about two minutes apart, so we don't have too long to wait."

"That seems...fast." Oh, who was she kidding? She didn't know jack about childbirth or contractions or any of that stuff. She'd been an only child, and her former fiancé had made damn sure she didn't have any close friends, so she'd never been around anyone—except in the most casual of circumstances—who'd been pregnant.

But Shawn nodded. "It is pretty fast. This baby wants to be out in the world, looks like."

"I guess that's a good thing?"

Sue moaned loudly from inside the hospital room, and Julia tried not to wince.

Shawn's mouth twitched, as if he was trying not to smile at her reaction. "Yeah, it's good. Ellen's not an anesthesiologist, so even though we have the meds here, she doesn't dare perform an epidural or anything. We have to do this the old-fashioned way."

Which, judging by the sounds Sue was currently making, felt about as good as having a backhoe repeatedly run over your foot. "And that's okay?"

"Women had children for thousands of years without epidurals. And she's doing great."

Easy for you to say, Julia thought. *You'll never have to worry about going through childbirth.*

Then again, neither would she, at the rate she was going. She'd never been one of those women with an overwhelming desire for children, although she had to admit part of that attitude might have stemmed from her less-than-ideal relationship with Ian. If she really wanted to help repopulate the earth, she should probably get her ass in gear.

She looked up at Shawn, taking in his warm brown eyes and friendly mouth. That mouth looked like it would know what it was doing. Maybe it really was time—

Ellen's voice carried out into the corridor. "Shawn, in here. *Now.*"

He flashed a grin at Julia. "Duty calls."

And he hurried back into the hospital room. What precisely Ellen needed him for, Julia couldn't quite tell, because they had a quick murmured exchange that was all but drowned out by Sue's continued groans. Julia waited outside, knowing it would be rude to try to peek inside. She wasn't a family member, or even a close friend of the about-to-be parents, only the person who was trying desperately to make sure this little outpost clung to some semblance of normality. Anyway, she was pretty sure she didn't even want to see what was going on in there....

After what seemed like an interminable period of moaning and groaning, broken by bouts of heavy breathing and Brian's low, encouraging voice, there came a brief silence, followed by the shrill, thin cries of a baby. Julia exhaled slowly, although she couldn't quite allow herself to relax. There were still so many things that could go wrong.

But then Shawn poked his head out through the doorway. His grin flashed white in the fluorescent light of the overhead fixtures. "I'd like to announce Los Alamos' newest resident. Addison Grace Nichols-Johanson."

Julia let out a shaky laugh. "That's a mouthful."

His smile didn't flicker. "Maybe. But I suppose that'll be her problem."

"And—" She hated to ask the question when Shawn was looking so cheerful, but it couldn't be avoided. "And she's okay?"

"As far as Ellen can tell. Seven pounds, twelve ounces. Sounds like she's got a good set of lungs on her, too."

"I hadn't noticed."

Shawn's grin broadened. "Uh-huh. Anyway, I think everything is under control here. Ellen said she'll stay for a few more hours, make sure everything's okay. But she told me I didn't need to hang around." He paused then, expression sobering slightly. His manner seemed almost diffident. "So...how about I buy you a drink to celebrate?"

At once Julia felt herself stiffen. That was just stupid, because she liked Shawn, dammit. And it was time she got herself together. Six months had passed since she'd come back here to Los Alamos. Plenty of time for Zahrias to appear in a puff of smoke or come riding up on a white horse, or whatever it was that djinn did. Okay, not exactly. Miles's devices would have kept the djinn from showing up within the borders of Los Alamos, but if Zahrias had really wanted to talk to her, they could have arranged something. Most likely he'd probably forgotten all about her, content to oversee his own little realm. Jessica had never mentioned him pairing off with anyone, so Julia had no reason to think those particular circumstances had changed.

Not that it really mattered one way or another. For whatever reason, he seemed content to live his life alone, but that didn't mean she had to.

"Sure," she told Shawn, summoning a smile from somewhere and putting it on. He looked pleasantly relieved in response, which meant her smile had to have appeared at least somewhat genuine. "I think I'd like that."

Zahrias pushed away from the desk where he'd been sitting and strode out into the hallway. On this mild autumn day, most of the windows in the house were open, along with the doors that allowed access to the interior courtyard of the structure. The building's design was one of the reasons he had chosen it for his own; his people often constructed their homes around central courtyards, and that similarity made this alien place seem a little more familiar.

Even so, he felt an unwelcome uneasiness thrumming along his veins. Whence it had come, he couldn't say, except that he found himself strangely unable to concentrate, restless. Boredom was not an emotional state the djinn usually experienced, for their lives were so long that they were used to the ebb and flow of excitement and calm, stimulation and silence. If it still seemed strange to him that his home was now here, in this world his people had coveted for so long, he supposed he would get used to it in a decade or two.

All was at peace. A peace hard-won, and not without its sacrifices, but he knew the community here was safe, and would remain that way. The elders who nominally ruled over his kind would not allow themselves to be circumvented again. His fellow djinn could continue to ravage and raid, hunting down mankind's last survivors, but they would never dare to come here.

Perhaps his unease merely arose from the impending birth of his brother Dani's child. Lauren, Dani's Chosen, could no longer assist Zahrias in the running of the Santa Fe community, since she was due any day now, but Zahrias hadn't yet selected her replacement. He could muddle on for another week or so before making a decision. Indeed, while he had thought Lauren indispensable at one time, now the djinn and their Chosen had all settled into an easy enough rhythm, enjoying the beauties of this world and its bounties, and he wasn't sure if his people needed all that much management anymore. No one took more than their due, and so far any disputes or quarrels had been few and far between.

He wouldn't attempt to explain such unprecedented harmony, for in general, the djinn tended to be quick to anger, easy to take offense. The peace that had settled over Santa Fe could be the result of realizing how close they had been to losing everything. If that was the truth of the matter, he knew he would not argue with it.

For some reason, though, Zahrias could not find that peace within himself. He had hoped that acting as leader here would give some shape and form to his days. Unfortunately, all he had done was surround himself with people who appeared to be infinitely happier than he.

The trees in the courtyard were just starting to turn, the leaves at their crowns beginning to ripple with deep gold. For some reason, seeing that warm shimmer in the wind made him think of her hair, the way it had blown around her face with the glinting shades of old gold coins.

No, he would not allow himself to think about her. He had done his best to banish her face from his memory, but thoughts of her would still come to him unbidden, as they did now. And with those thoughts, as always, a wave of guilt.

I saw her, when all the others were selecting their Chosen. I saw her, and wanted her, and did nothing, because I would not allow myself to be wounded by a mortal woman again. And because of my cowardice, she has suffered the kind of hurt that no woman should ever have to endure.

When Julia revealed to everyone precisely what that sorry specimen of a man had done to her, Zahrias had found himself so overcome by rage that it had taken all his strength, all his control, to keep himself from blasting Richard Margolis from the face of the earth. Even now, flames flickered wildly around Zahrias at the memory. But again, he had done nothing, because to reveal his anger would have been to let everyone around know that he was not quite so detached from the situation as he wished others to believe.

It seemed the more he tried not to think about Julia Innes, the more she occupied his thoughts.

He opened the door of wood and glass that allowed him entry into the courtyard. The breeze was brisk, ruffling through his hair, pulling stray strands from the clasp of red gold that held most of it away from his face. Usually, he found if he stepped out here and allowed himself a few moments with the wind and the sky, he could calm his thoughts. Now, though, his restlessness seemed only to intensify, as if the bright breeze bore on its wings invisible messengers of ill portent.

Perhaps you have spent too long within the walls of this city. The Chosen cannot venture too far forth unaccompanied, but we djinn do not share those restrictions.

Yes, he should go out. Not to walk, but to ride. His fellow djinn and their Chosen had taken over a stable near the edge of town and collected some of the stray horses in the area, partly for amusement, and partly because, sooner or later, the strange liquid that powered their vehicles would run out, and the horses would be their only viable mode of conveyance. True, he and the other djinn could move from place to place easily, and could take their Chosen with them as necessary, but it still never hurt to have other options.

While he would never admit it to anyone else, Zahrias found that caring for the horses and riding them around the land that was now his home had become his own form of meditation. He couldn't indulge as often as he would like, for it often seemed that some matter or another would keep him occupied at the center of town, but even so, he had been able to go out enough that he had familiarized himself with the contours of this land, so steady, so enduring and strong, so very unlike the ever-shifting planes of the world that had once been more a prison to the djinn than their home. They had endured it because they must, but this earth was so very much more appealing.

He nodded to himself, as if agreeing with his plan, and then reentered the house and closed the door to

the courtyard behind him. It wouldn't do to be gone
for too long, not with Dani's child about to make its
appearance, but even an hour would probably be sufficient. And if the child did decide to come in that hour,
well, someone could come to fetch him. A few miles
meant nothing to any of his people.

With that resolution fixed in his mind, he shut his
eyes and visualized the stables, the long row of build-
ings and the dry grass that surrounded them and the
sweeping vistas of far-off mountains to every side. In
less than the blink of an eye, he was there, standing
outside the stall that held his favorite horse, the huge
black stallion that Lilias' Chosen, Aidan, had named
Goliath.

No one seemed to be about, but Goliath's trough
held fresh water, and the bag in his stall bulged with
hay, so Zahrias knew someone had already been by
today to look in on the horses and make sure they'd
been cared for. In fact, several of the stalls were empty,
signaling that a few of Santa Fe's denizens had had the
same idea as he, deciding that this bright autumn day
was a perfect one for a ride.

Zahrias' mouth tightened at the possibility of
encountering one of those other riders. He had wished
for solitude, but at the moment, he saw no one else. It
would be easy enough to slip out before anyone else
returned, especially since he did not have to waste time

putting a saddle and bridle on his horse. A djinn had no need of such things.

He opened the door to the stall and Goliath ambled out, shaking his heavy mane, nostrils flaring at the scents carried on the wind. Clearly, he wanted to be outside as well, free of the confines of his stall.

With a show of agility that probably would have startled a human onlooker, but which Zahrias took for granted, he leaped onto the horse's back, settling himself behind the great beast's withers. On most occasions, he would whisper a word into Goliath's ears, letting the horse know where he wanted to go, but today Zahrias found he didn't much care where he went, as long as it was out and away.

Goliath lifted his head into the breeze, ears twitching. Then he turned and headed toward the rear of the property, where a gate opened onto empty hillsides dotted here and there with the squat dark green trees called juniper and the scrubby shapes of piñon pines.

Not that Goliath needed a gate. His pace increased, shifting from a slow canter to a hard gallop. Zahrias clung to the great beast's back, moving with each stride, letting the bright air stream past him.

And then they were over the fence, sailing above it almost as if the stallion had been given the gift of flight. They hit the ground running, the impact lessened by their forward momentum.

Yes. This was what he needed, to be free in the wind and the air, the scent of juniper and dry grass sharp in his nostrils. Out here, he didn't need to think about anything except the terrain beneath Goliath's hooves, the shifting patterns of dark and light as clouds drifted lazily above his head.

But then the stallion let out a harsh whinny and came to a sudden halt. Zahrias blinked, wondering what could have startled him so.

Not that he had to wonder for very long. For standing there amidst the brush, only a few handspans off, was his brother Dani, brows pulled together in worry and arms crossed against his chest. Unlike Zahrias, Dani had more or less adopted human garb, and wore a dark shirt and those stiff blue pants the mortals called "jeans."

Had the baby come? Zahrias could think of no other reason for being interrupted in such a fashion. He didn't bother to question how his brother could have found him; they were connected by blood, and so it was easy enough for them to track one another down.

"Is it the child?" he asked. "I had thought Lauren—"

"No," Dani replied, voice uncharacteristically harsh for him. "Lauren is fine. No, this is something far more troubling."

At that answer, Zahrias raised an eyebrow. Dani was not normally the sort much given to worry, and so for him to be troubled....

"What is it?"

Dani's dark eyes flickered with worry and a sort of baffled rage. "It's the prisoner. Margolis.

"He's escaped."

CHAPTER TWO

SEE? JULIA TOLD HERSELF. *THIS ISN'T SO BAD.*

She and Shawn Gutierrez sat in one of the booths at Pajarito's, the former gastropub that had somehow turned into the center of the revived Los Alamos community. By that point, it was almost four thirty, and people were beginning to trickle in after putting in their various shifts around town, whether that was cutting timber to store against the coming cold months, harvesting the last crops from the vegetable gardens they'd planted over the summer, or continuing with the grim but necessary process of going from empty house to empty house and gathering and cataloguing anything that would help the community survive the next winter. At least there were no dead bodies to contend with—the Dying had been a clean apocalypse, she'd give the djinn that much—but it still had to be difficult work, to enter the houses of people long dead and realize those little piles of gray dust used to be the inhabitants.

But she shouldn't be thinking about that now. She should be focusing on Shawn's easy grin, or remembering the exhausted, beautiful smile Sue Nichols had worn as she looked down at her newborn daughter. That smile had done something to Julia. Exactly what, she wasn't quite sure yet. But in that moment, she'd thought maybe it wouldn't be such a bad thing, bringing humanity back from the brink of extinction.

And if Shawn wanted to help her out with that....

"...going home tomorrow," he was saying.

Belatedly, she realized he must talking about Sue. "Isn't that kind of soon?"

"Not according to Ellen. She says there weren't any complications, and both mom and baby are fine, so there's no point in staying in the medical center after this one night."

Julia picked up her iced tea and took a sip. Right then she was wishing it could be some of her favorite, pinot grigio, but technically, she was still on duty until five, so....

Not that anyone else probably would have cared, since she worked seven days a week and never gave herself a break, but she was too much of a stickler to break that self-imposed rule. Anyway, depriving herself of a glass of wine only meant their supply would last that much longer. They'd been lucky, since a good amount had been delivered to the local grocery store and several of the restaurants right before the Dying began, but even so, supplies wouldn't last forever, even supplemented by what they managed to scrounge down in Española. Julia wondered if sending a group with one of Miles's devices to the Black Mesa winery on the north side of that town would be considered a frivolity. Probably not; it would be a long time before the community here was able to spare the resources to grow grapes for wine...if that was even possible at Los Alamos' elevation. She didn't know enough about viticulture to even guess.

"Well, I suppose Ellen knows best," she said. "I'm just glad that they're doing so well."

"You were worried about it, weren't you?"

Shawn hadn't bothered to say which "it," he was referring to, but Julia knew exactly what he meant. "It" was the elephant in the room, after all.

"How could I not be? I mean, I'd hoped that since we're all immune, any children we—that is, the people in the community—had would be immune as well. But I just didn't know." God, that sounded awful. She had to pray he hadn't read anything into that inadvertent "we."

If he had, Shawn didn't give any sign of it. "Well, that's understandable," he said easily. "I mean, no one really knows how the Heat worked, do they?"

He'd used the epithet given to the sickness because of the intense fevers it caused. No one much called it that anymore, since its aftermath—the Dying—was what had been burned into everyone's brains. "No," she replied. "If any doctors or epidemiologists survived the Dying, I haven't heard of them. We're lucky to have Ellen as it is."

Shawn nodded, expression growing somber. So far, everyone in the community seemed more or less healthy, and all Ellen had had to do during her tenure in Los Alamos was fix a few sprains and broken bones, and scrounge in the local pharmacy for a suitable replacement for Roger Garcia's asthma medication. Ellen and Shawn did great when it came to first aid sorts of problems, or even more complicated medical procedures like delivering a baby. But what if someone got really sick, got cancer or something? What then?

Then they'll probably die, Julia thought. We just don't have the facilities and the knowledge to treat something like that. Might as well be back in the Dark Ages.

The bitter thought crossed her mind that this was yet another problem the community in Santa Fe would never have to face. The djinn were all but immortal, and their Chosen also granted the gift of health and long life. They'd never have to worry about cancer or heart disease or any one of the hundreds of ailments that could strike frail humanity.

Being eternally young wasn't a bad deal, either. Jessica Monroe and all the other Chosen like her would be preserved forever at the age they'd been when their djinn selected them, but Julia knew her own clock was steadily ticking away. Her twenty-ninth birthday had come and gone in the bitter depths of January, and soon yet another birthday would be swinging back around to confront her once again.

In the time before the Dying, she hadn't thought that much about turning thirty. After all, in that careless world, thirty had been the new twenty. But she could see herself getting worn in service to the community here, fading away before she'd even had a chance to truly live —

"Hey," Shawn said gently. "You okay? You look as if you just went off to someplace not very pleasant."

Julia blinked, bringing herself back to here and now. It was damn stupid to be imagining such a bleak future when she was sitting here opposite the best-looking man in Los Alamos, a man who'd already indicated that he didn't think her faded at all. "I'm okay," she said, then picked up her iced tea and took a large swallow. "Just thinking about eventualities. Curse of the job, I guess."

"I guess," he echoed. His dark eyes scanned her face, and she hoped he couldn't see anything there of what she'd been thinking. "You work too hard."

"Don't we all?"

His shoulders lifted, and he drank some of his Coke. Julia knew he'd gotten the soft drink and not the beer he wanted after he realized she wouldn't be having any wine. "I don't know," he replied. "I sort of doubt the work I do in the motor pool is on a par with what you do every day to keep this place going."

"Don't forget about helping to deliver babies," she told him. Despite her earlier melancholy thoughts, she could feel a smile tugging at her lips.

"Mostly I stood there and watched. No big deal."

Julia knew he'd contributed a lot more than that— when Mitch Kosky broke his arm while cutting down trees in the forests around town, it had been Shawn who'd fashioned a crude splint and helped him down the mountainside so Ellen could treat the injury properly. And it was Shawn who'd organized a soft-ball league over the summer to keep people occupied during the long, warm days. Brent Sanderson had once called Julia the soul of the community, but she thought Shawn Gutierrez must be its heart.

And if heart and soul just happened to get together....

The walkie-talkie she always wore clipped to her belt buzzed then. She flashed an apologetic smile at Shawn and picked up the radio, hoping that whatever had prompted Natalie to contact her wouldn't be too serious. Julia was tired, and besides, if she hung out here for a few minutes longer, it would be after five and she wouldn't have any excuse not to order that glass of wine after all.

"Julia here."

No preamble from Natalie, only, "A djinn from the Santa Fe community named Dani just contacted me."

"And?" That sounded strange. Julia knew that Dani was Zahrias' younger brother, but usually it was his Chosen, Lauren, who handled communications. Then again, she was probably due to give birth any day now. Maybe Dani had taken over some of her duties.

"Bad news. He wanted to warn us that Captain Margolis managed to escape."

The interior of the restaurant was quite warm, but at those words, Julia could feel her body turn to ice. Literally. It was as if she couldn't speak, couldn't breathe, couldn't move.

"Julia?" A long pause, then Natalie's voice, worried even through the distortion of the little speaker from which it emerged. "Are you there, Julia?"

Somehow she managed to push down the button on the walkie-talkie. "I'm here, Natalie. Anything else?"

"Their leader, Zahrias, wants to talk to you. He's standing by on their radio."

Could she do that? Talk to the man she'd been mooning over not even an hour earlier? Right then it seemed as if her brain wasn't firing properly. Richard Margolis had escaped from his cell under the U.S.

Marshals' building, and Zahrias wanted to talk to her. Across the table, Shawn Gutierrez was staring at her with worried brown eyes.

"Um, sure. I mean, yes. I'll be over as fast as I can."

There probably was a way to patch his call through to her walkie-talkie, but Julia didn't know what it might be. Something else she should really ask Miles Odekirk about—if he wouldn't consider such a simple task beneath him.

"What's wrong?" Shawn asked as she grimly clipped the walkie-talkie back on her belt. When Margolis had ruled Los Alamos and she was his secretary, she'd worn office clothes—skirts and high-heeled boots. Now she was in jeans day in and day out.

"Bad news. Margolis has escaped."

Shock registered in Shawn's widened eyes. "What? How?"

"I don't know. I need to get back to the office so I can talk to Zahrias. Hopefully, he'll have more information."

"Jesus." Beneath his tan, Shawn looked ashen. As far as she knew, the former fireman hadn't had any run-ins with Margolis back in the day. Most likely, he was just worried on her behalf.

"It's okay," she said, tone a little too brisk. She knew she was over-compensating, but there wasn't much she could do about that. "I sort of doubt he'll come here and risk getting shot on sight."

"You'd think, but that guy was crazy—" Shawn broke off then. "Sorry. You're right. He wouldn't be stupid enough to come here. And really...." He stopped, and a sudden smile touched his lips.

"'Really' what?" she demanded, wondering what the hell he was smiling about. "I don't see anything amusing about all this."

"Really, where does he think he can go? Won't the other djinn hunt him down?"

God, she'd forgotten about that. They were protected here in Los Alamos by Miles's devices, and of course the other djinn knew the community at Santa Fe was off limits, but Richard Margolis wouldn't have any such safeguards. He'd be easy prey.

An answering smile lifted her mouth. "You're right, Shawn. He will be easy prey."

Thank goodness she had the radio in her office, though, and not out where anyone else could overhear what she was saying. Julia pulled the microphone toward her and said, "I'm here, Zahrias."

The deep, woodwind tones of his voice came through the speaker. "Julia."

Warmth flushed her cheeks. But she said steadily, "Zahrias, I've been told you have some bad news for me."

"I'm afraid so. It was discovered earlier today that Captain Margolis was missing from his cell."

Hearing it once more, spoken of so calmly, made Julia go cold all over again. Logically, she knew she was safe. Because they'd already had protocols in place in case of future disaster—although the former commander's escape was not an eventuality that had ever been discussed—the word had already gone out all over Los Alamos that Richard Margolis was loose. Two extra guards kept watch in the lobby of the municipal center where Julia now sat, and an extra vehicle had been assigned patrol duty. All this had happened while she was driving over here; her security team knew their stuff.

Anyway, she had to believe that Margolis wouldn't find too many sympathizers if he did somehow manage to make it back to Los Alamos safely. Yes, at one time he'd had most of the town on his side, because they were grateful to be someplace safe and weren't too worried about giving up a few liberties if it meant they'd make it through another day. But after Julia revealed what Margolis had done to her, any support he might have once possessed was gone as quickly as smoke blowing away in a strong breeze. No one wanted to be associated with a rapist.

She took a steadying breath and said, "How did it happen? I thought you had a guard watching him day and night."

"We did. He was left unattended for only a moment while the person watching him went to use the facilities. When he returned, Margolis was gone."

Great. Undone by somebody's pee break. Julia knew she wouldn't say that aloud, though, because it was ridiculous to expect someone to put in a day's shift watching the prisoner and not take a break sometime. The captive hadn't been held in some county jail's flimsy lockup, either, but a state-of-the-art facility faced in bulletproof glass and with full-spectrum laser monitoring. She hadn't seen the place for herself, having no desire to be in Margolis' company any longer than she had to, but Miles had explained the setup to her, since he was the one who'd reset the security measures so Zahrias' people could use them. There should have been no way for Richard Margolis to escape, even if his guard had gone up to the surface, ordered a Big Mac, and watched the midday news.

Okay, Big Macs and noon newscasts were things of the past, but still.

"How?" she asked.

"We are still assessing. At the moment, it seems as if he simply vanished. There was no sign that the biometric lock was tampered with. Only five people can open that lock—the four whose duty it was to guard the cell, and myself. They all swear that they did not touch it, and I know I did not."

Julia was silent for a moment, pondering what Zahrias had just told her. She didn't know the people who'd been assigned to guard the prisoner, but if Zahrias had chosen them, then she guessed their loyalty must be unimpeachable. On the other hand, Margolis was many things, but an expert jail-breaker he was not. And if he actually did possess the skill to get out of such a cell on his own, why do it now, six months after he'd been locked up, rather than immediately after he'd been imprisoned there?

Something definitely didn't smell right here.

The words startled her, even as they emerged from her mouth. "I want to talk to them. And I want to see the cell."

Zahrias sounded startled as well. "Julia, I do not think—"

"I think I have a right to speak to them. Margolis' escape could very well affect me more than it does anyone else." Maybe she was being irrational, but she'd always been the kind of person who needed to see someone's face when she spoke with them. They had these radios, but the Internet was dead, and Skype and Facetime along with it, and so the only way she'd be able to read their expressions was to do so in person.

"And how do you propose to do that?"

"I'll come to you—with an armed party," she added hastily, sensing that Zahrias was about to offer another protest. "We'll bring one of Miles's devices with us, just as we always do when we go out scavenging. Then we'll turn it off when we reach the border of Santa Fe, since we'll be under your protection at that point."

A long pause. "Very well. That should work. I assume you will be taking the northern approach into town?"

"Yes, down the 285." How prosaic that sounded, as if she was merely planning a brief lunch outing.

"Then we will all meet you at the U.S. Marshals' office. You know the way?"

She didn't exactly, but she didn't want to admit that to Zahrias. There were plenty of paper maps on hand here at the office, so she'd consult one of them. "Yes. Give me an hour or so to get everything set up, and then we'll head over."

Another one of those hesitations. "It will be late afternoon by the time you get here. Perhaps it would be better if you and your party stayed overnight. Yes, you will have one of Miles's devices to protect you, but I think it would be safer if you did not make the return journey after dark."

Journey. Something in her wanted to smile at his old-fashioned language, since he was talking about a trip of only a little more than thirty miles, all of it on paved roads that had been laboriously cleared of any abandoned vehicles. But they were also completely unlit roads. Maybe it would be better to stay in Santa Fe.

Giving you more time around Zahrias, she thought.

Right. He'd probably meet her at the U.S. Marshals', let her speak to the guards who'd been keeping watch on Margolis, and then disappear.

"Okay," she replied, hoping he hadn't noticed the way she'd paused before answering. "If it's not too much trouble."

"We have many unused hotel rooms here. I'll have my people get some ready for you. How many will be in your party?"

"No more than six," she replied. They couldn't fit any more than that in the Suburban she used for "official" business. "Which is probably overkill, but I'd rather be careful."

"I agree. Then we will see you in a few hours."

He ended the transmission then, and Julia sat in her chair, staring at the now-silent speakers of the ham radio setup. Well, she'd really put her foot in it this time, hadn't she? All these months she'd been more or less maintaining her cool, and now she'd made it so she'd have to go and see Zahrias in person. A lot of fun that was going to be, pretending that she only saw him as a fellow leader in this post-apocalyptic world. A colleague, so to speak.

Yeah, right.

She kept herself from sighing, then reached over for the phone so she could start making the necessary calls.

Julia Innes, coming to Santa Fe. Zahrias understood her desire to speak to the guards in person, for it was only when one looked a man in the face that one could see the truth of his words. The radio was a necessity, since there was no other way to communicate with the people in Los Alamos, but he disliked the device. It was too easy to hide what one was thinking when only spoken words were involved.

But perhaps it was just as well that he could not communicate with Julia easily or more often. For soon he would have to look at her, speak with her with only a few feet separating them, and that could prove to be difficult. He already had a hard enough time keeping her from his thoughts when the safety of miles separated them. What would he do when they were both in the same room?

Control yourself, he told himself harshly. *Far more is involved here than your desire for one mortal woman.*

That much was only the bitter truth. Everyone who had access to Margolis' cell swore that they'd had nothing to do with his escape, and Zahrias had no reason not to believe them, for the truth had all but shone from their faces and rung in their words. Something else was at work here, something he had yet to uncover.

It was human technology which had barred the door of that cell, and human technology could be just as frail as those who had invented it, yet....

Normally at a time like this, he would have had Lauren take care of making sure that accommodations were prepared for their expected visitors, but Dani had sent word that she had retired to her bed. No signs of labor yet, but she tired easily, and Miguel, the Chosen man who had taken on the duties of healer in their small community—not that they had much use for one, most days—had advised that she not get up again until after the baby was born.

So Zahrias went to Lilias, who he knew had more of an accommodating nature than many of his fellow djinn, and asked if she and her Chosen, Aidan, would assist him.

"If it is not too much of an imposition," Zahrias said politely as Lilias and Aidan met with him in the living room of their spacious home a few blocks from the plaza. "I thought a group of rooms at La Fonda—"

"Of course," Lilias said at once. "It will only take a few snaps of my fingers, after all, and I suppose you have enough to worry about, with that mortal somehow managing to escape."

There was the faintest trace of accusation in her words, and Zahrias raised an eyebrow.

Aidan looked annoyed on their leader's behalf. "Lilias, I talked to David, and he said nothing had been tampered with. It's like the *Enterprise* just beamed Margolis right out of there."

Zahrias had no idea what this *Enterprise* was that Aidan had spoken of, and, judging by the way Lilias' fine black brows drew together, she was equally mystified. But she appeared to brush the puzzle aside, saying, "It is no trouble, Zahrias. They will be here in a few hours? Be assured that everything will be ready far in advance of that time."

There was little he could do then but press his hands together and bow, then murmur a few words of thanks. After that he left, walking in the direction of the U.S. Marshals' building. He could have made himself appear there in the blink of an eye, but the afternoon air was fresh and fine and clean, and he hoped the walk would help to clear his head.

He would need a clear head when he met with Julia, just a few hours from now.

CHAPTER THREE

AFTER SHE BEGAN PUTTING TOGETHER A LIST OF the people she wanted to go with her to Santa Fe, Julia realized that the one person she really shouldn't leave out of the party was Miles Odekirk. He'd been the one to set up the security on Margolis' cell, and so he was probably the best person to look over the scene of the crime and see if he could find any clues as to how the former leader of Los Alamos had managed to escape.

So she radioed out to the labs and murmured a silent prayer under her breath that either he or Lindsay would pick up. Half the time they didn't; too involved in their work, Julia supposed. But today Lindsay was on the line soon enough.

"What's up?"

So she hadn't heard. The word had gone out, but to the people who patrolled the lab complex, not the labs themselves.

"Richard Margolis has escaped."

"*What?*"

At least Lindsay sounded suitably shocked. God knows what kind of reaction Miles would have had. Julia said, "I'm putting together a team to go to Santa Fe to get more information, and I need Miles to go, since he's the best person to try to figure out what happened."

"I don't think he's going to like that—we're really close to a breakthrough here—"

Julia prevented herself from letting out an annoyed huff. To hear Miles and Lindsay tell it, they were on the verge of a "breakthrough" every other week. The scientist was still attempting to modify his devices so they could ward off the bad djinn—the ones dedicated to hunting down the last of humanity's survivors—while tamping down the debilitating waves of energy that affected any friendly djinn within their sphere of influence. Julia knew his research was important, because it would make it much simpler for the people in Los Alamos and Santa Fe to interact with one another, but he had yet to see any real success.

"I understand that," she said. "But it's also really important to find out how Margolis was able to escape.

It's only one day, basically—we're going to stay over in Santa Fe tonight, for safety's sake, but I'm not imagining we'll need to spend too much time there."

"Okay," Lindsay replied. "I'll let him know. What time do you need us at the municipal center?"

"About forty minutes from now, if you can manage it."

"No problem. We'll swing by the house and get a few things on our way over. See you then."

"But shouldn't—" Julia began, then realized Lindsay had already cut off the transmission. She would have preferred to speak to Miles herself, but if Lindsay wanted to handle it, fine.

If they weren't there at the designated time...then Julia might have a few choice words on the subject of Lindsay's presumption. In the meantime, though, she had other things to worry about. After some deliberation, she'd decided she'd leave Shawn in charge during her absence. Taking him along could have gotten awkward, since she had absolutely no idea where things stood with him. And everyone liked and trusted Shawn, so he was a natural choice to watch over the town while she was gone.

In addition to Miles and Lindsay, Julia thought she'd bring Brent Sanderson with her. He wasn't the world's best shot, but he was Shawn's partner-in-crime in the motor pool. If, God forbid, anything went wrong with the Suburban during their round trip, Brent should be able to fix it. The last two members of the party would be Nancy Kovacs, the most experienced person on the Los Alamos security detail, and Eric Gold, who didn't look all that physically intimidating but who happened to be a black belt in taekwondo. Not that she really thought they'd be facing the kind of threat that would require true hand-to-hand combat, but Eric was also a crack shot...and Nancy's current boyfriend. If nothing else, Julia figured they might enjoy a night out in a Santa Fe hotel room.

Everyone assembled in the parking lot at the municipal center at a little past six. The drive would take about forty minutes, more or less, but even at the end of September, it would be some time before full dark arrived. Plenty of time to get safely to Santa Fe.

Miles Odekirk looked less than thrilled at being dragged away from his research. However, he didn't offer any protests, but only shoved the duffle bag he carried in with the rest of the backpacks and duffles and overnight bags everyone else had dumped in the rear cargo area, while Lindsay stood by, holding one of the djinn-repelling devices in her hand. There wasn't much conversation; everyone knew why they were there.

Julia got in behind the wheel, with Brent taking shotgun and everyone else getting into the second- and third-row seats. And after that they were off, driving along the mountain road that wound down out of Los

Alamos to join up with the highway that led to Santa Fe.

This would be the first time she'd actually left the town since she'd come back in the spring to assume her role as reluctant leader of the community. She'd been so consumed with making sure everything ran smoothly that she'd never volunteered to go on one of the scavenging missions in Española, although after a few months she did feel as if she was beginning to get a little stir-crazy. Albuquerque was her former home-town, and she wasn't used to being cooped up in a place that really didn't have very many resources. Also, the mountains that sheltered them at times felt almost intimidating, as if they were crowding in from all sides. Back in the wintertime, she hadn't noticed as much, but that could have simply been because the weather hadn't been very conducive to travel, and she'd been too busy focusing on all the busywork Margolis kept producing.

It did feel good to get out on the open road—and it was open, thanks to her crews expending a good deal of effort so the highway wouldn't remain littered with the abandoned vehicles of Heat victims who'd suc-cumbed to the disease even as they drove frantically to get away from it. From here it would be pretty much a straight shot down into the heart of Santa Fe, where the U.S. Marshals' building was located.

And where Zahrias would be waiting for her.

Waiting for your team, she reminded herself. Most likely he would be far more interested in hearing Miles Odekirk's insights than talking to her.

She wondered who else would be there; there were a few people she'd come to know while she lived among them so briefly before going back to Los Alamos. Probably not Jessica and Jace; the house they lived in was a good ways outside town, and Zahrias would have no reason to call them in on this matter. Unlike Miles, they most likely wouldn't be able to offer any particular insights as to how Margolis had managed to escape.

Eventually Julia came to the turnoff that led to Santa Fe's downtown. In the back seat, Lindsay fiddled with the device, shutting it down so it wouldn't affect the djinn they were about to meet.

Julia's eyes flickered from side to side as she drove, trying to take in the changed aspect of the town, which once had bustled with tourists and residents alike. Did the djinn keep the museums and shops open, so they might amuse themselves with looking at relics of a world long gone? She recalled that when she'd last been here, some of the stores had been open for people to take what they needed to furnish their houses, but the museums had been locked up, quiet and dark. The memory disturbed her for some reason, and she tried to put it aside. At least Santa Fe still had life and people, wasn't dead and empty like almost every other town on the face of the planet.

But not Los Alamos, she thought then with some pride. Getting that community going might have been Richard Margolis' one and only good deed. For all she knew, he'd done it for selfish reasons, to have someplace where he could be master, but the fact remained that the town was doing well, thanks to the protection Miles Odekirk's devices provided and the resilience of its inhabitants. They might be mere mortals, but they'd done well for themselves.

The streets around them now were empty. Julia supposed the djinn didn't have much need for cars when they could simply "blink" themselves from place to place, and maybe they did the same thing for their Chosen. She did notice a few people out on the sidewalks, probably enjoying the last of the bright afternoon before it was time to go in for their evening meals. Had Phillip, the man who'd acted as chef up in Taos when the group was sequestered in a resort there, opened a restaurant where humans and djinn could mingle and be social?

So many questions. But she wasn't here to simply satisfy her idle curiosity.

She pulled the Suburban into one of the spots in front of the U.S. Marshals' building, a handsome stone structure with a sort of obelisk standing guard out front. For some reason she'd been expecting a modern glass building, but she should have known nothing so out of place would have been allowed near Santa Fe's historic downtown.

As soon as everyone got out of the SUV, the front doors to the building opened, and Zahrias and a man Julia didn't recognize emerged. Not that she really had eyes for anyone except the djinn leader. He wore his usual garb of an open silk robe over his full silken pants, that robe revealing the sculpted muscles of his chest and stomach.

Julia swallowed, then lifted her head and approached him and his party, while her own companions trailed along behind her. Vanity had made her touch up the light cosmetics she wore and make sure her hair was brushed, but if she'd changed out of the jeans and T-shirt and leather jacket she was wearing earlier that afternoon, someone might have noticed. Besides, she doubted that Zahrias cared what she looked like.

"Welcome," he said. "Was it a smooth journey?"

"Yes, thank you," she replied. Somehow his formality made this first encounter after so many months a little easier. "Clear roads all the way."

At that moment, Miles nudged his way forward, Lindsay at his elbow. "I'd like to see the cell—"

Something that might have been a hint of a smile pulled at the corner of Zahrias' mouth. "Of course, Dr. Odekirk. Let us show you." He turned toward Julia. "It is rather confined down there, however, so if some of your people could remain up here—"

"Sure," she said. "Miles and Lindsay can come with us, and everyone else can keep an eye on the Suburban."

One of the djinn's eyebrows lifted. "I assure you, your vehicle is quite safe here."

"I'm sure it is," she replied, trying to ignore the unwelcome thrill that went through her as Zahrias' dark eyes met hers. "But it'll give them something to do."

Brent Sanderson shot her the side-eye at that remark, but he didn't say anything, and Nancy and Eric seemed content to stand on the steps and watch the sun set. So Julia followed Zahrias inside as his sole companion fell in with them.

"This is David," the djinn leader said, indicating the mortal who was with him, an extremely good-looking man of about twenty-five, with dark hair and bright blue eyes. "He was the one on duty when Margolis disappeared."

David obviously wasn't too happy to be introduced that way. His jaw tightened, and he gave a reluctant nod. "I was gone a minute, max."

"I don't think anyone's blaming you," Julia said, making sure she sounded calm and composed, even though part of her wanted to scream at him for going to take a bathroom break and thus giving Margolis the opening he needed.

They took the elevator —the electricity in Santa Fe seemed to be functioning normally, with none of the rationing her people were forced to use in Los Alamos—and descended several floors. Julia was beginning to wonder just how deeply the jail cell in question was buried when the elevator finally stopped and its doors opened on a bleak hallway painted institutional gray.

"This way," Zahrias said, leading them to a short corridor that terminated in a single chamber.

Looking at it, Julia couldn't help but be reminded of Hannibal Lecter's cell in *The Silence of the Lambs*—this room was also fronted by glass, not bars, and larger than she'd imagined. The similarity ended there, however, because otherwise it looked sleek and modern, the bed with its flat mattress somehow attached to one wall, the basin and toilet set up in the same way. On the bed was a thick abandoned paperback, although she couldn't make out the title from where she stood.

On the wall next to the cell was a panel with a few blinking lights and a surface of smooth black glass. She guessed that must be the biometric scanner.

Miles went to it at once, then put his thumb on the glass. The cell door opened smoothly.

"Hey," David said in injured tones. "I thought only Zahrias or one of us four guards could open that thing."

"I programmed my thumbprint into it when I was testing the device," Miles responded, sounding somewhat testy.

Despite the situation, Julia couldn't help grinning. "Well, mystery solved. Miles did it."

Zahrias shook his head, as if to show that he wasn't amused by her comment, and Miles said indignantly, "I most certainly did not. I was working in my lab, thirty-five miles away from here. Lindsay can attest to that fact."

Lindsay looked like she was trying to stifle her own grin. "I think she was kidding, Miles."

"That is not something you should joke about." He narrowed his eyes behind his glasses and then transferred his attention to Zahrias. "At any rate, it seems the biometric scanner is working normally. Let us inspect the door mechanism. Lindsay, if you could—"

She moved forward at his gesture. "What do you need?"

"I'm going to open and close the door several more times, using the biometric scanner. Keep an eye out for anything that looks out of alignment, indicating that the door might have been tampered with."

She nodded, then crossed her arms and waited while Miles engaged the scanner once more. The cell door slid open smoothly. Julia couldn't see anything wrong with it, but she'd be the first to admit that she was no expert.

"I'm not noticing anything," Lindsay said after this operation was performed several more times.

"Neither am I." Miles pushed his glasses up on his nose and turned back to the watching group. "So if the door wasn't tampered with, then the most logical explanation is that Captain Margolis had an accomplice of some kind."

"If you're suggesting—" David spluttered, hands balling into fists as he shot an angry glare at the scientist.

Julia hoped that Zahrias would contain the situation, because David looked like he could pound Miles into the ground like a tent stake. Apparently the djinn leader was having the same thought, because he stepped forward and said sternly, "That is a theory I cannot support. All of the guards, both human and djinn, who were set to watch over Margolis owed their loyalty only to this community. They would have no reason to do such a thing."

During the confrontation, Lindsay had said nothing, apparently confident that Zahrias wouldn't let matters get too out of hand. Julia remembered that Lindsay had spent a good deal of time around him, since she had been Chosen back then and had lived with the djinn community for months. She must have had a fairly accurate idea of what Zahrias would and would not put up with.

Now she said, "All right, maybe not any of the guards, but what about someone else here in Santa Fe? Maybe they could have reprogrammed the lock."

"Who?" Zahrias inquired, looking almost amused. "You lived among us for some time, Lindsay. You were the only one of our Chosen with any true scientific or mechanical aptitude. Perhaps you would have the skill to do such a thing, but can you say the same of any of your former compatriots?"

She hesitated, then shook her head. "No. And actually, I don't think even I could have done it. That is, I watched Miles set it up, so maybe now I could manage the job, but before that, trying to figure it out on my own?" Her shoulders lifted. "No way."

"So does that put us back to square one?" Julia asked. Frustration had seeped into her tone, but right then she didn't much care.

"No," Miles said, returning his attention to the cell. "The answer has to be here somewhere."

"And if anyone can find it, you will," Zahrias said. "But we are coming to the time of our evening meal, and perhaps this is something you can revisit in the morning. Surely you would like to be shown where you will be staying tonight."

"Later," Miles replied with an irritated wave of his hand. Lindsay looked exasperated, but clearly she knew better than to bother contradicting him. "Have someone bring us a tray or something."

Once again Zahrias' mouth quirked. "If that is your wish. But surely the rest of your party should be accommodated—"

"Yes, thank you," Julia put in quickly, before Miles could start making decisions for the rest of the team. "I don't want to interrupt the other three guards if they're having dinner, but if I could talk to them tomorrow morning?"

"Of course. That was already my plan."

She should have thought of that. Yes, she needed to speak with them, but making them delay their evening meal or otherwise interrupt their evening wouldn't put Margolis back in his cell. Those conversations could wait a few hours.

Besides, her stomach was reminding her that she hadn't really eaten lunch today, only a few slices of toast and half an apple around ten in the morning. Best to let Miles continue with his investigation—although she doubted he would turn up anything—while the rest of them got something to eat.

"Thank you, Zahrias," she said. "Then please, show us where we'll be staying."

He had chosen the La Fonda hotel because of its central location and because he knew Julia and several of her party were familiar with it. They seemed more than pleased with the group of rooms he had secured for them, and perhaps a little surprised that they should be ready on such short notice.

"I really wasn't expecting this," Julia told him as the hard-faced blonde woman who had accompanied her went into the room she'd been assigned—accompanied by a trim, compact man whose calm, appraising eyes told Zahrias he was not quite as innocuous as he seemed. A warrior, like the woman he was with. Nancy, that was what Julia had called her.

"It is the least we could do," Zahrias said. It was more difficult than he'd thought, to stand here next to her and force himself not to gaze too long at the fullness of her mouth, or the way the light seemed to shimmer along the lengths of her unbound hair. She was dressed plainly, but the slightly oversized leather jacket she wore couldn't quite hide the curves of her body. "You would not have had to come here at all, were it not for our negligence."

"That might be a bit harsh—" she began, but he shook his head.

"Yes, negligence, even if it was not intentional. These days we do not dine in a group, as we did back in Taos, but Phillip has come here to the hotel to prepare a meal for you so you may all eat in the dining room downstairs."

Julia nodded. Was that a flicker of disappointment he saw in her clear blue-gray eyes, the color of the morning sky just before the sun rose? No, he must be imagining things. He could see no reason why she would be disappointed to be so accommodated, unless...

...unless she had wished to dine with him alone.

He pushed that thought aside. There could be nothing between them. She had her duty to the people of Los Alamos, just as he had his duty to the djinn and Chosen who lived in Santa Fe.

"That sounds wonderful, Zahrias," she said. "Thank you."

Her words sounded sincere enough, but he noted the briefest of hesitations before she spoke. From the very first time he'd met her, he had sensed something about Julia that was almost too controlled, as if she had to measure every word and every deed before she spoke or acted. Now she seemed even more restrained. Was that because of the situation they now found themselves in...or because she was having a difficult time being around him once again?

If it was the latter possibility, he could understand her restraint all too well, for he found himself holding back, knowing they had never shared one word that could not be safely overheard by another. He wanted her, but he would not allow himself to have her—even if she wanted him just as fiercely.

"You are more than welcome," he said, knowing as he spoke that he sounded too stiff, too formal. But what else could he do? "I will leave you now, so that you may settle yourselves before dinner, but I will come for you in the morning so you may speak with the other guards. I assume that the tenth hour of the morning would not be too early?"

"Not too early at all." A flicker of a smile played around her mouth, and Zahrias had to force himself not to stare at her lips, so full, so soft. "I'm usually up hours before that."

"I will see you then." He bowed slightly, then turned away and strode off down the corridor toward the elevator. That contraption was not his destination, however; he merely wished to be out of sight before he used his powers to transport himself from the hotel to the library in the house he now occupied. For some reason, he did not wish Julia to see him disappear in such a way, for it would only reinforce how very different they were from one another.

Zahrias did not quite wish to ponder why that fact should bother him so much.

"He's an odd one, isn't he?" Brent Sanderson remarked.

Julia sat with Brent because Nancy and Eric had paired themselves off at a table for two over in the corner, clearly not wanting to squander this rare chance for a romantic meal together, and Miles and Lindsay were still nowhere to be found. Julia had to hope they'd eat something at some point, but she supposed that wasn't her problem. They were grown adults, and she wasn't their babysitter.

Anyway, the food was amazing. Julia didn't know how Phillip had managed to throw together stuffed quail and rice and steamed fall vegetables, accompanied by the kind of fresh-baked bread she hadn't tasted since the world ended, but she wouldn't argue with the end result.

If only she could have shared it with someone other than Brent.

Not that she didn't like Brent. She liked him very much. He was a good man, and an important part of the Los Alamos community. But he was certainly no Zahrias.

"Well," she said, making sure she sounded as unconcerned as possible, "he *is* a djinn, after all."

"True." Brent sipped some of his wine, looking as if he wanted to grimace but wouldn't allow himself to. She had a feeling he was more a beer guy, but of course Phillip would never dream of allowing someone to drink a Budweiser with one of his finely crafted meals and had served a truly lovely pinot noir from the hotel's cellars to accompany their dinner. "Maybe that's it. I haven't really been around them much—just that little bit in the spring when Margolis dragged us all over here. Although the one Jessica is with seems like a nice guy."

"He is," Julia replied. There was an understatement. Jace was strong, determined, and passionately devoted to the woman he had chosen. Jessica Monroe was one lucky girl. "Most of them are."

Brent raised an eyebrow at that remark.

"All right, the ones here in Santa Fe," she amended. "Obviously, there's a whole group of them who aren't nice people at all. But the ones who tried to save humanity, who're with their Chosen—they're good. Different from us, but good."

"If you say so." Brent scooped up a forkful of rice and chewed before adding, "Just between you and me, I'll be glad to be back in Los Alamos. It feels weird to be here."

His commented startled her a bit. "Weird how?"

A lift of his thin shoulders. "I don't know. Just...I mean, look at this dining room."

"What about it?"

"It's like...nothing changed. The lights are on, and they've lit the little candles on the tables, and we're eating a meal that could be right off a menu from before." He didn't elaborate on what he meant by "before." He didn't have to. Everyone's existence had been forever divided between now and the world before the Heat. "But the only reason it's like that here is because this town is run by djinn, and they can use their powers for whatever they want, including making it seem like the world is the same as it always was."

Julia picked up her glass and sipped some wine. Lush fruit spilled over her tongue, so much more complex than anything they had back in Los Alamos. "You say that like it's a bad thing."

A pause then, while Brent's brows knitted together, as if he was wrestling with a thought he wasn't sure he quite knew how to articulate. "But...I think it is. The world *has* changed—changed because of them, even if the ones here in Santa Fe didn't have anything to do with the Dying. We need to acknowledge that so we can move forward. Because all the candlelit dinners in the world can't change the fact that nothing will ever be the same again."

Abruptly, Julia set down her glass. The wine she had just drunk seemed to turn bitter on her tongue, although she knew it hadn't changed—she had. Or at least her thoughts had. "No, it won't be the same," she said at length, after she had sat there, silent, for a long moment, one finger tracing the curved edge of the wine glass's base. "I guess I was hoping it would be okay to pretend a little bit, though."

Brent's face fell. "I'm sorry, Julia. I—I didn't mean to spoil your dinner or anything. I mean, it must be tough enough for you, what with Margolis—"

"I don't want to talk about him," she cut in. "Because that *will* spoil my dinner. Let's talk about something else."

"Like?"

"I don't know. Like...what's your best guess on how our gasoline supplies will hold up this winter?"

Brent shook his head. "You call that stimulating dinner conversation?"

"It's important, isn't it?" She'd been tracking their gas supplies on her endless spreadsheets, but since he was in charge of the motor pool and did the actual dispensing of the precious fuel, he had a better idea of how seriously people were taking her efforts at conservation.

"Well, yeah." He pushed some rice around on his plate, then said, "I think we'll be okay. We've yet to tap all the gas stations in Española, and there's stuff in some of the outlying areas as well if we need it. And then everything in Albuquerque, if we decide to venture that far afield—"

He went on, plain, honest features serious as he weighed their various options. Julia let him keep talking, because then she didn't have to speak, could nod at the appropriate intervals and act as if she was absorbing everything he had to say. The subject was an important one, and deserved her attention. She couldn't seem to make herself focus, however. Her thoughts kept straying to Zahrias.

She would see him the next morning. That wasn't so long from now. And then....

And then you'll try to remember why the hell you're here, she told herself grimly. *Get a goddamn grip.*

With a frown, she poured herself some more wine. Coming here was starting to seem like a very bad idea.

CHAPTER FOUR

BY THE TIME ZAHRIAS SHOWED UP AT THE HOTEL to collect her, Julia thought she'd more or less gotten her thoughts together. She wouldn't let herself thrill at the sound of his voice, or do anything but briefly note that he wore yet another of his open embroidered robes, even though the weather had clouded up and the air had a distinct bite to it as they exited the hotel lobby.

He probably doesn't even notice, she thought. *He's a fire elemental, after all. He could probably stand bare-chested in a blizzard and not bat an eyelash.*

And she promptly pushed that mental image as far from her thoughts as she could. Bad enough that his clothing revealed as much as it did. But to think of him with that robe gone, showing the heavy muscles in his chest and arms and shoulders....

She'd been right. Coming here was not a good idea at all.

Somehow she managed to keep it together as they went back to the U.S. Marshals' building. Zahrias seemed to think that she would want to check in on Miles and Lindsay before sitting down with the other three guards, the ones who hadn't been on duty when Margolis escaped. Julia went along with Zahrias' wishes, even though her policy had always been to let Miles do more or less what he wanted and then wait for him—or, more often, Lindsay—to report on his findings.

The two of them looked cross and rumpled enough to have spent the night down in the bowels of the building, although Julia hoped that wasn't the case. Lindsay was propped up against the wall, arms folded over her chest, while Miles had his iPad attached to the biometric scanner next to the door. The scowl he wore was fierce in the extreme.

"That good?" Julia asked.

Miles didn't even look up at her. "No, it's not good at all. I can't find any evidence of tampering. No one has altered the programming of the scanner, and the door itself is also untouched."

"All of which has to point to someone on the out-side helping him," Lindsay added. "And someone who's got to be a djinn. There's no human being in Santa Fe who could've gotten Margolis out of there without leaving any trace at all."

That was a prospect Julia hadn't really wanted to contemplate. Why on earth would one of Zahrias' people want to let Margolis out? They knew that he'd tortured Jace, had outright killed Natila, one of their own. Julia sent a sideways glance at Zahrias, whose brows were drawn together, his dark eyes seeming to smolder in an echo of the flames that flickered in and out of existence around him.

"I cannot believe that," he said at length, voice taut with pent-up anger. "My people's hatred of Margolis runs deep. They will never forget what he did to Natila."

A sudden thought came to Julia. Seeing the forbidding frown on Zahrias' features, she almost held her tongue. But surely they'd need to explore every possibility...even the unpleasant ones. "What if—" she began, then broke off, wondering if they'd all think she had gone too far.

"What if what?" Lindsay asked, pushing herself away from the wall.

Julia glanced at Zahrias. His frown was still in place, had etched itself deeper, if anything. But even that scowl couldn't distort the symmetry of his features. She pulled in a breath and said, "What if one of the djinn here in Santa Fe did release him...so they could get their revenge for what he did to Natila and Jace?"

A long silence greeted her question. Miles looked up from his iPad, expression both curious and surprised, as if he wished he'd thought of that theory. Lindsay's gaze shifted to Zahrias and then back to Julia, startled.

Finally, however, the djinn leader shook his head. "No, I do not think that is the explanation. Not," he went on, lifting a hand when Julia began to open her mouth, "because I do not believe none of them are capable of such a thing, but because if they had truly wished to seek vengeance for Margolis' wrongdoings, they would have done so long before now. Also, I live among them and see them every day. While they may still hold anger in their hearts toward him, they have all appeared to accept his punishment. A life in the four walls of a prison cell is no life at all, perhaps far worse than a swift death might have been."

Julia wished she could argue with him, but, as he had just said, he lived here and knew the people who now looked to him as their leader. Zahrias was many things, but she didn't believe he lacked in perception. If one of the djinn here in Santa Fe had harbored such a murderous fury toward Margolis that they had broken him out just to kill him, Zahrias would have known.

"Then I guess we're back to nothing," she said, feeling far more tired than she should have, given the comfortable room she'd slept in the night before and the excellent breakfast she'd eaten before coming here.

But she still had the three remaining guards to interview. Maybe they'd be able to provide some insights. She lifted her chin and looked over at Zahrias. He still wore that same troubled expression, although it seemed to soften slightly as their eyes met.

Her breath caught. Damn, she really needed to figure out a way to keep herself from reacting to him every time they were in the same room. At least Miles and Lindsay didn't seem to have noticed anything; Miles had returned to typing on his iPad's screen, and Lindsay just looked annoyed, as if she thought she must be overlooking something obvious.

"Let us hope not," Zahrias said then. "Come—I'll take you to speak with the other guards now."

Weariness was evident in the droop of Julia's shoulders, but she seemed businesslike enough as she sat down at the long table in one of the building's conference rooms and folded her hands on top of the pale wood surface. Zahrias sat down next to her, trying to keep himself from breathing in the subtle perfume that seemed to waft gently from her hair. To be this close was almost intoxicating. Perhaps he should not have sat so close. But no, that would have been far too obvious. It made sense that the two of them would sit thus, while the three guards they wished to question arranged themselves across the table.

Two djinn, one human. Zahrias could see Julia's eyes flicker with surprise as she realized one of the djinn guards was female; apparently she hadn't been expecting that. Alshira had lost her Chosen, Clay, to the rogue djinn Khalim and his followers. She had no reason to stay here in Santa Fe, but she did, mourning the untimely death of her lover. And when Zahrias had put out the call, saying he needed those who could give up something of their lives so that Margolis would be guarded at all times, she had been among the first to answer his request. The other djinn was Murrah, whose Chosen, Martine, had been captured and abused by Khalim. Zahrias knew the two lovers had had a difficult time becoming one with another again, and so Murrah had accepted guard duty as a way of giving Martine more time to come to terms with what had happened to her.

And the fourth guard, Lewis Turnbull. His djinn lover had not been overly happy about Lewis taking on guard duty, but he'd insisted. Why? Was it so he could wait for an opportunity to free the captive? Why Lewis would want to do such a thing, Zahrias had no idea, but he would be the first to admit that he did not always understand mortals' thought processes. At the same time, he had allowed Lewis to take the position, hoping that by doing so he would show that he trusted the mortals in his community as much as he trusted the djinn.

Julia spoke then. "I appreciate you coming here to discuss Margolis' escape. I realize that none of you were on duty when he disappeared, but I thought speaking with you might help me understand what might have happened."

"I understand," Alshira said. Unlike most djinn women, who allowed their hair to flow free, Alshira's long black locks were drawn back into a severe braid. She had taken Clay's death hard. Zahrias had not counseled her to look for a replacement. Where would she even begin such a search, when the rest of their kind were busy making sure that no humans who were not already chosen had been scoured from the earth?

"And I," Murrah put in, his voice a soft rumble.

"Anything I can do to help you find out what happened," Lewis said. His mouth looked tense, although Zahrias knew that could have been for any number of reasons.

Julia smiled at all of them. What must it cost her, to appear pleasant and polite, when the man who had violated her was now free? Zahrias didn't know. What he did know was that he would show Margolis no mercy if he should encounter the mortal ever again. The man's neck would be snapped like a twig before he had a chance to open his mouth.

"Thank you," she said, still smiling. "I guess this question is for all of you. Did you notice anything different about Margolis over the past few days or even weeks, something that might signal he was planning an escape?"

The three guards exchanged glances. Alshira spoke first. "No. He read a good deal. We would bring him books from the town library, but only one at a time. He did not speak to me much. He does not like djinn, I think."

If anything, Alshira had understated the case. Margolis' pathological hatred of djinn was well known. While Zahrias could understand that antipathy, he thought it entirely misdirected. The djinn here in Santa Fe would have left him alone...if only he had possessed the presence of mind to leave them alone as well. His treatment of Jasreel and Natila, however, could not be overlooked.

"Yes, that much was obvious," Murrah said. "He did not like to say anything to me. Even when he wanted a new book from the library, he would write down his request on a slip of paper and give it to me so he would not have to speak."

"Paper?" Julia echoed. "He had paper with him in his cell?"

"Yes," Murrah replied. "He had a little book and a pencil. To write down his thoughts, I believe. I saw him writing in it a good deal."

"There was nothing like that in his cell," Julia said. Her tone sounded almost accusatory, and Zahrias caught the quick, sidelong glance she sent him through her thick eyelashes.

"No," Zahrias told her. He had inspected the cell himself, and the only thing there besides the furnishings was the one paperbound book Margolis had left lying open on the bed. "It is true that we did allow him his diary. But he must have taken it with him wherever he went."

Julia did not look very pleased by that revelation. Not that Zahrias could blame her, for Margolis' diary might have contained a good deal of useful information, including the identity of the person who had helped him to escape. However, whatever that mortal's faults, stupidity was not one of them. He would never have left anything incriminating behind where his captors might find it.

But then he saw her shoulders lift. Her gaze fastened on Lewis Turnbull. "What about you? Did he ever speak with you?"

Lewis hesitated. "Sometimes."

"About?"

The mortal's features hardened. He was a muscular man with thick, close-cropped brown hair and blue eyes. Perhaps a woman might have found him handsome. Clearly, his djinn partner Rosala thought he was. "About how I could be a traitor to my kind."

Julia didn't flinch at the sharp tone in the man's voice. "Because you're with a djinn?"

"Yes, ma'am."

Something about her mouth seemed to soften then. Zahrias wished he could have been the one who had prompted that easing of the tension in her face. But then, he wished for many things, most of which would never come true.

"Did that bother you?"

"No, ma'am."

Her head tilted to one side, and a few heavy locks of dark gold hair slipped over her shoulder. Allah, what hair that woman had. It made Zahrias want to bury his face in it, breathe it in. Breathe *her* in.

"Which branch were you, Lewis?"

He didn't pretend to misunderstand. "Army reserve, same as Margolis." A pause, and then Lewis added, "Well, not the same as Margolis, but you take my meaning."

"I do. Did Margolis give you any crap about that? I mean, on top of being a traitor to your race?"

"Yes, ma'am, he did. Not that I paid him any mind, because as far as I was concerned, he'd forfeited his right to a high horse because of what he did to Natila and Jace, what he did to—"

"Thanks for that, Lewis." The interruption was done so smoothly that perhaps some people might not have even noticed, but Zahrias knew that Julia had spoken in the way she did because she wanted no reminders here of the atrocities Margolis had visited on her. Rage flared within him, but he knew he had to keep it tamped down. It wouldn't do for the others in the room to realize his anger toward Margolis was a little too personal.

Lewis leaned forward over the table, his hands flat on the smooth surface. "That's why I volunteered for guard duty, ma'am. I felt like—like he'd made me look bad, made everyone who served look bad. The least I could do was keep an eye on him and make sure he couldn't hurt anyone ever again."

To either side of the mortal man, Alshira and Murrah nodded. Their expressions were equally grim. Zahrias could see nothing in either of their aspects that would suggest they had been complicit in Margolis' escape.

It seemed that Julia was thinking more or less the same thing, for she settled back in her seat and let out a breath that wasn't quite a sigh. "Thank you, Lewis," she said. Her voice was calm enough, but Zahrias thought he could hear the faintest tremor behind it. It seemed obvious enough to him that she had hoped one of the guards would betray him- or herself, give something away to prove that Margolis had been assisted in his escape.

"We wish we could tell you more," Alshira added, her tone gentler than it normally was these days. "But truly, the prisoner did not wish to speak to us. He always seemed...preoccupied."

"Preoccupied?" Julia asked.

"As if his thoughts were elsewhere. Which I suppose I can understand, for if one is confined to a cell
only a few handspans wide and deep, then what else
can one do but cast one's thoughts someplace else?"

A nod, and then Julia turned toward him. Her face
was almost too calm. He knew she must be struggling
with her disappointment, for truly he had felt that
same too-calm expression on his own features more
often than he would like.

"I can't think of anything else," she said. "So...."

"So that will be all for now," he said, addressing his
words to the three guards who watched them. "Thank
you for coming to speak with us."

They all nodded and murmured commonplaces
that more or less stated they did not mind at all. Then
they got up and let themselves out of the room.

"Well, damn," Julia said, once only she and Zahrias
remained. "I was hoping one of them would incrimi-
nate themselves. That is, it would have been awful, but
at least then we would have known what happened."

"I understand," he replied, and he did. Loose ends
set him on edge. Seeing the worried look in her eyes,
he went on, "I do not know if this will reassure you
or not, but my people have been scouring the area
around Santa Fe and have found no trace of Margolis.
Wherever he went, it is nowhere near here."

"I suppose that's some reassurance." She pushed her chair away from the table and stood. "Now I suppose I should see how Miles is getting on. If he's not making any progress, then we should probably pack our things and get back to Los Alamos. Obviously, we're not doing any good here."

A pang went through Zahrias at these words, but he made himself nod. He could not protest her leaving, not without betraying how much he wanted her to stay.

They left the conference room and headed downstairs, where Lindsay was now crawling around on the floor of the cell and appearing to take some kind of measurements, and Miles was still tapping away on that flat-screened contraption he appeared unwilling to let go. Lindsay shot a long-suffering glance up at Zahrias and Julia as they approached but didn't say anything. If Miles had even noticed their arrival, he gave no sign of it.

"Um, Miles," Julia ventured after a few awkward seconds had passed.

"What?" he snapped.

Zahrias wanted to tell him to keep a civil tongue in his head when speaking to Julia Innes, but he forbore. Everyone seemed to ignore the scientist's rudeness, perhaps because otherwise, he had proved to be quite useful.

"I've talked to the other guards, and they don't have anything to contribute, either. I really think we need to pack it in and go home."

That statement did cause Miles Odekirk to lift his head and give Julia a narrow-eyed glare from behind the spectacles he wore. "Now?"

"Well, yes. I mean, as soon as we can get all our stuff together."

"That would not be prudent."

Julia's eyebrows lifted. "Why not?"

"Because I am unwilling to give up after so little time has passed. One more night here couldn't make that much of a difference, could it?"

"Most of a day and then a night," she pointed out. "Since it's not even noon yet."

"All the better. That may give me enough time."

She shifted her weight from one foot to the other, clearly uncomfortable. Was she concerned about spending that much time away from Los Alamos...or was she simply worried about what might occur if she extended her stay here in Santa Fe?

Zahrias hardly dared to breathe. Logically, he knew it would be better if she packed up and left this afternoon, removing all temptation from his world. But he knew he wanted her to stay. All the intervening months since he had last seen her now seemed empty, barren. She brought light and life to every room she inhabited. Would it be so terrible after all, if something happened between them?

At length she gave a reluctant nod. "Okay, Miles. One more night. But after that we really have to go. All right?"

"Hmm." Now that she'd relented, Odekirk had already transferred his attention back to the device he held.

A rueful shrug, and Julia turned toward Zahrias. "I'm sorry—it looks as if we'll have to prevail on your hospitality for another night."

"It is no intrusion, I assure you." A thought came to him, one he hoped would please her. "Since you are extending your stay, perhaps you would like to visit with Jasreel and Jessica? I am sure they would be happy to see you."

A sunrise of a smile spread over her features. "Oh, that would be wonderful. I wished I might be able to see them, but I knew we had more important things to do."

"Then let me contact Jasreel. Such a visit should make the time pass more swiftly."

Still smiling, Julia nodded.

And if I give you to them for the afternoon, Zahrias thought, surely they will not mind if I borrow you for dinner....

Jessica and Jace's home was like a little slice of heaven on earth. Julia had heard her friend talk about the house with longing, even when she and Jace were ensconced in a high-end place only a few blocks from the Plaza, and at the time Julia could only wonder what it was about the house well outside the outskirts of town that made it so special. Now that she was here, though, she could understand what Jessica had meant. Every piece in the house seemed to have been chosen particularly to work with its pueblo architecture, but the charm of the place went far beyond the interior decoration.

No, there was something about the way the breeze ruffled the gold-crowned aspens that ringed the property, and the way the warm late-September light slanted through the windows, glowing on the terra-cotta tiles that covered the floors. Everything was neat and clean and tidy, from the house itself to the vegetable garden off to the side and the large walled yard with its complement of goats. Even though they probably hadn't lit a fire in months, the place still smelled faintly of wood smoke, welcoming, familiar.

Both Jace and Jessica had already heard the news about Margolis' escape, but they also seemed to realize that Julia didn't want to discuss the subject, not on this gold-washed afternoon where the clouds from earlier that morning seemed to have dissipated, along with the tension in her neck and shoulders. Maybe that was a result of telling herself she simply couldn't do any more than she already had, and to let it go and relax. Or maybe it was just being here in this magical spot that seemed so far away from any of her problems.

"We're making some really good goat cheese now, too," Jessica said. The three of them had retired to the living room after Jessica had given Julia the nickel tour of the property. A bottle of white wine, nicely chilled, sat on the coffee table. The wine was from Black Mesa winery, reinforcing Julia's idea that she really needed to get an expedition out there one of these days to load up on supplies for Los Alamos. "Jace has been talking about getting some sheep, too."

"You ever think you'd end up as a farmer?" Julia asked him, only slightly teasing. Truth was, they all needed to be farmers now. The days of walking into a supermarket and getting anything you wanted were long gone.

"No," Jace said with a grin, "but it appears I have some talent for it. And Jessica tends to accommodate my whims."

"Only because they're usually damn smart ideas," she replied.

"So you don't mind being so far away from the others?"

Jessica and Jace glanced at each other briefly, and then they both shook their heads. "Not really," she said. "After all, we can be in town in the blink of an eye, and we go in once or twice a week to bring Phillip some of our latest offerings, or to check in with every-one. But they're still...." She let the words hang there, as if she wasn't quite sure of the best way to express what she was trying to say.

"They're still living like djinn," Jace explained. His tone was even. Julia couldn't sense any condemnation in his words, but somehow she could tell he was slightly frustrated with his fellow elementals. "They think I'm a fool for working the land like a mortal. Why bother, when I can just snap my fingers and have whatever I want?"

"Is that how it works?" Julia inquired, intrigued. She'd seen various djinn use their powers on occasion, but she still didn't have a very good idea as to how they managed to keep Santa Fe functioning, with power and food and anything else its small band of residents might need.

"More or less," Jace said with a shrug. "That is, they can't conjure the materials out of nothing, but as long as the raw ingredients exist somewhere in this world, they can make their meals and their clothes appear as if from nowhere. They provide the power that runs the lights and keeps the water flowing and the heat on. To an elemental, it's a mere trickle, something we don't even notice giving away."

"Must be nice," Julia remarked, trying not to sound envious. After all, she knew that everyone in Los Alamos was lucky to have electric lights and warm showers—even if those showers were limited to five minutes each.

"It is…on the surface. But it's also a crutch. The djinn have taken this world for their own, but they don't seem too eager to live in it with any respect for its resources."

"Besides," Jessica added with a grin, "chopping wood and herding goats has given Jace some awesome muscles."

"I had those already," he protested, and Jessica chuckled.

Watching them, Julia felt another stab of envy. They seemed so easy with one another, even more so than the djinn she'd seen with their Chosen in Santa Fe. Maybe it was because Jace and Jessica interacted with one another as equals, not as a magical being and the mortal he'd deigned to choose. Whatever the reason, she knew they were both damn lucky, for multiple reasons.

And Julia—well, she supposed she'd get her life figured out sooner or later. Being around Zahrias had been difficult, but she didn't think she'd done anything to arouse his suspicions or make him believe that she saw him as anything other than a colleague. True, he'd asked to have dinner with her tonight, but he'd quickly added that he thought it would give them the opportunity to discuss how their respective communities were faring. Nothing in his voice or expression had seemed to indicate he expected anything more than that.

"So," Jessica said, abandoning the topic of Jace's muscles, "you're having dinner with Zahrias tonight. What are you going to wear?"

"What I have on," Julia replied calmly. "We're just going to discuss business."

"Uh-huh."

Jace chuckled, then sobered as Julia lifted an eyebrow in his direction. After retrieving his wine glass, he settled back against the sofa cushions, apparently content to let the women argue this one.

"Zahrias is a very formal person," Jessica said. "I don't know how he'd feel about a dinner guest showing up in jeans."

"Well, that's all I brought," Julia told her, feeling irritated. "Have you forgotten the reason why I'm here in Santa Fe in the first place?"

The smile faded from Jessica's lips. "No, I hadn't forgotten," she said quietly. "But you've done everything you could on that front, so you might as well make a good impression tonight. Hang on."

She got up from the sofa and headed down the hall that led to the bedrooms. Once they were alone, Julia turned to Jace. "Do you know what she's up to?"

"Not at all. But I suppose we'll find out in a minute."

As they did, because Jessica returned a few minutes later carrying some lengths of teal-colored fabric draped over one arm. In her other hand, she had a pair of high-heeled brown boots. Julia stared at them for a moment, and then shook her head in recognition.

"Where on earth did you get those?"

"I rescued them after I saw that you'd left them behind when you went back to Los Alamos." Jessica laid the top and its matching skirt down on the cushion of the love seat where Julia was sitting. "And the jewelry. I stuck it in the skirt pocket."

"Jessica, I—" Breaking off, Julia could only shake her head. Yes, she had left the lovely outfit behind when she vacated the townhouse where she'd been living in Santa Fe. She hadn't seen any reason to bring the clothes with her, since she'd known she'd be too busy running Los Alamos to worry about having any fancy outfits.

Besides, she could recall all too well the sudden flash of admiration, quickly hidden, that she'd seen in Zahrias' eyes when he first saw her wearing those clothes.

"Just take them," Jessica said. "You don't want to offend Zahrias, do you?"

No, Julia supposed she didn't.

CHAPTER FIVE

Dᴜʀɪɴɢ ᴛʜᴇ ᴡᴀʀᴍ sᴜᴍᴍᴇʀ ᴍᴏɴᴛʜs, Zᴀʜʀɪᴀs had enjoyed sitting at the table in the courtyard and consuming his meals there, but he knew the nights now were too cold for such an arrangement to be comfortable for Julia. Instead, he planned to sit down with her in the dining room. The table seemed small and somewhat mean to him, as it could only accommodate twelve and no more, but since it would only be the two of them, he supposed that didn't matter.

He recalled that she had enjoyed the meals Phillip prepared, and so he enlisted the mortal man to create the menu and prepare the dishes. Not wishing to impose too much on that worthy individual, Zahrias made sure that Phillip could do all the cooking during the afternoon and be done in time to prepare another fine meal for Julia's party so they wouldn't feel too abandoned. It would be easy enough to keep everything warm until the appointed hour.

Besides that, Zahrias made sure the table was covered in a fine cloth of ivory linen, and two place settings of porcelain were laid out just so, along with oversized goblets of blown glass. The dining room had a fine sideboard of dark carved wood, and he collected candle holders from throughout the house and set them there.

Would she think it too much? Difficult to say. He always dined by candlelight because he enjoyed it, but he couldn't guess what Julia's reaction might be. Humans seemed to think of candles as "romantic," rather than as a useful alternative to harsh electric light. Ah, well. In his heart of hearts, he rather hoped she might get the wrong impression.

Jace had promised to bring Julia back to her hotel once she was done with her visit, and so Zahrias had little to do except wait for the appointed hour. He revisited the dining room several times to make sure that everything was just as it should be, and spent a great deal of time deciding on the best wine to accompany the elk tenderloin Phillip had prepared. The people who had owned this house were long gone, but they had left behind a very impressive wine cellar.

In the end, Zahrias chose a cabernet franc and opened it to let it air. Just as he was setting the bottle down, the doorbell rang.

Djinn had no need of watches, for they sensed the passage of time as easily as they breathed. Mortal divisions of time were more difficult, but Zahrias had become accustomed enough to them to know that Julia was right there at the hour he had specified.

He went to the door and opened it, then did his best to keep from staring. For Julia was not wearing the jeans and leather jacket she'd had on earlier, but a flowing ensemble in a dark teal tone that brought out the burnished highlights in her golden hair. It looked vaguely familiar to him, and he realized he'd seen her wear that outfit once before, back in Taos before the community had relocated here to Santa Fe. Had she brought it with her? No, that seemed unlikely. Julia had thought she would be back in Los Alamos by now. She certainly wouldn't have packed anything so impractical.

"Good evening," he said, relieved that his tone sounded smooth enough. Perhaps she hadn't noticed anything amiss about his reaction.

"Good evening, Zahrias," she replied calmly, stepping into the foyer as he moved aside to let her enter. Once he'd shut the door, she added, "I hope you don't think this is a bit much. Jessica was reading me the riot act about showing up for dinner in jeans."

"Not at all," he assured her. "It was kind of her to think that a dinner here required more formal attire. How are she and Jace?"

"Very well. That's quite the setup they have out there."

"Yes, they've made quite a success of their little farm." Zahrias realized that they still stood in the foyer, and so he gestured toward the dining room. "If you would follow me—"

Julia trailed along behind him as he led her toward their destination. Although she was silent, he could sense the way she was looking around her, taking in her surroundings. According to Jessica, this was quite an impressive house, as things were reckoned here. It seemed small compared to his residence back in the djinn world, but he still would never go back there willingly. At least the sky above this house was blue, and the air fresh to breathe. No wonder his people had coveted this world so much. For himself, well...he would not lie to himself and say that he had not wished to live here, but never at the price the human race had paid.

Her eyes did widen as she entered the dining room. "It's—it's beautiful."

"I'm glad you like it." He went to the place where he wished her to sit and pulled out her chair. Human etiquette; a djinn would have moved the chair with the power of his mind, but he didn't want his actions to discomfit her.

At least, not any more than he had to. After they were both seated and he had poured a measure of wine into each of their glasses, he snapped his fingers once, and the meal Phillip had prepared appeared on the table before them.

Julia blinked. "Now I see what Jace was talking about."

"Indeed? And what did Jace say?" Zahrias was fond of his cousin, but Jasreel did have some very odd notions.

A slight flush tinged Julia's cheeks. "Oh, just that the djinn like to make things easy on themselves."

And what, pray, is wrong with that? But because Zahrias didn't wish to provoke his companion, he replied calmly, "That does sound like something Jasreel would say. Would it make you feel better to know that Phillip prepared this meal? All I did was bring it here from the kitchen."

"Oh, well, in that case...." She reached for her wine glass, then paused, slender fingers wrapped around the stem.

Zahrias thought he understood her hesitation. He lifted his own wine glass and nodded toward her. There were many things he wished he could say in this moment, but he settled for the one he guessed she would find the least worrisome. "To the continued health of both our communities."

"To our health." She raised her glass and drank, giving perhaps the faintest of appreciative nods before she set the glass back down. "Speaking of which, how is Lauren doing?"

He was surprised Julia had thought to ask, but then he realized that she had been communicating with Jessica for many months before returning here to Santa Fe, and so probably knew more of the doings in his community than he had guessed. "Well enough. She has been confined to her bed, since our healer thinks it best that she doesn't exert herself, but her health is good, and the baby seems to be faring well, if somewhat reluctant to make an entrance. We had thought he would be here by now."

"He?" Julia asked. "So you know the sex of the child?"

"No. A slip of the tongue. Perhaps it is only that I think the child will be a boy, as we have few girl children in my family."

She appeared to consider that reply, then nodded. "Well, it would be convenient."

"Convenient?"

Her lips curved in a smile, even as she reached for her wine glass once again. "We just had our first baby in Los Alamos, a girl. So if Lauren and Dani were to have a boy...."

She didn't complete the sentence, but Zahrias understood. By necessity, the two communities must keep their distance for now, but perhaps one day it would be possible for the mortals and djinn and their half-blood children from his community to mingle with the children of Los Alamos, and create a new society that was not either/or, but which included all.

He thought he liked the sound of that.

"It could be a good thing for all of us," he said. "But now, perhaps we should eat."

"Oh, yes. I wouldn't want Phillip's food to get cold."

There was no possibility of that happening, but Zahrias didn't bother to object. Instead, he speared several of the elk medallions with the serving fork and placed them on Julia's plate, then added some of the delicate, thinly sliced potatoes layered with cream and cheese, and long spears of asparagus braised in a sweet wine-based sauce.

"This all looks amazing," she said, staring down at the food on her plate. "So, did Phillip's djinn choose him specifically because he's a Cordon Bleu chef?"

"I know nothing of this Cordon Bleu," Zahrias replied. "But I believe she chose him because she thought he was the mortal in this area best suited for her."

"And all the rest of you benefited from that."

Zahrias couldn't argue with that. Before he had come here to live in this world, he hadn't thought he could eat anything more appetizing than the delicately seasoned dishes of his own people. After sampling Phillip's food for the first time, however, Zahrias realized he might have to admit he'd been wrong in thinking mortal cuisine could never match that of the djinn. "Yes, we did benefit, a great deal."

Julia smiled and fell silent then, clearly intent on enjoying the food that had been set before her. Zahrias followed her lead and ate quietly for a few moments, pausing in between bites to take sips of his wine. Yes, that cabernet franc had been an excellent choice.

Then he asked, "And how are you faring in Los Alamos? Is there anything the community here in Santa Fe can assist you with?"

A flash of surprise in those long-lashed eyes of hers. "We're doing quite well, but thank you for the offer. We had more luck than we'd thought with our vegetable gardens, so we were able to grow a good deal of our food and have managed to put more than we'd hoped aside for the winter." She paused for a moment, seeming to contemplate the bounty on the plate in front of her. "I think we're okay in terms of supplies, but...."

"But?" He wondered what worried her so much that a frown marred her clear brow.

She shifted in her chair so she was turned more toward him. The candlelight shimmered against the fall of her hair, and something about the way the shadows fell over her only seemed to emphasize the enticing curve of her breasts under the silken fabric of her top. Now it was harder than ever for Zahrias to meet her gaze calmly, to arrange an expression on his face that was merely one of concerned interest and nothing more.

"We've been lucky so far," she said. "I don't know if it's that we were all immune to the Heat because overall we have very good immune systems, but we haven't had to deal with any real illnesses. Allergies, Roger Garcia's asthma, but that's about it. The medical center in Los Alamos was pretty well stocked, thank God. But in a few years, those medicines might not be as effective anymore. I suppose that's what really worries me. What if one of us gets sick...really sick? We're really lucky that we have Ellen—she used to be a nurse—with us, but even she can do only so much. Sooner or later we're going to come up against something she can't fix." Julia paused then and gave Zahrias a rueful smile. "Sorry about that. I didn't mean to dump all over you."

"It is fine," he reassured her. Truly, because his own people never had to worry about illness and disease, he'd forgotten what a very great risk those ailments could be to the mortals who'd managed to survive thus far. "We both have our responsibilities, and I think it is important that we can discuss our challenges frankly with one another."

"Well, that's my challenge," she said. "Or at least one of them. It must be a lot easier to be immortal."

"We are not precisely immortal," Zahrias replied, although he made sure to keep his tone neutral so it wouldn't sound as if he was correcting her. "We are exceptionally long-lived, true, and we cannot become ill, but we can still die."

"Of course," Julia murmured, her expression darkening. No doubt she was thinking of Natila, dead at Margolis' hands.

"Yes," he said, "As you know, through injury or accident...or treachery." He spoke quickly, hoping she would not ask for more details. The history of the djinn was a long and bloody one.

"I would assume that's not common, though."

"No." Should he tell her more, speak of the greatest reason why his people were no strangers to death? He found he did not wish to keep secrets from her. "Far more common are those who weary of unending life and wish to move on to the next world. They choose the path of the *aljar al-nawim.*"

"The what?"

"In your tongue, it means 'the draught of the dark sleep.' A subtle poison that brings a calm and painless death."

Shock registered in her eyes, the candle flames shimmering against the darkness of her pupils. "They commit suicide?"

"It does not have quite the same negative connotations as the act does in your world. For those who feel they have nothing left to feel or experience, it is the better path, rather than to remain here and simply... endure."

Julia was silent for a moment, appearing to absorb his words. She reached for her glass and drank—more deeply this time, rather than the small sips she had been taking earlier. Still in silence, she swirled the remainder of the liquid in the goblet, watching as the glow from the candles awoke deep garnet-colored shimmers within the wine.

At last she spoke. "Do your Chosen know about this?"

"I cannot say. That is something for each of my people to discuss individually with those they have selected for their partners. Besides, every djinn here is young as my people count these things. They are very far away from the point where they would consider pursuing the dark sleep, especially now that they have partners whose welfare they must consider. I do not think you have anything to fear on their behalf."

A nod as she absorbed this explanation. Whether she believed him, Zahrias couldn't say for sure, but he had only been telling her the truth as he saw it. He supposed the subject would have come up at one point or another, but in that moment he only wished he could have avoided speaking of it this evening. Julia now looked very solemn, her thoughts clearly running in pathways she hadn't previously explored.

Wishing to do something, he picked up the wine bottle and poured more of the cabernet franc into

Julia's glass, then topped off his own. As she watched, her expression seemed to relax somewhat.

Relieved, he said, "I am glad to hear that your community is doing so well. But I also know that your winters here are harsh. Last year, of course, we could not offer any assistance, but now that Los Alamos is under your care—"

"Thank you for that. It's good to know we're not alone. And maybe if Miles keeps fiddling with it, he'll finally come up with a way to modify his devices so they still block djinn powers without making you all feel like you're about to keel over. It would be nice if it was easier for us to visit."

Having suffered the effects of being around those devices for an extended period, Zahrias had to agree. True, he did not like the idea of not being able to use his powers, but he thought he could suffer that lack for a short time if it meant being able to go to Los Alamos so he could see the community for himself. He had to admit to some curiosity about how the world's only remaining all-mortal town functioned on a day-to-day basis.

For he knew Los Alamos was the only place in the world where humans who were not Chosen still lived. That was a truth he had kept to himself, for he knew it would do little good to let the people in the town know there were no others like them. The rest of the djinn had completed their cleansing operations some months back. Oh, he guessed that a human survived here and there, hidden and hunted, but even those holdouts' days were numbered. It was only because of Miles Odekirk's miraculous devices that the thousand or so who now called Los Alamos home still lived and breathed.

"I think many of us would like that," he said. Then he gestured toward the platter with the elk tenderloins. "Would you like some more?"

She shook her head. "No, thank you. It was marvelous, but I suppose I'm not used to eating such rich food."

No, they probably served simpler fare where she had come from. When he'd asked Phillip to prepare the meal, Zahrias had decided against offering a sweet course, since he himself did not care for sweets, and he thought the meal on its own should be sufficient to satisfy his guest. Now that seemed to be the case, but he wondered if he had made a misstep. If Julia wished to have nothing else, what would prevent her from leaving now and returning to her hotel?

He lifted the wine bottle and held it up so he could see how much remained of its contents. At least a third. Perhaps he could at least persuade her to stay long enough to finish the wine.

She seemed to understand what he was thinking, for she said, "That wine was lovely, though. I suppose it would be a shame to waste it."

Relief coursed through him. So she was willing to stay a while longer. "Perhaps it would be more comfortable in the living room—"

A nod, and then she lifted the napkin from her lap, folded it, and placed it on the table next to her plate. "That sounds like a wonderful idea."

Oh, God, this was crazy. When she'd told Zahrias she was full, Julia knew she should have then progressed to saying that she'd had a lovely time but that she really needed to get back to the hotel. Which was a complete lie, because what was she going to do once she got there? Scare up Brent Sanderson and ask him if he'd like to play a game of Scrabble? With no cable TV and no Internet, the list of options for occupying oneself in a hotel room these days was pretty damn short.

All right, Nancy and her beau Eric probably were having a fine time of it, but that particular activity wasn't really an option for Julia.

Wine glass in hand, she followed Zahrias as he led her from the dining room to the living room, a large space with fourteen-foot ceilings and a rounded kiva-style fireplace in the corner. The furniture wasn't particularly Southwest in style, though, but more modern—a pair of sleek bone-colored leather couches, a glass and metal coffee table. The art that covered the walls was abstract, blocks of color in dark salmon and turquoise, with hints of gold leaf. Did Zahrias prefer that sort of thing, or had he merely taken the house as he'd found it, not bothering to give it any touches that would make it his?

Maybe someday she'd have the courage to ask.

He waved a hand in the direction of the fireplace, and at once the logs piled in the hearth roared to life, sending some welcome heat into the room. Julia wouldn't say she'd exactly been cold since she entered the house, but she could tell that Zahrias didn't need his surroundings to be a perfect seventy-two degrees, either.

Since she wasn't sure what she should do, she sipped some more wine from the glass she carried as he set the bottle on the coffee table. Sitting down on one of the couches seemed fraught with complications. Would he sit next to her, and what might that mean? On the other hand, if he chose the sofa opposite hers, that would seem to indicate he'd only had her come over for dinner out of politeness.

Well, if he was really intending a seduction, he probably would have chosen slightly different topics of dinner conversation, she told herself. *Letting me know how some of the djinn off themselves when they get bored with life probably wasn't the best way of getting me in the mood.*

Actually, his revelation had fascinated her. She'd never stopped to think what it might be like to be blessed—or in some cases cursed—with unending life. After a while, it might start to get pretty old. Still, having someone close to you who chose to drink the draught of the dark sleep had to be terrible for the people left behind.

Zahrias paused a few feet away from her, wine glass in his hand. The light from the fire behind him framed his form, silhouetting him in a warm glow. She realized then that she hadn't seen any of the little dancing flames around him since she'd gotten here. Had he suppressed them on purpose, unsure as to whether they would make her uneasy, or did they only appear when he was angry or feeling some other strong emotion?

"So you will be returning to Los Alamos tomorrow?" he asked.

She couldn't detect anything of regret in his tone. On the other hand, he sounded almost too casual, as if he was forcing himself to bring up a topic he really didn't want to discuss but knew would have to be addressed at some point.

Or maybe she was just indulging herself.

"Yes," she replied. "I spoke to Shawn Gutierrez—he's been holding down the fort for me—this morning to let him know we'd be staying here for one more day, and he was all right with that, but I could tell he didn't want to be stuck in charge for much longer."

"It can be difficult to find adequate lieutenants," Zahrias said then. "I can rely on Dani to manage things for me if necessary, but he is going to be rather preoccupied very soon."

She had no doubt of that. "So...are djinn babies any different from human babies?"

"If you're asking whether they cry less or whether their diapers need to be changed less, I fear the answer is no."

Was that a hint of a smile touching Zahrias' mouth? Yes, she thought it was. She wished he would smile more often, because it brought a warm light to his dark eyes that seemed to illumine his whole face.

Julia found herself smiling in return. Then she realized maybe that had been a miscalculation, because his expression sobered, even as his gaze fastened on hers, eyes locked so she couldn't look away...not that she wanted to.

Deliberately, he set his glass down on the coffee table next to the wine bottle before taking a step toward her. Then another. Now she could see little flickers of flame beginning to dance around him, as if he couldn't hold them back any longer.

He was so close, not even an arm's length away. Was she still breathing? She couldn't tell for sure. The room was absolutely quiet, even the logs in the hearth not crackling away, although she could have sworn she'd heard one of them give a loud pop not a moment earlier.

His voice was hardly more than a harsh whisper. "I swore to myself I would not do this."

"Do what?" she asked. But of course she knew the answer.

"This."

Then he was right there, his arms going around her, pulling her close, his mouth on hers, tasting her, and heat seemed to explode in her core, in the very center of her being. She was melting into him, tasting the darkness of the wine on his tongue, breathing in something sharp and aromatic, possibly a perfume that clung to his heavy silken robes.

God, he was strong. Not because he was holding her too tightly, but more that she could feel the heaviness of the muscles in his arms and chest, the coiled power there. She'd never been with a man who felt like this. Ian, her late fiancé, had been in shape, but lean and slim, a runner and a tennis player. And Margolis—

No, she wouldn't think about him. She hadn't been with him, anyway, only forced to endure his touch. Better to let herself drown in Zahrias' kiss, to drink in every sensation, from the brush of his hair against her cheek to the heat that seemed to pulse from every inch of his flesh.

Very gently, he lifted his mouth from hers. His hands cupped her face, so tender, fingers warm and strong against her skin.

"You are so very beautiful," he murmured.

A shudder went through her. She wished she could speak, but no words seemed right in that moment. *He* was right, perfect and strong and amazing. And yet she knew this was wrong. It had to be. If he really wanted her this badly, then why come to her now? Why not save her when the Heat began, the way Jace had saved Jessica?

Somehow she found her voice. "I don't—I don't understand."

His brows drew together, even as he lifted his hands from her face, settling them instead on her shoulders. "What don't you understand?"

"Why now?"

Something flickered in those dark eyes. Not an echo of the flames that danced around him, flames that did not burn, but some emotion she couldn't quite read.

Finally he said, "Because I could not find the will to withstand you any longer."

He made it sound as if she was a drug habit he'd been trying to kick. She pulled in a breath. "So...what? You wanted me all along, but wouldn't allow yourself to be with a mortal?"

"It is more complicated than that."

God, she hated it when men made that kind of excuse. She shrugged her shoulders out of his grasp, and he let go, stepping back a pace. "It always is," she said bitterly. "But I'd still like to hear the reason why you would say that."

His face went very still. "If that is what you wish."

One kiss, and they were already arguing. That seemed to be par for the course where her love life was concerned. But she wouldn't back down. She needed to know the truth...needed to know why Zahrias was only coming to her now. If she'd been Chosen, she wouldn't have had to endure last winter in Los Alamos. Wouldn't have had to endure Margolis....

"It is what I wish," she said.

Zahrias turned away from her and retrieved his wine glass, then swallowed a too-large mouthful. Something about the act startled Julia, made her realize that he was not quite as self-assured as he wanted her to believe. "I'm surprised Jessica said nothing of it to you, but very well. Many years ago, I bound myself to a mortal woman. But she could not reconcile herself to the life of an immortal, of seeing her friends and family pass from the world, leaving her behind. And so eventually she took her life, so that she might be with them."

This terrible story was related in calm, even tones, as if it had all happened to someone else. All the heat that had washed through Julia's body a few moments earlier now disappeared, replaced by a creeping chill.

"So you see why I might resist the attraction to another mortal woman. Not to say that you are anything like Evangeline, but I could not allow myself to take that risk."

Evangeline. A beautiful name, but Julia hated the long-dead woman in that moment, hated her for her selfishness. How could she have done such a thing to someone as strong and good and noble as Zahrias?

"And yet you took that risk now."

"Because even I cannot resist forever. At least, not when it comes to you, Julia."

On his lips, her name was both a caress and a plea. Hearing it, she wanted to go back to him, to lay her head on his shoulder and tell him she understood. But while some part of her did understand, beneath the understanding burned an anger that he couldn't get beyond his past to come to her at a time when it would have mattered. Before Margolis had laid his hands on her, and fractured a piece of her soul.

"Maybe you should have," she told him. "Because what exactly did you think was going to happen next?"

He didn't exactly recoil, but she saw his back stiffen. Jaw tight, he replied, "I had hoped that was something we could discuss together."

Once upon a time, maybe such a thing would have been possible. She wanted him—even now she could feel how her body ached for him. But he'd made his move too late. He could have saved her from so much... but he hadn't.

She had to get out of here. Back to the hotel, where she could hide until it was time to leave the next morning. Then she could run away to Los Alamos and pretend that none of this had ever happened. In time she might even be able to forget.

"Thank you for dinner," she said, then turned and headed for the door.

Zahrias didn't try to stop her.

CHAPTER SIX

THE DOOR CLOSED. SOFTLY, BUT THE SOUND OF IT was like thunder in his ears.

Zahrias stood in the center of the living room, watching where she had gone, but somehow unable to move. It was as though he thought if he only remained still enough, that terrible scene would be erased, and he could go on as he always had.

Worse, he could still taste her on his tongue, smell the scent of her hair. His body throbbed with need for her, and he could do nothing about it.

What did you expect? he thought then. Once she knew the truth of the matter, she would despise him for his weakness, for not being able to move past his pain to claim her for his own at a time when doing so would have made a difference. One might argue that if she hadn't been in Los Alamos to help them, both Jasreel and Jessica might have perished at Margolis' hands, but that had to be cold comfort to a woman who had been despoiled by that very same monster.

A monster who was now on the loose.

Anger flashed through him, terrible and quick as the lightning storms that swept over this country at the height of the summer monsoon season. In answer to that anger, the wine bottle flew across the room and smashed itself in the hearth. The flames there sputtered and then flared up more brightly, consuming the alcohol spattered over the logs.

Useless display...and a waste of good wine. He realized he could have used that wine to dull the ache of Julia's departure. And true, he could have summoned another bottle, but it would not have been the one he had just broken. Like Julia, the cabernet franc had been perfect in its way, not something he could easily replace. Nor would he wish to. They were meant to be savored as their own unique selves.

He wondered then if perhaps he could have said something—anything—to keep her from going, but when the moment came, he had not been able to summon the words to his lips.

In time, perhaps he would heal. She would be gone, and he could return to the life he had constructed here for himself. It had been foolish to think he could have anything more than that.

Ah, well. At least he had had many decades to learn how to live alone.

Sleep was not Julia's friend that night, but eventually she drifted off, more because she knew she had to be somewhat functional the next day, no matter what had happened between her and Zahrias. The problem was, she could still feel his arms around her, the strength and heat of his flesh. Her body yearned for him, even though she knew being with him was not an option. It was—all right, she wasn't so irrational as to think it was his fault that Margolis had raped her, but one couldn't argue that she would never have been around the commander in the first place if Zahrias had only claimed her at the same time the rest of the djinn selected their Chosen.

And when she awoke the next morning, she was irritable from lack of sleep and knew she looked terrible. She'd packed a few cosmetics, but they weren't enough to hide the shadows under her eyes or her reddened eyelids. If anyone asked, she'd just say she'd had an allergic reaction to the detergent they used to wash the sheets here or something.

However, no one did ask. She ate breakfast with Brent Sanderson, but he seemed to be looking at his eggs or into his coffee mug or out the window of the restaurant—anywhere except directly at her. He knew she'd had dinner with Zahrias the night before, but clearly he wasn't going to ask her about it.

After they were done with breakfast, she told Brent and Nancy and Eric to make sure they were ready to go. No point in dragging them over to the U.S. Marshals' building; she'd head there herself and collect Miles and Lindsay, then be on the road home by nine o'clock. She hadn't seen any djinn hanging around, but that didn't surprise her too much.

The only awkward moment had been when Phillip himself brought out their breakfasts, and asked Julia how she had liked the elk tenderloin the night before. She stammered that she thought it was amazing, and thanked him for preparing for such a wonderful meal. If he'd noticed anything about her appearance or manner that seemed off, he didn't show it. Thank God for small favors.

She went over to the U.S. Marshals' building soon afterward. Murrah, the big djinn who'd been one of Margolis' guards, was loitering around the place and offered to take her down in the elevator. Julia knew the way well enough, but she thought refusing him would be rude, and so she allowed him to get in the elevator car with her and guide her to the cell in the lowest sub-basement, after which he waited off to one side like the world's most oversized bellhop.

As she'd expected, Miles and Lindsay were already there. By that point, it seemed as if Lindsay had given up any pretext at working and was propped up against one wall, a mug of coffee in her hands and a frown pulling at her brows. Miles, of course, was still tapping away at his iPad. Julia wondered if he slept with that thing...or if he slept at all. Poor Lindsay.

"Okay, troops," Julia said, hoping she sounded at least halfway authoritative. If only she wasn't so damn tired. "Time to pack it in. We're heading back to Los Alamos."

An expression of relief crossed Lindsay's features, but Miles only shook his head. "I'm still tabulating—"

"I'm getting the impression that there isn't anything *to* tabulate," Julia broke in. "It's okay to admit every once in a while that you're flummoxed."

"I am not flummoxed," Miles protested. "I am gathering data. Because you aren't a scientist, perhaps you don't—"

"You're right. I'm not a scientist." Usually Julia tried to be a little more patient with Miles, because she knew his contributions to the Los Alamos community were what had kept everyone there alive, but at that moment she'd had it. She wanted to go home and get the hell out of Santa Fe. Maybe once she was back in familiar surroundings she'd be able to forget that kiss she'd shared with Zahrias. She had to. Otherwise, Shawn Gutierrez's prospects were looking pretty bleak. "But I am the leader of our group, and I'm saying we're going home."

Miles's lips compressed. "Lindsay, tell her we're not done."

"*You're* not done, Miles. I was done yesterday." Lindsay lifted the coffee mug she held to her lips and drained the remainder of its contents. Her expression softened as she looked over at her companion. "Sweetie, there just isn't anything to find here."

Julia didn't have time to reflect on the incongruity of Miles Odekirk being referred to as "sweetie." Without looking back at Murrah—for all she knew, the djinn would report their entire conversation to Zahrias after this was all over—she said, "I think you need to listen to Lindsay, Miles. You've been over and over the same ground ever since we got here. There's just nothing to find."

"I'm staying," he said mulishly. "You go, if you feel it necessary to go back to Los Alamos. Lindsay can go with you."

"Oh, no way," Lindsay said at once. "If I leave you here, I just know you'll forget to eat, and I doubt anyone is going to hang around to babysit you. If you're staying, then I'm staying, too."

Crazy, the both of them. The universe had been kind in allowing them to find each other. Too bad it hadn't been nearly as kind to her. Julia shoved that self-pitying thought aside. "So how are you supposed to get home whenever you decide you *are* done? We only brought the one device with us."

Miles didn't blink. "We can keep in contact by radio. When I feel we've sufficiently exhausted our options here, I'll let you know, and you can send a team to retrieve us."

Using up more fuel and putting more people at risk. But maybe that was being a little harsh. The drive over here had certainly been uneventful. Yes, it would waste some gas to come back and get Miles and Lindsay, but Julia was certainly in no position to drag them away from their work. Maybe if she'd brought Eric along with her this morning, he could have karate-chopped the two of them into submission or whatever, but she wasn't quite ready to go to that extreme.

"Fine," she said with a sigh. "I'll let Zahrias know that you're staying."

There, she thought. *You were able to say his name without flinching. You can do this.*

Miles nodded and turned back to his iPad. As if to trying to apologize for his rudeness, Lindsay flashed her a smile and mouthed *thank you.* Julia nodded and turned away from them, letting Murrah push the button to open the elevator door. They rode up in silence, but she thanked him as she left and headed back to the La Fonda hotel.

The rest of her team was already waiting in the lobby with their meager baggage. Julia debated whether to go over to Zahrias' house to inform him they were leaving, or whether to take the coward's way out and slip off before he could notice. She wasn't given that option, however, because as soon as they went outside and began putting their backpacks and duffles in the back of the Suburban, the djinn leader appeared, seemingly from nowhere. At least, Julia hadn't seen him walk up, but she supposed he could have just popped in from nowhere in that disconcerting way the djinn had.

He didn't seem to have weathered the night much better than she. His eyes also looked shadowed, and his mouth was grim. But he nodded at them all pleasantly enough, although he appeared confused when he realized that Lindsay and Miles were not with them.

"Our mad scientist is still tabulating," Julia explained, all too aware of the watching eyes of her companions as she and Zahrias shared this exchange. Had she sounded casual enough? Too casual? Nothing to do but forge ahead. "So he and Lindsay are staying behind so they can keep working. We'll send someone to fetch them when they're done. I hope it's not too much of an imposition."

"Not at all," Zahrias replied. "They're welcome to stay for as long as they wish."

This would have been easier if he'd been acting like a jerk. Then Julia could tell herself that her anger with him was entirely justified. But there he was, grave and courteous and handsome, playing the polite host. "I appreciate that," she said. "Hopefully, it will only be for a day or so more. I honestly don't know what it is that Miles thinks he can find, but when he digs his heels in, it's best not to argue."

"As I said, he and Lindsay can remain for as long as they deem necessary." Zahrias' gaze flickered past the remainder of her group, then returned to her. His eyes were cool and dark, betraying nothing. "Have a safe journey back to Los Alamos."

"Thank you," she said, an empty politeness. Of course they'd have a safe trip back. The day was bright and fine, and the device would keep them safe from any djinn interference. They'd be in Los Alamos within the hour.

She nodded toward her team, and they all climbed into the Suburban, Nancy and Eric in the back seat, Brent taking shotgun once again. Feeling Zahrias' eyes on her the entire time, Julia got into the driver's seat and shut the door. Was there something else she should have said? Probably not. The best thing now was just to get the hell out of here.

After retrieving her sunglasses from where she'd looped them around the rearview mirror, she pulled away from the curb in front of the hotel and headed back to Paseo de Peralta so she could get them back on the highway. One good thing about the apocalypse; you could ignore the maze of one-way streets around Santa Fe's plaza and go any direction that was the fastest. No one else seemed to be driving that morning, so Julia could do what she wanted.

All right, not exactly. What she really wanted right then was to turn the Suburban around so she could go back and tell Zahrias that she'd screwed up, that she wasn't really angry with him. Except...she was. Sort of. It was more that intellectually she could understand his reticence about approaching her, but her gut wasn't quite ready to forgive him. And her libido seemed to want to tell both her brain and her gut to take a hike so she could fall into his arms again.

Goddamn it.

Jaw tense, she maneuvered her way out of downtown Santa Fe and got them headed north on Highway 285. The roadway here wasn't quite as clear as it was on the 502, since the Los Alamos group used that highway to get to and from Española, but it was all right as long as she kept her speeds down below fifty miles an hour. And once they were back on the 502, she'd be able to push it up to sixty-five.

They were coming up to the turnoff for the highway. Off to the right was a casino complex, its parking lot still filled with cars that the Los Alamos scavenging teams hadn't deemed suitable to acquire.

Julia slowed down to take the curve that led them back under the 285 and then west on the 502. In the seat next to her, Brent was watching the scenery go by with half-lidded eyes; he'd probably been on this route a number of times already, since he'd been one of Margolis' chief vehicle-scroungers back when they were all scouring the area for every four-wheel-drive truck and SUV they could get their hands on.

A roaring sound filled her ears. Beneath her fingers, the steering wheel jerked violently. Julia tightened her grip and hung on, thinking they must have blown a tire. But no, the whole Suburban shuddered and seemed to leap up off the pavement, flying into the air even as she felt it tipping sideways, starting to roll. Black smoke surrounded them, accompanied by flames that blew up and out, hitting the roof and walls of the underpass.

We're going to crash, she thought, quite calmly. Then a red-tinged darkness rushed up and swallowed her.

"You are looking quite thunderous today," Dani remarked after Zahrias had let his brother into the house. "Weren't you supposed to have dinner with Julia Innes last night?"

"I did have dinner with her," Zahrias said heavily. She'd been gone less than half an hour, and already her absence weighed on him, making it difficult to think. Foolish, he knew. He had functioned quite well without her all these months, so what was the problem now?

The problem was that he had kissed her, and so now he knew exactly what he had been missing.

"From the look on your face, I would hazard a guess that it did not go well."

Sometimes Dani could be too perceptive. But then, he had always been the one who enjoyed being around others, who liked understanding their moods and motivations. His was entirely too sunny a nature for a djinn. However, that nature had stood him in good stead when it came time to establish this mixed mortal/djinn community. The humans felt they could confide in him, for he did not seem quite so alien to them.

"It...did not go as I had hoped," Zahrias replied.

"She does not share your attraction?"

"Not precisely." No, that was not the problem at all. He knew well enough when a woman reacted to him, and Julia had been responsive, eager...until he confessed to her that he had kept himself from reaching out to her earlier because of the tragedies in his past.

Dani lifted a skeptical eyebrow. Although Zahrias did not have as many conquests in his past as other djinn his age might, he certainly had never lacked for female companions. "So is it that she doesn't wish to be with you, or is it something else?"

Zahrias waved an impatient hand. Sometimes his brother could be too inquisitive for his own good.

And the wound of Julia's rejection was still too raw for Zahrias to want to discuss what had happened. Instead, he went to the sideboard and poured two glasses of wine from the bottle that sat there. Dani's eyebrows lifted almost imperceptibly.

Clearly, the younger djinn had been spending too much time around humans. Yes, it might not yet be the hour for the midday meal, but the djinn did not follow mortal rules that governed when it might or might not be the proper time to imbibe. Alcohol affected elementals, true, but not to the same extent as it did humans.

"How does Lauren fare?" Zahrias asked. The question was an obvious deflection, and he knew Dani would see it as such, but he needed to move the discussion away from Julia.

"As well as can be expected," Dani replied. From the glint in his eyes, he knew exactly what his brother was doing...but he would not argue the point. "She frets over being confined to her bed, but Miguel says that is what's best for her. The pains she was experiencing have subsided, now that she isn't moving around as much, and so everything should be fine."

"Should" being the most important word in that sentence. Lauren's partnership with Dani meant that she enjoyed the same robust health as the rest of the djinn, but even so, complications from mixed births such as these were not completely unknown. That was how Jasreel had lost his own mother, when she'd attempted to give another child to the djinn man who had claimed her. At least the universe had been kind and had granted Jasreel full djinn powers, thus ensuring that his father would take the motherless boy and raise him as one of their own, despite his half-blood status.

But Zahrias would not speak of such things to his brother. Dani knew Jasreel's history as well as he himself did. Perhaps it was recalling how Jasreel had lost his mother that made Dani unusually tense now. The situation was quite different, though. True, Miguel was not a true healer, but he had spent the last six months reading about pregnancy and childbirth in the many books the mortals had left behind, and he was probably far better suited to deliver a child than the healers back in the time when Jasreel was born, so many centuries ago.

Zahrias handed one of the glasses of wine to his brother. "Since Lauren is the active, busy sort, I can see why she would chafe at being so confined. However, perhaps you should remind her that she will be very busy very soon, and so perhaps she should enjoy the quiet time she has now, even if it is being forced on her."

A grin, and Dani lifted his glass. "Wise words, brother. I will be sure to tell her that."

Raising his glass as well, Zahrias didn't quite smile. Somehow he couldn't find it within him to do so. Perhaps in a few days he would be more inclined, once the memory of Julia's lips against his had faded. In the meantime, well, there was plenty of wine.

Her ears were ringing, and people groaned all around her. Julia opened her eyes, but nothing in the world seemed to make sense right then. After she blinked once or twice, she realized everything seemed wrong because the Suburban was on its side, the windshield a spiderweb of cracks, Brent Sanderson dangling next to her, held in place only by his seatbelt. Bright blood from a gash along his scalp obscured half his face.

"Brent?" she croaked.

He didn't move. Shit.

Her fingers shook as she fumbled with the buckle of her own seatbelt. After a few abortive tries, she got it loose. Since she was already lying smashed up against the driver-side window, she didn't have to worry about falling.

What the hell had happened? Her first thought had been a blown tire, but no tire should have erupted like that, with flame and smoke. Had there been some kind of explosive lying in the roadway? No, that didn't make sense. Teams from Los Alamos had come this way before; they would have cleared anything dangerous.

Well, she could figure that out later. From the back seat, she heard more groans. "Eric? Nancy?"

Eric's voice. "We're okay. Banged up, but okay."

Thank God for that at least. "Can you move?"

Nancy let out a soft moan. "I think my arm's broken. And I dropped the device."

"It's okay," Julia reassured her. "It's got to be in the car somewhere. We can find it after we get ourselves out of here."

"I can climb out through the passenger side," Eric said then. "There's glass everywhere, though."

"Hang on," Julia told him. The last thing she needed was for him to slice up his hands while trying to extricate himself from the vehicle. "The windshield's already smashed, but I can push it out of the way."

"Brent?" Nancy asked.

"He's passed out, I think. His window's broken, too—looks like some shrapnel or whatever it was got it. But I think he's breathing."

"Shit."

"What happened?" Eric again.

Julia was about to tell him that she had no frigging clue when Nancy spoke again. "If I didn't know better, I'd say someone hit us with an RPG or a rocket launcher or something."

"That's impossible," she said.

It definitely sounded impossible. Julia could maybe believe it had been some kind of djinn attack—if it weren't that Miles's device should have kept any djinn in the area at least a quarter-mile away from them.

Anyway, that didn't matter right now. What mattered was getting out of the Suburban. She didn't smell gasoline, but that didn't mean much. It could still be leaking somewhere.

Her spirit quailed at the thought of having to limp back to Santa Fe for help, but first things first. She dumped her useless wallet and cosmetics bags and the other items from her purse—miraculously, it was still wedged next to her on the seat—and then used the empty leather bag to wrap around her hand so she could punch the windshield out of the way. Maybe it would have been better to kick it out, but with the angle she was lying at, she didn't know if she could have gotten enough leverage. Anyway, the shattered safety glass did fall away after her second blow, landing with a crunch on the pavement.

Climbing out past the steering wheel was trickier than she'd thought, and she knew she'd picked up a few more bruises along the way, but eventually, Julia was able to push her way through the windshield opening. She landed on her hands, skinning her palms. Could have been worse, though. At least she hadn't cut them on any broken glass.

She bit back a moan as she straightened, feeling wrenched muscles protest the movement. No doubt tomorrow she'd be one big walking bruise. But at least she was still alive.

A strange, acrid scent hung in the air below the overpass. Smoke, yes, but with a weird chemical tinge to it. Julia didn't think she'd ever smelled something like it before. Well, she'd have to worry about that later.

The Suburban lay on its side like some prehistoric monster felled in combat. From that angle, it seemed impossibly tall to her. There was no way she could climb up there to free Brent, or help Eric out his window. Maybe if she could grab the axle somehow, pull on it so the SUV would fall back down into its normal position. A maneuver like that would jostle everyone inside, and Julia winced at what it might do to Nancy's broken arm, but she didn't know what else to try. She couldn't leave them as they were.

"You all still doing okay in there?" she called out.

Eric and Nancy answered in the affirmative, but nothing from Brent. This was bad.

Biting her lip, Julia began to circle the Suburban, looking for the best angle of attack. It was probably crazy to think that she could tip over a three-ton beast like that when she weighed about a hundred and twenty pounds wringing wet, but she had to do something.

Glass crunched behind her and Julia whirled, a wild hope racing through her that Zahrias had somehow been watching over them, was even now approaching to offer his assistance.

But that hope died a horrible death as her gaze met that of Richard Margolis. He held a semi-automatic pistol in his hand, the business end pointed directly at her heart.

"Hello, Julia," he said.

CHAPTER SEVEN

No. This was impossible. Margolis couldn't be standing there only a few paces away, a gloating smile on his thin lips.

But yet...there he was.

"You look surprised," he said. "You really shouldn't be. You knew about the National Guard armory in Santa Fe—after all, you helped me set up an expedition to retrieve guns and ammunition there last fall."

Her brain and her mouth didn't seem to want to work in concert. Surely she should say something—anything—but her thoughts just kept chasing around each other. *Margolis is here. Margolis is here.* He couldn't be here...

...and yet he was.

"What you didn't know," he went on in that same conversational tone, "was that the armory also had a cache of shoulder-launched missiles. The hardest part was finding one that wouldn't completely destroy the vehicle you were driving. I didn't want that, of course."

Of course.

The Suburban shifted, and Julia saw why in the next second—Eric must have heard her talking to Margolis, and so had pushed himself up into the passenger-side window, ignoring the broken glass. What he hoped to accomplish, she wasn't sure.

And in the next second, it didn't matter, because Margolis had lifted the gleaming gun he held and shot off a quick round, hitting Eric squarely in the head. His body slumped over the window opening, blood from the wound in his temple mingling with the blood that spilled from cuts inflicted by the window's shattered glass.

Inside the SUV, a woman cried out in despair and rage.

Julia wanted to scream as well. But for some reason she could only stand there, stricken and immobile, as if Margolis' stare had been that of a gorgon, turning her to stone forever. Smiling at her lack of reaction, the commander walked past her and approached the front end of the upended Suburban. He grasped the bumper with his free hand and pulled, hard. The SUV tipped back over into a more or less upright position, although two of its tires noisily collapsed as soon as the full weight of the vehicle landed on them. Barely a second later, another gunshot rang out, this time coming from within the vehicle. Nancy might have been mourning the loss of her lover, but her grief hadn't slowed down her reaction time.

Unfortunately, the bullet went wide and slammed into the concrete wall of the underpass, spraying dust everywhere. Still moving calmly, Margolis went around to the driver's side and fired again, and that was the end of Nancy's attempt at vengeance.

"That's better," Margolis said. Then he moved forward so he was even with the front seat, and peered inside and frowned. "Your friend doesn't look so good."

It couldn't be possible that Margolis actually cared about Brent's condition—not after what the commander had just done to Eric and Nancy. At last Julia found her voice. "Leave him alone."

"That wouldn't be very Christian, would it? The man looks concussed. Probably suffered brain damage from that head trauma. The best thing to do would be to put him out of his misery."

God, she needed to get her mind working again. Thinking desperately, she said, "Captain, that's Brent Sanderson. You know Brent. You were friends." Well, they had been, once upon a time before Brent realized what kind of a person Richard Margolis actually was.

But she didn't think it would be a good idea to mention any of that. The former commander didn't seem to be firing on all cylinders, so to speak. Maybe he wouldn't remember that Brent had given up on him, had lent his support to Julia instead.

Margolis' head swiveled toward her. He stared at her for a moment with flat, dark eyes, then said, "I don't have any friends."

Blam!

The pistol roared again, but Julia didn't bother to cover her ears. Trying to deaden the sound wouldn't change what she'd just seen. Brent was dead. How could Brent be dead? He was one of the good guys. He was supposed to continue his not-quite flirtation with Norma Gomez, the town's teacher, and then one day start a family with her. He couldn't be sitting there, still strapped into his seat, with dark blood trickling from a bullet hole in his head.

Julia jammed her fist into her mouth to keep herself from screaming—or maybe it was simply to push back the bile she felt rising in the back of her throat. In mute agony, she watched as Margolis stuck the pistol into the waistband of the camouflage pants he wore, then began digging around inside the SUV. What the hell was he up to?

A minute later, Julia saw what he'd been prospecting for. He backed out of the Suburban, left hand clutching a small dark box not much bigger than his palm.

The djinn-repelling device they'd carried with them.

"There," Margolis said. "Gotcha." He turned it over, then pressed the switch on the bottom to turn it off.

Julia's voice finally reasserted itself. "What the hell are you doing?"

The commander smiled. "Keeping a promise."

The ground rumbled beneath her feet. Julia wanted to run, but where could she go? Margolis could drill her between the shoulder blades before she got ten feet away, and even if she somehow managed to evade his shots, there was no running from a djinn.

And then the roadway seemed to erupt in a geyser of dirt and broken asphalt. Standing before them was a tall, black-haired djinn Julia had never seen before, his dark eyes flashing as he took her in.

Julia thought she had seen the face of evil before— certainly in Margolis' features when he leered down at her just before violating her as she lay in her cell below the municipal center in Los Alamos, and again when the rogue djinn Khalim had invaded Taos and attempted to take the town for himself. But something about the gloating expression this new djinn wore made Julia want to quail in fear, to cover her eyes so she wouldn't have to look at him anymore.

"I did as you asked, Qadim," Margolis said. "Can I have her now?"

The waiting was, as the old saying went, the hardest part. Dani had drunk perhaps two swallows of his wine before he seemed to go rigid, eyes widening. Then he had exclaimed, "It is time!" and blinked out of the room, wine glass still clutched in his hand.

Zahrias knew they would not remain in the home that Dani and Lauren had taken as their own. Miguel had made it clear that the baby needed to be born in the hospital, where he would have access to any specialized equipment or medicines he might need. So Zahrias went there as well, blinking himself into the waiting room of the maternity ward. Dani was nowhere in evidence, which meant he must be in the delivery room with his Chosen.

The location of that delivery room soon became clear enough, for Zahrias could hear Lauren's cries and moans coming from the hallway to the left. Perhaps it was foolish for him to sit here and wait when he could do nothing, but this child would be his niece or nephew, and he thought it his duty to be here for the birth.

To Zahrias' surprise, Jasreel and Jessica appeared only a few minutes after he arrived.

"Dani reached out to me," Jasreel explained, while Jessica offered a tentative smile.

"After all, there should be friends and family in the waiting room, right?" she said. "Jace is family, and Lauren and I have gotten to be pretty good friends, especially after—" She broke off awkwardly.

Zahrias knew she must be referring to Julia and her return to Los Alamos. The two women had been close, at least as far as he could tell, and Jessica had probably missed having a good female friend here in town. He braced himself, waiting for the inevitable question.

"How was your dinner?"

"Excellent," he said, his tone short. "Phillip always prepares very good meals."

A confused expression passed over Jessica's face, and then she bit her lip and exchanged a sidelong glance with Jasreel. No doubt they were sharing a quick subvocal conversation, probably attempting to analyze what had gone wrong.

Having Dani pry into such a thing was bad enough, but if Jessica and Jace started probing the same subject, it would be intolerable. As a brother, Dani had some right to ask questions about Zahrias' personal affairs, but Jessica and Jasreel did not possess those same privileges. Yes, he and Jasreel were cousins. That did not mean Jasreel could make any inquiries he liked.

Apparently the younger djinn knew that as well, because he gave Jessica a final quelling glance, and she settled back in her chair with a sigh.

"Have they decided on any names?" Jasreel asked.

An innocuous enough change of subject. Zahrias wanted to sigh as well, only in relief, not exasperation. "I don't believe they had yet made a final determination. Dani wanted a djinn name, while Lauren expressed her preference for something, as she put it, 'a little more pronounceable.'"

"Well, let's hope they don't go for a hyphenate," Jessica said. "Can you imagine having to go through life named Jaden-Danilar or whatever?"

"I am sure that common sense will prevail." Or rather, he was fairly certain that Dani would have the last word. Lauren could be strong-minded about certain things, but Zahrias had noticed that she tended to defer to his brother on important matters.

Another series of moans and cries carried down the corridor, and Jessica winced. "Sounds like Miguel decided against the epidural."

"If you're referring to one of your drugs, then yes, he discussed the matter with Dani and Lauren, and they all decided together that it would be too risky, since he wasn't trained in its use. However, I believe Lauren has been practicing a certain method of breathing—"

"Lamaze," Jessica supplied. After glancing down the corridor, and flinching once again as another guttural groan traveled down toward them, she added, "That doesn't sound like it's going so well."

Zahrias was inclined to agree with her. However, he had been present at other births, and he knew that one could not always judge how they were progressing merely based on the volume of the crying involved. Lauren was a strong, healthy young woman, and Miguel claimed he knew what he was doing. This would all be fine.

"Goddamn you, Dani—I *told* you I wanted to wait!" traveled down the corridor, followed by a low murmur of male voices.

Jasreel shook his head, but at that same time, a lopsided smile tugged at his lips. "And people wonder why Jessica and I didn't run out and immediately start a family once everything seemed to calm down."

Had others in the community been asking about that? The djinn were usually slow to have children, considering they had so much time to play with. Humans seemed to have a different take on the subject, however. Then again, Lilias had just informed him that she and Aidan would be having a child of their own sometime next spring.

"Wise," Zahrias said, "considering we don't precisely know how calm things are. With Margolis on the loose—"

Jasreel's smile immediately slipped away, and Jessica reached out and took his hand. They sat very close to one another on the angular metal-and-fabric couch, their legs not quite touching. Seeing their casual intimacy made a twinge of jealousy go through Zahrias. The two of them made it look so easy. But no, they had gone through their own trials to get to where they were now. Could he ever persuade Julia that perhaps one day they, too, might be able to share such closeness, such easiness with one another?

"Any progress on that?" Jessica asked.

Zahrias didn't bother to shake his head. He was sure the frown he wore was answer enough. "Miles says he is still 'tabulating,' whatever that means. I fear he is just too stubborn to give up his investigation. Certainly there is no evidence to show how Margolis escaped, and even less to indicate where he might have gone."

"Are you—" The words trailed off, and Jessica shot a sideways glance at Jasreel. His shoulders lifted slightly. That small gesture seemed to be what she'd required to continue, though, for she asked, "Are you sure it was safe, sending Julia off like that?"

"Like what?" Zahrias responded, his tone harsher than he'd intended. Jessica didn't blink, however, but only gazed at him steadily, waiting to hear what else he had to say on the subject. "She left with the same guards she brought with her. They were traveling over roads they traversed only the day before yesterday. If Margolis was out there somewhere, waiting to pounce, he could have gotten her on her journey here. Not that I believe he is out there," he added, because the look of worry still hadn't left Jessica's eyes. "The man is many things, but I don't believe he is a fool. He would want to put as much distance between us and himself as possible."

"You're probably right," Jessica said, and she pushed up against Jasreel, who dropped an arm around her. "I just wish—"

"What do you wish, beloved?" he asked.

Her dark gaze was fixed, not on the doorway that opened on the corridor, but on the opposite wall—the western one. Somewhere, miles beyond, Julia would be driving home to Los Alamos.

"I just wish I didn't feel in my bones as if something was wrong."

Julia didn't recognize the house. How could she? It was somewhere in the Pojoaque Valley, maybe a mile from the ill-fated underpass where Margolis had attacked her group with his rocket launcher. A gracious place, built to feel old even if it wasn't, with its beamed ceilings and wooden floors and arched doorways, the sort of house someone would use to escape the world.

Unfortunately, that seemed to be Margolis' intended purpose for it as well.

Qadim—the djinn—hadn't directly replied to the commander's request back in the tunnel, but had only said, in a deep, harsh voice, "Take her to the house." Then he'd disappeared with much less fanfare than the manner in which he had arrived, blinking out of existence in the peculiar way that djinn had.

Margolis had grasped her by the arm and dragged her to a black pickup truck parked just beyond the underpass. After pushing her into the passenger seat, he went and got behind the wheel, then gunned the engine and drove them past the wreckage of the Suburban, heading deeper into Pojoaque.

She hadn't spoken, hadn't asked where he was taking her. What difference did it make, really? Her people were dead. They'd died trying to find the man who now held her captive. In that moment, she could only thank God for Miles's stubbornness, his insistence on staying in Santa Fe. Otherwise, he and Lindsay would probably be dead, too.

A tiny whimper of misery pushed its way past Julia's lips. Margolis didn't seem to hear, however; he had the windows rolled down, and the noise was probably sufficient to keep him from noticing any sound she had made. Experimentally, she put her hand on the door handle, wondering if she had the courage to open it and jump out, even though they were racketing along at around fifty miles an hour. But of course it was locked.

If Margolis noticed, he didn't say anything. Maybe she should have been studying his expression for cues as to what he planned to do next, but Julia couldn't bear to look at him. So she sat quietly in her seat, watching as they headed out into the country and the road grew narrower, crowded on either side with oaks and cottonwoods. Then Margolis turned the truck down a narrow lane that clearly led to a private property of some sort. At last they pulled up in front of the house, which was painted a warm ochre shade and surrounded by more trees.

They'd gone inside. Margolis pointed at a chair in the family room, which was located right off the kitchen, and said, "Sit."

So she did. He seemed restless; he ran a hand through his gray-streaked dark hair, which was longer than she remembered. Probably the Santa Fe contingent hadn't been too worried about maintaining the buzz cut he preferred. At length he shrugged out of the green army jacket he wore and flung it on the couch. Underneath he had on a black T-shirt.

Disconcerted, Julia saw that he had a series of small scratches, less than an inch long, cut into the skin of both his forearms. The cuts were far too regular to have occurred due to some sort of accident.

He seemed to catch her staring, because he said, "I wanted to keep track of how many days they kept me locked up in there. One hundred and eighty-nine, in case you were wondering."

Holy hell. Julia had no idea what kind of a man Richard Margolis had been before the Dying—whether he'd had a family, people he cared about, some kind of stable life—but it definitely had done a number on his head. Even when she was working for him, she'd gotten the impression that something was off, but as long as everything was going well in his world, he seemed to more or less maintain some kind of mental equilibrium. After Jessica and Evony and Jace escaped, though, he'd gone off the deep end...or so Julia had thought. Now she realized he'd still been wading in the shallow end of the pool compared to who he'd become after being imprisoned by the djinn in Santa Fe.

Since she had no way to reply to his statement without making it sound as if she thought he was crazy—because she did—she decided to avoid that subject altogether. "May I please have a glass of water? I'm feeling kind of wiped."

There. She wanted him to think she was weak, had been more shaken up by the attack on her party than she actually was. Not to say that she wasn't aching all over at the moment, and grieving inside, but if he gave her an opening, she sure as hell was going to take it.

He watched her for a moment, dark eyes appraising. She couldn't quite make herself meet his gaze. That was probably all right, though. He'd be expecting her to be cowed, fearful of him. After all, she knew exactly what he was capable of.

After an agonizing pause, he nodded and went into the kitchen, then opened the refrigerator and pulled out a plastic bottle of water. So he had power here. Did the house have solar panels on the roof or somewhere else on the property, or were things here djinn-powered like they were back in Santa Fe?

"Here," he said, handing it to her. His fingers touched hers as she took the bottle from him, and she forced herself not to shudder. He'd done that on purpose, she knew.

Julia didn't bother to thank him. In silence, she unscrewed the cap and took a long swallow of water. It was cold and felt good going down her throat. She drank more, maybe about a third of the bottle's contents, and then put the cap back on.

The whole time, Margolis had been standing there, watching her. The greedy gleam in his eyes made her want to vomit, but she knew she couldn't lose it now. Even if the worst happened.

And if it did, well, she'd survived him once before, and she'd survive him again. "Who's Qadim?" she asked abruptly.

Margolis didn't blink. Something about his dark, flat stare made her think of a snake. "An earth elemental."

"Yeah, I kind of got that part. How do you know him? Last I checked, you weren't exactly on what I'd call friendly terms with the djinn."

A couch was positioned to the left of the armchair where she sat. Margolis lowered himself onto the sofa and smiled slightly. "He helped me."

"Helped you? Is that how you got out of the cell at the U.S. Marshals' building?"

At her mention of the place where he'd been held captive for six months, Margolis' brows drew together. "Yes."

Julia had to wonder how this Qadim had managed that stunt. True, djinn could blink themselves from place to place without batting an eyelash, and apparently they could take humans for ride-alongs when they did so, but shouldn't the other djinn in Santa Fe have sensed the presence of an elemental who wasn't part of their group? She had to admit she wasn't quite sure how all that worked.

"But...why?" Margolis' main obsession had been finding a way to get revenge on the djinn, hence his waterboarding experiments on Jace and Natila. Julia couldn't figure out why one of the djinn would willingly work with someone whose goal in life was to kill as many of their kind as possible.

Margolis reached over and took her hand. She had to force herself not to snatch it back. But they were alone together here, and she didn't want to provoke him. If he was talking, then he wasn't doing...other things.

Even so, she couldn't prevent the shudder that went over her at his touch. His flesh was warm and rough, and he ran his index finger over the cut on the back of her hand. The wound stung slightly, and she flinched.

"He promised me things," Margolis said. "You among them."

Somehow, Julia managed to choke back the bile that had begun to rise in the back of her throat. "I'm not his to promise."

"Oh, but you are."

Qadim's voice came from the doorway that led from the kitchen into the dining room. He seemed to fill the space, head almost touching the curved arch of the opening. Then he walked toward them, stopping a few feet away from where Julia and Margolis sat.

She would never have said that Margolis was a comforting presence, but right then she was almost glad that he sat by her and held her hand. At least that way he seemed to provide something of a buffer between her and the djinn.

Here, in the prosaic surroundings of the country house, Qadim seemed even more frightening to her. He had to be more than six and a half feet tall, his shoulders proportionately broad. Like Zahrias, he had jet-black hair and black eyes, but the resemblance stopped there. His nose was long, his mouth a cruel line. Gold hoops glimmered in both his ears, and his clothing, similar in style to what Zahrias wore, was the deep shades of earth, brown and black and iron gray.

Wearing an amused expression, he gazed down at the two of them. Something in those black, black eyes flickered as he took in the way Margolis' hand had closed around hers, and his mouth compressed.

"I did not say you could have her yet."

At once Margolis let go of Julia's fingers. She wasn't sure she should be relieved that he was no longer touching her, or worried by the way he so quickly reacted to Qadim's words.

Even though he had let go of her, the commander still managed to voice a protest. "I have done everything you asked—"

"Peace," Qadim rumbled, and Margolis subsided. The djinn turned his gaze on Julia, and she had to fight to keep herself from looking away. Something about his expression made the blood in her veins turn to ice. Tone musing, he went on, "Yes, I can see why he would want you. For a daughter of men, you are quite beautiful, aren't you?"

How could she respond to that question? Demurring would probably only anger him. Agreeing would make her sound impossibly conceited. Besides, which "he" was Qadim referring to? If he'd meant Margolis, wouldn't he have referred to him by name?

But what other "he" could he mean?

Oh, no....

Swallowing, Julia said, "If you say so."

Qadim's eyes narrowed. Then he glanced over at Margolis. "Leave us. I wish to speak to her alone."

That request—well, command, judging by Qadim's tone—didn't sit too well with Margolis. He scowled and got up from the couch, saying, "I brought her here. I don't think—"

"That is correct," Qadim interposed, the rumble of his deep voice effectively burying the commander's protests. "You do not think. You do as I say. Now go."

Still with his forehead etched in a frown, Margolis stalked out of the room. Julia sat frozen in her chair, wishing she could flee. Not that the djinn would probably allow her to take two steps before he stopped her.

"Better," he went on, once the sound of Margolis' footsteps had disappeared. Julia wondered how big the house actually was. "Come with me."

That didn't sound good. She doubted protesting that she wanted to stay right here would go over too well with Qadim, however, and so she got up from her chair. "Where are we going?"

He smiled, and she wished he hadn't. Most people's smiles improved their faces, but she couldn't say the same for the earth elemental. "Not far."

Moving away from her, he went to a set of French doors a few feet behind the couch. They opened on a courtyard where the trees seemed about to overwhelm their planters and dead plants filled the various terra-cotta pots set around the space. Seeing them, Julia couldn't help but think how pretty they must have been once upon a time, when someone lived here and tended the flowers that grew there once. All gone now, all dead.

In the center of the courtyard was a raised fountain, its interior lined with brightly painted Mexican tiles in shades of green and red and blue. Qadim snapped his fingers, and the fountain came to life, water splashing merrily away under the bright afternoon sun.

"Aren't you an earth elemental?" Julia inquired, and then wished she had kept her mouth shut. Maybe asking questions about their abilities angered the djinn.

But Qadim only went to the fountain and trailed a hand through the water before turning to face her. "Yes, but this was a small trick. The element at my command had nothing to do with it."

"Ah." She'd seen evidence before that the djinn seemed able to perform small bits of magic seemingly unconnected to the elements they claimed as their own, but she still had no idea how any of it actually worked. Right then, she was only glad that the fountain had distracted Qadim, because at least that way he was a good yard or so away from her. Crossing her arms, she said, "So...you freed Margolis."

"I did."

"Why?"

"Because he was necessary."

That sounded ominous. It was entirely possible that she shouldn't be asking these questions, that doing so would only annoy Qadim, but Julia couldn't seem to stop herself. In her mind, she kept hearing the echoes of Margolis' pistol firing, each shot the death knell of a friend. She had to know what had provoked all of that terrible violence. "Necessary for what?"

Qadim didn't answer immediately, but only stood where he was, back to the fountain, which continued to dance blithely away behind him. Then he stepped toward her, closing the distance between them. The breeze caught at the somber patterned silk of his robe, blowing it so one edge brushed against her leg. Julia tried not to shudder.

"I asked myself, 'What is the one thing that will draw him out?' For he has hidden himself among his people, cowering down there in Santa Fe as he does the elders' bidding. He has no reason to leave, to make himself vulnerable."

She'd worried for the last few minutes who this "he" was that Qadim kept referring to, but now she thought she knew.

"Zahrias," she whispered.

Another one of those sharp-edged smiles twisted Qadim's features. "Very good, Julia. Yes, Zahrias al-Harith. He has managed to make himself look like quite a martyr, playing the solitary, noble leader, but I heard whispers of rumors, whispers that he was not quite as indifferent as he seemed. That a certain mortal woman had caught his eye, even though he did not have the courage to make her his Chosen."

The djinn reached out and ran one hand down her tangled hair, slowly, deliberately. Julia held herself still, knowing that any sign of disgust would only amuse him.

Or worse, titillate him.

Qadim's smile disappeared, but he didn't appear angry, or annoyed. He gave the briefest of nods, as if her lack of reaction had confirmed something for him. "So if the woman he wants is taken—and taken by the one man Zahrias knows will do her harm, because that harm has already been visited on her before—then the fearless leader must step forth to rescue her, must he not? And then I will be able to take my own revenge upon him."

"Revenge for what?" Julia asked, making sure she sounded cold, almost uninterested, as if his words meant very little to her...as if his touch hadn't made her feel like vomiting up everything she'd eaten for the past few days.

"That, I think, is no concern of yours." Qadim paused then, as though stopping to take stock of her appearance for the first time. An expression of false solicitude passed over his harsh features. "But you have had a wearying time, and suffered some injury. Margolis said his device would not hurt you, but it seems he was wrong in that estimation."

"I'm fine."

"No, I am not quite sure you are. You must appear in the very best of health when Zahrias sees you."

"Really?" Julia asked, not bothering to keep the scorn out of her voice. "You'd think I'd make much more convincing bait if I looked a little banged up."

"No. He must feel the pain of everything he is losing. You will have a hot bath, a good meal, a good night's sleep. Then you will be ready to face Zahrias."

Was he crazy? Well, considering he'd teamed up Margolis to enact this so-called revenge on Zahrias, then yes, Qadim probably was crazy. Julia shook her head. "If you think I'm going to sit in a bathtub with Margolis on the other side of the door—"

"He will not come near you. He will not molest you in any way."

Considering the way Margolis jumped at Qadim's commands, Julia thought maybe the djinn's confidence wasn't entirely misplaced. Still....

"He knows he will have to answer to me if he touches you without my leave."

Those words didn't exactly reassure her, but she had to admit that Qadim had the upper hand here. He could blast Margolis into the next dimension without batting an eye. It seemed for the moment that the commander was willing to follow his djinn partner's orders, since he clearly thought if he did everything right, he would get Julia as his reward.

But she wasn't the reward. She was the bait, the honey trap.

And there didn't seem to be a damn thing she could do about it.

CHAPTER EIGHT

Zahrias watched as Jessica smiled down at Santa Fe's newest arrival, but there was a certain question in her eyes. "He looks just like a human baby."

Dani crossed his arms and raised an eyebrow at her. "Do we djinn not look like humans?"

"Well...." Her expression turned sly. "You look like perfect movie-star humans. I'll grant you that."

Sitting in her hospital bed with Santa Fe's newest arrival bundled in her arms, Lauren shook her head. She appeared pale but composed, now that the ordeal was over. "What did you think he was going to look like—a bug-eyed alien or something?"

"Of course not." Jessica leaned over and gave Lauren's hand a squeeze. "I just didn't know if djinn babies pooped rainbows or something."

"They most decidedly do not," Zahrias remarked dryly. "As I'm sure Lauren will find out in due time."

"I don't care what he poops," Lauren said. "I'm just glad he has ten fingers and ten toes."

"And the nicest head of black hair I've ever seen on a baby," Jessica added.

"I'm actually a little disappointed about that," Dani remarked, although the expression on his face didn't reveal anything except pride in his new son. "I was hoping for red hair like yours, Lauren. Maybe next time."

"Years from now," she replied. "I don't think I want to go through that again anytime soon. And maybe by then, Miguel will have figured out how to do an epidural."

"Of course, my darling," Dani said, then bent down to kiss her gently on her cheek.

Watching them, Zahrias couldn't help but be happy for his brother and the woman he had chosen—but at the same time, an odd little pain struck him somewhere near his heart. Would he ever stand there like that, gazing down with loving eyes at the mother of his child?

The way things were going, probably not.

He wondered then if anyone had heard from Julia and the Los Alamos contingent. They should have been back to their mountain stronghold several hours ago. Dani was usually the one to man the radio, since he had a most un-djinn-like fascination with the device, but he had been involved with far more important matters this afternoon. And, because of his distraction, he probably hadn't assigned anyone else to monitor the radio and answer any incoming transmissions.

It seemed a shame to leave now, but truly, Lauren probably needed to rest and not have friends and family constantly hovering over her. He could return in the morning to check on her and the baby.

He excused himself, saying that he needed to follow up on the Los Alamos party and see how they had fared on their trip home. At his words, Jessica seemed to stiffen, the happy light in her eyes dimming.

"Can Jace and I tag along? Just—just to say hi."

Zahrias thought her motives were most likely somewhat more complex than that, but he nodded. "Of course. And Lauren, Dani, I will come by again in the morning."

"That may be your last visit here," Dani said. "Miguel told us that Lauren might be able to go home tomorrow afternoon if all continues to go well."

"Even better. I'm sure you'd both find that situation far more comfortable." Zahrias offered Lauren a final encouraging smile before transporting himself to the art museum, where the small office that had once been used by the facility's support staff now contained the radio equipment. Why exactly Dani had decided to have it set up there, Zahrias didn't know for sure.

The museum did have a certain charm, and perhaps his brother enjoyed being surrounded by things of beauty, rather than the sterile atmosphere of an office building.

Jace and Jessica arrived only a few seconds after he did, popping into the doorway. The couple had their arms wrapped around each other—the only way a human could be transported by a djinn was to have close physical contact—but they extricated themselves soon enough, approaching Zahrias as he stood next to the radio.

He'd operated it a few times before, since Dani had insisted that he know how to use the device, even if doing such a thing was not part of his daily routine. Reaching out, he picked up the handset and toggled the switch that would turn it on. Since it was always set to the one band the two communities used to communicate, he did not have to make any adjustments.

A faint crackle came through the speakers, and he spoke, knowing the connection was now open. "Los Alamos, this is Zahrias from Santa Fe. Are you receiving?"

At once a woman's voice, warm and friendly, responded. "Zahrias, this is Amanda Garson. We're receiving. What can we do for you?"

"We wanted to confirm the safe arrival of Julia Innes' party. They headed out some hours ago, but we were rather occupied here with the birth of my brother's child, and I only now have had the opportunity to follow up on our visitors."

A long pause. Then Amanda said, sounding a little puzzled, "Congratulations on the baby. But Julia's party hasn't gotten here yet. What time did you say they left?"

"I didn't," Zahrias replied, a band of tension seeming to tighten itself around his forehead. It was still difficult for him to think in the tiny pieces mortals used to measure time, but he'd gotten better at it during his tenure here in Santa Fe. "But I believe they left sometime before eleven this morning."

"Which means they should've gotten here by noon," Amanda said, worry clear in her voice. "Shit. I mean, sorry, Zahrias. Maybe—maybe they stopped to scavenge in Española on the way home, since they had one of the devices with them and it would save us having to send out another party anytime soon. Julia's efficient that way."

Of course. That sounded like a perfectly rational explanation. True, Julia had said nothing of such a plan to him, but why should she? The two of them were barely speaking when they parted. The mere thought of their icy leave-taking was enough to make him want to wince, although he didn't.

Even so, doubt niggled at the back of his head, only serving to increase the sensation of pressure bearing down on his forehead and temples. He asked Amanda, "Is there someone you can confirm that with?"

"Sure. Do you mind waiting a few minutes? I'll scare up Shawn Gutierrez and ask him. Julia left him in charge."

"Take as long as you need," Zahrias told her. "I can wait."

The speakers on the radio went silent, except for the soft, ever-present hiss of background noise. Standing a few paces off, Jace and Jessica exchanged worried glances.

"This doesn't feel good," Jessica said at length. "I was getting the heebie-jeebies earlier, but I didn't want to say anything because of Lauren...." Words seemed to fail her, and she shook her head.

"I'm sure it will be all right," Jace told her, then took her hand in his, offering unspoken comfort. Even as he spoke, though, his dark eyes flickered toward Zahrias, as if looking for reassurance there.

Unfortunately, Zahrias had no reassurances to give. As Jessica had said, this didn't feel good. Yes, one could argue that the ever-practical Julia would not pass up an opportunity to gather more supplies for her community, but surely she or someone else in the group would have mentioned those plans to someone, if that had truly been their intention.

A man's voice came over the speaker, pleasant but tense, with just a faint trace of the accent that Zahrias had come to associate with those of Mexican descent. "This is Shawn. Amanda just told me what's going on. I suppose it's possible Julia decided to go into Española if she left Santa Fe that early in the day, but I find it hard to believe that she wouldn't have let someone know what she planned to do."

"So she said nothing to you?"

"No. Last I talked with her, she said they were coming back today but that Miles and Lindsay were staying in Santa Fe." The man's voice sharpened. "They *are* still there with you, aren't they?"

"Yes," Zahrias said, trying to sound confident and not at all concerned, although he wasn't sure how successful he was being. "Still at the U.S. Marshals' building, as far as I know, unless Lindsay convinced Miles to stop for dinner."

"Well, that's something." A pause, and then Shawn said, "I'd better send someone out to look for them."

"Can you afford to do that? How many devices do you have?"

Shawn chuckled, but there was very little humor in the sound. "Plenty. Miles and Lindsay were like a factory with those things over the summer. So it's no hardship to send one out with a search party. And we'll try to raise the CB in the Suburban."

"CB?" Zahrias wasn't sure he'd heard the term before.

"Citizens' band radio. We made sure to put them in all the vehicles we use for going out and scavenging, or even that we know could be going outside the borders of Los Alamos for any reason. Since we can't use our cell phones, it's the next best way to stay in touch."

"Of course."

"Anyway, we'll send someone out and let you know. I'm sure it's nothing." Even as he said the words, however, Shawn didn't sound very confident of that fact.

"Thank you. And if you need us to go out and look—"

"Thanks for the offer, Zahrias, but we're okay. They're our people."

"Of course," Zahrias said again. He didn't quite like the unspoken subtext in Shawn Gutierrez's words, that the party had been comprised of people from Los Alamos, and therefore not any concern of the djinn and their Chosen in Santa Fe. But he knew that protesting further would most likely just make Shawn dig his heels in that much more. Better to let his search party do their work. If they located Julia and her group, then the problem was solved. And if not—

If not, he'd have to pray that they weren't too late to find out what had really happened to them.

Despite Qadim's reassurances that she would be left alone, Julia hesitated for a long time, staring down at the water in the sunken bathtub with its surround of slate tiles. Wisps of steam curled up from the bath, seeming to beckon her in.

Oh, the hell with it. She'd taken the chair from the vanity area of the bathroom and wedged it up under the doorknob, so even if Margolis got any funny ideas, he wouldn't be able to get very far. And she ached in every limb. Soaking in the bath would help.

Well, it might help with the various pains in her body. She doubted it would do much to soothe the dull, throbbing hurt in her heart.

Mouth set, she bent down and untied the laces on her hiking boots, then pulled them off, along with her socks. Next were her jacket and her jeans, then her T-shirt. She paused for a long moment, and finally unhooked her bra and slipped out of her panties. Since she didn't have anything else to change into, she'd have to put them back on, but at least her body would be clean.

Sort of.

She lowered herself into the water, clenching her teeth as the heat of the water shocked against her bare flesh. In a moment, though, she became acclimated enough that she could relax, could let the warmth surrounding her work with her instead of against her.

There were bottles of shampoo and conditioner and body wash sitting on the ledge next to the tub. All high-end stuff, too, based on the labels. Julia wondered whose house this had been, whether they had lived here full-time or whether the property was simply a vacation getaway. There were lots of places like that tucked in and around Santa Fe, toys of rich people to be lived in for a few weeks out of the year and then ignored.

Well, whoever had owned the house was now long gone. Why Qadim had decided to use this place as his hideaway, Julia had no idea, except that it wasn't visible from the road, but still fairly close to the ambush site. And it was large; she didn't have a clear idea of the scope of the place, since she'd only seen a few rooms, but she guessed it had to be upwards of four thousand square feet. Way above her pay grade in her former life. She thought about the condo she'd scrimped and saved to buy, and which her ex-fiancé had cajoled her into selling. Two bedrooms, one bath, barely a thousand square feet. The whole thing would have fit into the kitchen/family room combo in this place.

Which was only a way of attempting to distract herself from the reality of her situation, that she was merely here to lure Zahrias out so Qadim could kill him. No, the big djinn hadn't said as much, but she could read between the lines. What bad blood in their past had brought them to this point? Certainly she'd never heard Zahrias mention Qadim, but why would he? They hadn't discussed very much that was personal, and Zahrias had a long, long history behind him. This current plot could be based on a slight that had occurred centuries earlier.

She had to think of some way to get out of here, to get away before Qadim could use her to bring Zahrias to his doom. But maybe she was selling him short. Yes, Qadim was big, the biggest djinn she'd yet seen, but bigger didn't always mean more skilled. Surely Zahrias was in charge of Santa Fe at least partially because he knew how to take care of himself and the people he had sworn to serve. But if Qadim got the drop on him....

Scowling, she rinsed the shampoo from her hair, then worked in a good dollop of the conditioner. Just another distraction, something to concentrate on rather than the echo of Nancy's scream against the concrete walls of the underpass, the ear-piercing sounds of Margolis' pistol firing again and again. Had he gotten some perverse pleasure out of killing Brent and Nancy and Eric, or had he not even given them that much thought, only seeing them as obstacles that stood between him and the woman he desired?

Despite the hot bath water, Julia shivered. She was taking too long. At any minute, he could be at the door, knocking on it, talking to her through it while imagining her naked in the bath.

God. She rinsed out the conditioner, then grabbed a towel from the rack next to the bathtub. Working quickly, she dried herself off and wrapped a second towel around her hair. As she paused to send a nervous glance in the direction of the door, a chill went down her spine.

Her duffle bag was sitting on the seat of the chair she'd tucked up under the doorknob.

The last she'd seen it, that bag had been stowed in the cargo area of the Suburban. And she knew Margolis hadn't brought it with them, because he'd marched her straight to his pickup truck and driven away.

Which meant that Qadim must have retrieved it, then blinked it into the bathroom while she was bathing.

Better than him marching in with it, but even so, Julia couldn't help feeling violated. After all, he could have left the duffle in the bedroom that was attached to the bath. The djinn had already informed her she would be sleeping in that room tonight.

No, he probably enjoyed having the duffle show up in here because it would send her off-balance, make her start to wonder if he could somehow see through the door or the walls, see her naked body....

Stop it, she told herself. *He wants you to torture yourself. So don't.*

Mouth pressed into a grim line, she retrieved the duffle and set it on top of the long tiled counter that stretched across one entire wall of the bathroom. Right then she should just be glad that she'd packed extra underwear and another set of clean clothes. She wouldn't have to change into her dirty and rumpled clothing after all.

She pulled on panties and a bra, then slipped into the jeans and long-sleeved T-shirt she had folded at the bottom of the duffle. All her toiletries were there, too—deodorant and toothpaste and moisturizer.

There was a blow dryer in one of the bathroom drawers. The house clearly had electricity, so she could dry her hair if she wanted to. But should she waste time on that lengthy process? Then again, her hair would take forever to air-dry. She couldn't guarantee that it wouldn't still be damp by the time she went to bed; outside the window, the world was dim and dusky, the sunset come and gone while she was in the bath.

Incongruously, her stomach growled. It didn't seem to care that she had lost three friends that afternoon, or that she was locked in an isolated country house with a madman and a scheming djinn. Qadim hadn't said anything about feeding her dinner, but surely he must intend to, if his words about making sure she would be in decent shape to see Zahrias the next day were to be believed.

Grimly, she plugged in the blow dryer and then went to work on her hair. Since it reached nearly to her waist, the process took a while. The entire time, she tried to analyze what she had seen of the house so far, if there was any chance to get away without either Margolis or Qadim noticing. This bathroom and its connected bedroom were on the second floor, and faced away from the road. The bathroom window was tiny, and she knew she'd never fit through it. But maybe the bedroom?

Julia finished with her hair and put the dryer back in the drawer where she'd found it. Afterward, she went to the door and pulled the chair out from under the knob, then headed into the bedroom. Yes, it had French doors that opened onto a balcony. She went to them at once and jiggled on the handles. Locked. Of course.

She could break through the glass, but that would make so much noise that any chance of slipping away undetected would be ruined. Would the element of surprise be enough to help her get away? She'd be on foot, and Margolis had his truck. And she had no idea whether she'd be able to evade Qadim's pursuit or not. Djinn seemed to know when mortals were around, or they wouldn't have been able to so mercilessly hunt down those Immune who weren't lucky enough to find sanctuary in Los Alamos.

"It is cold," Qadim said from behind her. "You will not need to open those tonight."

She whirled. The djinn stood just inside the doorway that opened onto the upstairs hall. In his hands he held a wad of gleaming golden fabric. As her gaze fell on it, he extended it to her.

"You will wear this for dinner."

Again, a shiver ran down her spine. Ignoring it, she said, "I'm already dressed, thank you."

"What you're wearing is not suitable. You will wear this."

Outright defiance didn't sound like a very good idea at the moment. She stepped forward and took the fabric from him, but didn't unfold it to see what it actually was. "I wasn't aware there was a dress code."

His heavy-lidded black eyes, overshadowed by his brows, seemed to narrow further. "You will meet me in the dining room in a quarter-hour. Don't be late." He turned and went out into the hallway, then closed the bedroom door behind him.

Wonderful. At this point, she had no idea as to what Qadim's intentions toward her might be. Certainly during their conversation in the courtyard, he'd given no indication that he was interested in her personally, only in her usefulness in luring Zahrias here.

He isn't interested, she told herself. *He's just messing with you. Showing who's in control, playing little head games.*

The thought actually reassured her somewhat. Not because she appreciated Qadim's maneuvers, but better that than the alternative.

Repressing a shiver, she went to the door and engaged the lock, then finally unfolded the garment he had given her.

It was actually two pieces of clothing, a long fitted tunic with high slits up the sides, and billowy full trousers in a style that she'd seen both male and female djinn wear. The fabric was a supple silk woven in a subtle geometric pattern in shades of light and dark gold. Intricate beadwork surrounded the neckline and cuffs of the tunic.

The ensemble was actually breathtakingly beautiful, but Julia couldn't take much pleasure in the thought of wearing it. Now, if Zahrias was the one to see her in these clothes, rather than Qadim or Margolis....

She pushed that thought aside, then hastily stripped off her T-shirt and jeans and climbed into the shimmering silken outfit. It fit her perfectly, hugging her curves. How Qadim had managed that feat, she wasn't sure and probably didn't want to know.

Something sparkled at her from the top of the dresser. She went toward it, and saw the sparkle had come from a pair of long, dangling earrings in heavy gold, set with what looked like diamonds. Was she supposed to wear those, too?

It sure seemed that way. Julia removed the small silver hoops she wore all the time, and put in the gold earrings instead. When she stared at her reflection in the mirror above the dresser, a vision in gold looked back at her. All gold, from her loose hair to the clothing she wore. Something about that image disturbed her, and she turned away quickly.

What she was supposed to put on her feet, she had no idea. The hiking boots she'd been wearing didn't seem like a very good match for the fancy clothing she had on. Well, she supposed she could go barefoot; the house's flooring was a combination of slate tile and wood, but rugs were scattered everywhere, so it should be all right. It wasn't as if she'd have an opportunity to make a break for it, not with Qadim apparently breathing down her neck every time she turned around.

But when she opened the door to step into the hallway, she saw a pair of gold beaded slippers sitting immediately outside. Had the djinn forgotten to give them to her, or had he wanted her to find them separately, the way she had with the earrings?

Pondering Qadim's thought processes was probably a fruitless endeavor. Julia stepped into the slippers and noted that they fit her just as well as the rest of the ensemble did. Well, at least she wouldn't have to go barefoot. That was something.

She descended the stairs, fighting the sense of wrongness that seemed to surround her with every step. How could she be so calm when she should be running away, doing whatever she could to get out of here?

Because she knew she had no choice. The djinn were scary enough when they were being friendly. She had no chance of besting someone like Qadim. All she could do was go along and pray that somehow Zahrias would have the upper hand when he finally did confront his old enemy.

"My God."

Margolis' voice. Julia halted on the bottom step and saw that the commander was standing in the foyer, staring at her as if he'd never seen her before. Well, she supposed he hadn't—not looking like this, anyway.

"I guess Qadim wanted me dressed for dinner," she said, trying to sound casual. Margolis' attention was never welcome, but now, in this silky getup that clung to her body and was more low-cut than anything she'd dared to wear in years, it almost seemed as if his hands were moving over her once again, even though he stood a good ten feet from her.

He frowned. "It looks that way. He didn't say anything to me about it."

Trouble in paradise. Maybe if she could get Qadim and Margolis quarreling with one another....

She shrugged. "I guess not. Which way is the dining room?"

The commander pointed to the hallway to his left. "First opening on the right."

Not that she really needed the direction, because as soon as she began to turn, Qadim appeared in the corridor. "I am glad to see that you are punctual, Julia. That pleases me."

The last thing she wanted was to please Qadim. However, his words seemed to annoy Margolis, which she found encouraging.

"Do I get to have dinner, too?" the commander asked, the faintest of whines entering his voice. "You neglected to mention it to me."

"I fear that only two places have been set. You will have to do for yourself."

Margolis' hands, hanging at his sides, balled into fists. "I think you're forgetting that I brought her here to you. And you promised me—"

He didn't have the opportunity to complete the sentence, because the words were suddenly choked off, and an invisible hand seemed to grasp him by the throat, then push him up against the wall and hold him there. His eyes bulged, and his face began to turn red.

Shocked, Julia began to step forward. Qadim's gaze flickered toward her, and she stopped where she was. Not that she really cared too much about helping Margolis—she'd only reacted on instinct.

The djinn spoke. "I think you are forgetting your place, mortal. You will get your due at a time of my choosing, and no sooner. Do not disturb me again this night, or it will go badly for you."

In the next instant, the invisible hand that had been holding Margolis up against the wall seemed to release him. He slid down, but braced himself at the last minute so he wouldn't crumple to an ignominious heap on the floor. In silence, he turned and stalked off toward the kitchen—but not before sending a final baleful glance in Qadim's direction. Julia knew she wouldn't want to be on the receiving end of such a glare, but the djinn appeared supremely unconcerned.

"Come," he said, extending a hand.

The last thing Julia wanted to do was take it, but she knew she had little choice. Especially not after the show of force she'd just witnessed. Swallowing, she came toward Qadim and laid her hand in his, and tried to ignore the unwelcome heat of his flesh. Strange how that same warmth had been so attractive in Zahrias.

Qadim led her into the dining room, a large chamber with an equally large table. As he had informed Margolis, only two places were set at that table. In one corner of the room was a small kiva-style fireplace where a fire crackled away, combating some of the chill she could feel seeping in through the French doors. Maybe they opened onto the courtyard, but it was too dark outside to tell for sure.

"Sit," the djinn commanded her, pointing to the place setting to the right of the one at the head of the table.

Arguing would be futile, so she did as he'd instructed. At least the wrought-iron light fixture overhead had been switched on; a trio of pillar candles in coordinating wrought-iron holders flickered at the center of the table, but clearly Qadim hadn't intended this to be a romantic candlelit dinner. Once again she had the impression that he had set all this up to both annoy Margolis and discomfit her.

A bottle of wine was already airing on the table, and Qadim picked it up and poured some into her glass, and slightly more into his own. She couldn't see the label, but the wine was dark, almost opaque, with just the faintest garnet flicker when the firelight caught it.

"To settling old scores," the djinn said, holding up his wine glass.

Julia didn't move. "You can't honestly expect me to drink to that."

A smile played around his thin lips. "Ah, perhaps not. Then to new friends?"

She didn't like the sound of that much better, but she decided not to force the issue. Wrapping her fingers around the stem of her glass, she raised it as well. "To new friends."

The wine was heavy, with a tinge of earth to it. Well, she supposed it made sense that an earth elemental would choose something with that particular quality. Julia didn't think she cared for it very much, but that was probably just as well. Then she wouldn't be tempted to have more than one glass, if even that.

In the next moment, platters of food appeared on the table. By that point, she was a little more used to the way Qadim showed off with displays of his power, but it still startled her. So different from Zahrias, who seemed to take care not to do anything that she'd find off-putting. Yes, she knew he wielded power she couldn't completely understand, but he never made a spectacle of it.

She didn't recognize everything that had been placed before her, but it all smelled good. Some kind of rice dish with golden raisins and slivers of almonds, and hunks of meat so richly seasoned and dark with sauce that it took her a moment to realize it was only chicken. A salad of finely chopped lettuce with sesame seeds in an aromatic dressing. Flat bread that reminded her of naan, only delicately seasoned with saffron.

"Is this djinn food?" she asked.

"Yes. Do you like it?"

At least she could be honest about that. "It's very good."

He appeared pleased by her reply, because he nodded, smiling slightly. "I am glad to hear that. More wine?"

Julia hadn't intended to drink anything more than the one glass, but for some reason she nodded and held out her wine glass so he could refill it. The smile still lingered on his lips.

Really, she didn't know why she'd thought him unattractive. His nose was long, his lips thin, but for some reason they seemed to work together to make a pleasing combination. And his brows were heavy, but the lashes surrounding his eyes were thick and black, so thick she could almost believe they weren't real—except of course they were.

Looking at him, she could feel a strange warmth throbbing low in her belly. Need, she realized foggily. Desire.

She wanted him.

No, she couldn't want him. She wanted Zahrias. But wait—she didn't want Zahrias, because he was weak. A coward. He should have claimed her back when it would have made a difference.

Suddenly, Qadim wasn't in his chair anymore. He was standing next to her, his robes brushing against her arm. Just that feathery touch was enough to make her heart begin to pound.

Then he bent and pushed her hair out of the way, head lowering so he could lay his lips against the exposed skin of her neck. All her nerve endings seemed to light on fire, and she moaned.

"Yes, my beauty," he murmured. "You want this, don't you?"

She did. She wanted him. How was that possible? He was evil—he'd sent Margolis to fetch her, Margolis, who'd killed her friends. And yet her body didn't seem to care about any of that. It thrummed with need. She had to have him. It had been so very long since....

No. The word seemed to come from somewhere deep within her. *This isn't you. This is Qadim, using his powers to make you think you want him. Remember what Jessica told you about the djinn glamour.*

It was like trying to recall a story she'd heard a hundred years ago, but Julia pushed against the fog in her brain, remembering how Jessica had revealed to her that some of the djinn had used these powers of attraction to get their Chosen to bond with them more easily. Now Qadim was doing the same thing, and she'd almost fallen into his trap.

"No," she said aloud, laying her hands flat on the table. Feeling the solid surface beneath her palms helped to steady her. "I'm not going to fall for your djinn mind tricks, Qadim, so don't bother."

At once he straightened, then crossed his arms across his chest. His dark eyes bored into her. "How is it that you are able to do this?"

"Because I know what you djinn are capable of."

A long pause, during which Julia thought for sure he must be able to hear the panicky beating of her heart. Defying him like this was dangerous, but she couldn't—*wouldn't*—give in to him. The very thought made her ill.

Then an improbable smile touched the corners of his mouth. "Interesting. I've never before encountered a mortal who was able to withstand a djinn's glamour."

"There's a first time for everything," she said, and reached for her glass of wine and took a sip, hoping she looked casual and unconcerned. Unfortunately, her hand gave a betraying shake, and she quickly set the glass back down.

During this exchange, Qadim had remained standing next to her. After watching her closely for a few more seconds, however, he returned to his chair and sat. Still wearing that faint smile, he poured more wine into his own glass. "You impress me, Julia Innes. Shall we make a bargain, you and I?"

"What?" she asked, tone guarded. Anything he was offering couldn't be good.

He wrapped his fingers around the stem of his wine glass. The ring of gold and tiger-eye he wore on his pinky seemed to glare at her balefully. "When I best Zahrias tomorrow—"

"*If* you best him."

A lift of one eyebrow. "Very well. If I best him, I will give you a choice. You can have Margolis...or me."

He was serious. She had a feeling the commander wouldn't be very happy to hear about this new wrinkle, considering that Qadim had promised her to him. But the alternative....

No, she wouldn't allow herself to think about that. About all she could do now was pray that Zahrias really would be able to beat this bastard. Otherwise, her own fate would be an unhappy one, no matter which choice she made.

And, judging by the amused expression on Qadim's face, he seemed to know that as well.

CHAPTER NINE

ONE WOULD THINK THAT WITH ALMOST ALL OF eternity to play with, waiting would become easier, but as the minutes stretched past, Zahrias began to wonder if he would go mad trying to figure out what might have happened to Julia and her party. At one point Jessica slipped out of the office at the museum, saying she'd better scare up some food, since it was getting late and they all needed to eat something. All Zahrias could do was think that he certainly had no appetite at the moment. Even so, he had to acknowledge to himself that she was only trying to help.

She returned sometime later with a bag of those odd bread and meat inventions that mortals referred to as sandwiches, as well as a big insulated container of coffee.

"Since we don't know how long this is going to take," she explained.

Right then, Zahrias thought his nerves would have appreciated a good glass of wine rather than the coffee, but he didn't say so. At any rate, coffee was one of this world's vices that he'd come to appreciate, so he murmured his thanks as she poured some into a mug she'd gotten from the museum's gift shop.

The sandwiches proved to be tasty enough. Where Jessica had gotten them, he didn't know for sure, but he guessed she had probably gone to Phillip for the ingredients, even if she'd put them together herself. The three of them ate in silence for a few moments, although Zahrias noticed the way Jasreel and Jessica would flicker a quick glance at the silent radio equipment from time to time, as if willing the Los Alamos people to make contact.

But no call came through. Jasreel silently gathered up the paper the sandwiches had been wrapped in and discarded it in the trash can that sat in one corner of the room. As he did so, Jessica poured some more coffee into Zahrias' mug.

"Maybe I should have scared up some brandy to put in that," she said, offering him a smile.

But he could see the strain in her dark eyes, despite the smile. She was doing her best to cover up her worry, he could tell. Unfortunately, that best didn't seem to be sufficient at the moment.

Then the radio crackled, and Shawn Gutierrez's voice came through the speakers. "Santa Fe? Are you there?"

Zahrias immediately picked up the handset. "We're here. What news do you have?"

"Nothing good." The mortal's voice sounded tight, too controlled, as if he was doing everything he could to hide how troubled he actually was. "We traced the route Julia would have taken to come back to Los Alamos and found the wreckage of her Suburban in an underpass in Pojoaque."

Jessica gasped, and Jasreel reached out to take her hand.

"Wreckage?" Zahrias demanded. He had to push aside an image of Julia's SUV a crumpled heap, her body broken inside. "She had an accident?"

"Oh, this was no accident," Shawn said, sounding grim. "There were scorch marks on the asphalt, and parts of it were melted. The Suburban was blackened underneath, like it had been hit with a rocket or something."

A rocket? What in the world....

Jessica seemed to be one step ahead of him. She came close enough so she could speak into the microphone. "Like someone hit them with an RPG or something?"

"Yeah, it looked that way. And who do we all know who could use something like that?"

Margolis. Of course. Zahrias was on his feet before he even realized what he was doing. "Where was this exactly?"

"Where the 502 crosses under the 285. It—"

But Zahrias had no intention of waiting to hear anything else. He could go see for himself.

He had never been to the location in question, but that didn't matter. His people could send themselves pretty much where they pleased on this plane, as long as they had a general idea. During his time here, he had studied maps of the region; he knew more or less where to go.

The night was a black one, for the moon had yet to rise. But Zahrias summoned his flames to him, and they served well enough to illuminate the underpass where Shawn Gutierrez had said that Julia's Suburban was located.

Or what was left of it, at any rate. Two of the tires were flat, and black marks marred the undercarriage. In places, the paint looked blistered. The windshield was gone, although Zahrias could see where its remains had been pushed off to one side.

And there was blood. None on the driver's side, for which Zahrias murmured a silent prayer of thanks, but gruesome stains marked the upholstery of the passenger seat, and the back seat as well. But no bodies.

Glass crunched behind him, and he turned, fists clenching. But it was only Jasreel and Jessica. The other djinn had clearly been holding his Chosen so he could transport her here with him; as Zahrias watched, Jasreel unclasped his arms from Jessica's waist, allowing her to step away from him. She glanced around, taking in the wreckage, then approached Zahrias.

"Maybe someday I'll get used to the way you djinn can pop in and out like that," she said. "But you should have waited to hear what else Shawn had to say."

"And what was that?"

"His search party took the bodies back with them. *Three* bodies, Zahrias. Julia wasn't one of them."

Relief at her words, yes, but if Julia wasn't here, then that meant Margolis must have her. Zahrias nodded, since he wasn't sure he trusted himself to speak. Just the thought of that monster having her in his grasp once again was enough to turn his blood to fire.

Jessica must have come to the same conclusion, because she said, "I know. It's awful. But at least she's still alive."

"We *think* she's alive," Zahrias replied bitterly. "We know nothing for sure."

"All right, you have a point. But it really looks like he targeted the SUV in a way that wouldn't completely blow it up. Margolis wanted her to survive."

Zahrias would have to take her word for that, since he knew very little of how such devices worked. He was about to say as much when Jasreel called over to the two of them.

"I think you'd better take a look at this."

Frowning, Zahrias turned toward the other djinn and looked where he was pointing. A portion of the asphalt was not so much torn up as exploded outward, as if something had come boiling up from beneath it. As he approached the spot in question and stared down at it, cold washed over him. Only an earth elemental could have created that kind of destruction.

An earth elemental....

No.

"What is it?" Jessica asked. Clearly, she had noticed some shift in his expression.

"This was caused by a djinn," Jasreel told her.

"A djinn?" she said blankly. "One of ours? But—"

"No," Zahrias cut in. "Not one of our community. Someone I had hoped never to meet again."

Now both Jasreel and Jessica looked puzzled. That was only to be expected; Zahrias and Jasreel were cousins, but there was a good deal the younger djinn didn't know about his past.

"His name is Qadim al-Syan. An earth elemental, as you can see from the way he made his entrance here. No real need for that, of course, but Qadim always did like to show off."

"How do you know him?" Jasreel asked.

"I was...involved with his sister." At that reply, both Jessica and Jasreel looked startled, and Zahrias went on, hating to reveal this much of his past but knowing he must, "It was very long ago. Long before I met Evangeline and tried to make a life with her. I was young and foolish, and soon realized that Lyanna—Qadim's sister—and I would not do well together. So I ended our attachment, but she did not take it well."

"What happened?" Jessica this time, her tone gentle but her eyes curious. No doubt anything she might learn of djinn society would fascinate her.

Zahrias glanced over at Jasreel. "How much have you told her of our ways?"

"Some. As much as she has asked about. It does not seem to have much relevance to our lives now, to the way we djinn have devoted ourselves to our Chosen."

"Ah." It was true that those of the One Thousand, the djinn who had committed themselves to saving what they could of humanity, had known they must attach themselves to that one mortal forever, because if the connection was ever broken, the gifts of long life and abundant health that the djinn provided to their Chosen would also be taken away. But it was not always so with his people. Addressing his next words to Jessica, Zahrias said, "It is not generally our way to be with one person throughout our lives, for we recognize that to cleave to another being for that length of time is unrealistic. However, there is always a special significance given to the first person we are intimate with, and the expectation that those relationships should last longer, and be dissolved gently."

"But I take it yours wasn't?" Jessica said. "Dissolved gently, I mean."

"As gently as I could." He wished he didn't have to speak of this. For, whatever their differences, he had not meant to hurt Lyanna. But the same fire that had first attracted him made her, by nature, difficult to deal with. She had wanted to spend centuries with him, to bear his children. And he'd realized early on that the last thing he wanted was to have any offspring with her, for that would have tied them together for eternity, even if they took other lovers later on. "She did not take the rejection well, and her brother even worse. In his mind, I had ruined her, for in those situations, it should be the woman who breaks things off, so she might save face. Qadim felt that I had made his sister look like someone that no man would ever wish to be with."

Jessica's brows drew together, and she glanced over at Jasreel briefly before she spoke. "That's being a bit extreme, isn't it?"

"We might think so, but...." Zahrias let the words die away, then shook his head. "Qadim is not known for his moderate nature. Indeed, he wished to challenge me over this perceived insult, but our families intervened, saying that would cause an even greater scandal. We all went our separate ways, and I thought that was the end of the matter."

A matter that should have ended centuries before. Zahrias had not given any thought to Lyanna for more years than he could count. After all, he had heard that she did seem to recover at some point, and had many liaisons, although she had never begun a family with any of her conquests. When the news of her numerous lovers reached his ears, he put aside any guilt he might have felt over the way things had ended between them, and eventually put her from his mind, save to idly wonder now and again how she was faring.

Unfortunately, it did not seem as if Qadim had forgotten the slight Zahrias had made his sister suffer, imagined or no. That Julia might now be in such a vengeful djinn's hands....

"There's one thing I don't understand," Jasreel said then.

"Only one?" Zahrias responded. The bitterness was clear in his tone; he had made no attempt to mask it.

"For the moment, yes." The younger djinn hesitated, as if he was wrestling with the best way to phrase what he intended to say next. "Putting aside for the moment the question of why Qadim is working with Margolis at all, I have to wonder how he would have known of your attachment to Julia in the first place."

"I have no attachment to her," Zahrias said stiffly. This was unbearable; he had no desire to speak of such things, even to sympathetic listeners.

Jessica's head tilted to one side. "Come on, Zahrias. You're among friends here."

Would he have to lay bare his heart, when he had tried to keep it hidden even from himself? Yes, he supposed he could count Jessica and Jasreel as his friends now, although he had never been close with his cousin before they came here to dwell on the mortal plane.

As they watched him, he let out the smallest of sighs. "Very well. I do feel...something...for her. I have tried to ignore it, because I know she feels bound to her duty in Los Alamos, and I have no idea how she would respond to any overtures I made." For the moment, he saw no reason to disclose what had passed between him and Julia only the day before. Yes, they hadn't parted on good terms, but somehow that kiss he had shared with Julia still felt sacred.

To his surprise, Jessica reached out and laid a hand on his arm. "Zahrias, I never thought I'd say this to you, but you're being kind of a dumbass."

"I beg your pardon?" he said, certain he should be offended, although the exact meaning of the epithet eluded him.

"You two have been so busy dancing around each other that neither of you seem to realize that you've actually been dancing *with* each other the whole time. Julia's just as interested in you as you are in her, but she went off to Los Alamos last spring because you basically goaded her into it."

"I did not—" Zahrias began, but she wouldn't allow him to get any further than that.

"Oh, yes, you did, with that remark about how Los Alamos would be lucky to have her. When you said that, she knew she had to go. Because if you'd wanted to be with her, you would have made sure someone else got nominated to run things over there. She didn't think she had any hope."

Was that really what had happened? At the time, he'd been fighting his attraction to her, had told himself that he could not allow himself to become involved with a mortal. So perhaps he had subconsciously chosen to say something which would make it clear to her that there was no hope of a future with him.

"I—" He broke off there, realizing that his attempts to avoid future pain had only caused a great deal more. "I am a very great fool."

"That's being a little harsh," Jasreel said. "The important thing now is to find out where Qadim could have taken her."

"True." That was better. If he could focus on the logistics of getting her back, then perhaps he wouldn't be able to think about everything he'd done wrong…

…or what Qadim might be doing to her at this very moment. The earth elemental might be thinking that because Zahrias had ruined his sister, he might as well do the same thing to the woman Zahrias loved.

The woman he loved. He hadn't allowed himself to think of Julia in such a way, but he knew then that he did love her. Loved her strength and her intelligence and her beauty, the sweet fire of her lips. He had to get to her. Somehow.

Jessica asked, worry clear in her voice, "He wouldn't—he wouldn't have taken her to the djinn world, would he?"

Immediately, both Jasreel and Zahrias shook their heads. Jasreel spoke, saying, "No, that's impossible. I've told you that mortals can't exist there for more than an hour or two. I don't think he'd risk her that way, since it's clear he's using her to get back at Zahrias. He'd stay close, I think, because this area has been designated for the Santa Fe group and their Chosen, and so there isn't any risk of coming up against those of our people who are still out hunting the Immune."

Zahrias hadn't even thought of that, but it was true. Julia was not Chosen, and so would be seen as fair game by the djinn who'd made it their duty to ensure that the world was cleansed of any remaining humans. No doubt Qadim would try to protect her, lest his chance at revenge be taken away, but that couldn't be entirely guaranteed. Jasreel was right—they had to be somewhere close by.

"What is this place?" Zahrias asked then, extending a hand toward the black night beyond the underpass, which was still illuminated by the ghostly flames he had summoned.

Jessica appeared a little startled. "What, you mean Pojoaque? I don't know that much about it. Semi-rural at best, I guess. There are houses and ranches. Not a lot. But still...."

She didn't complete the sentence, but Zahrias thought he knew what she was driving at. Even in a sparsely populated place like this, there were probably several hundred empty houses or other structures where Qadim could be holed up with Julia. Where Margolis fit in with all this, Zahrias didn't know for sure. Clearly, he had been the one to mount the attack on Julia's party. But why? Had Qadim promised the former commander of Los Alamos that he would have Julia, if he only did as Qadim ordered?

That theory made a sickening sort of sense. Zahrias' only comfort was that he very much doubted the earth elemental would honor his promise. Why give up his prize to a lowly human, when he could enjoy her himself?

"We will find her," Jasreel said. Perhaps Zahrias' inner turmoil had been too clearly reflected on his face, and so his cousin was saying what he could to offer comfort. "But it still worries me that Qadim somehow knew taking her would be the best way to wound you. Is it possible he's been in contact with someone in Santa Fe?"

Zahrias did not want to contemplate such a prospect, for it would mean they had a traitor among them...or, at the very least, a djinn whose loyalty was questionable. "I cannot say. It is possible that one of our people might have a family connection with him. I do not know the genealogy of everyone there."

"Well, it's worth looking into," Jessica said. "But later. The most important thing now is to find this Qadim." She glanced from Jasreel to Zahrias, her gaze speculative. "Or, more to the point, find Julia. Aren't you djinn able to sense when a mortal is around? You never seem to have a problem tracking down people when you need to."

Unfortunately, the situation wasn't quite as simple as that. "In most cases, I would say yes, but things are more complicated now because we are dealing with an earth elemental."

"I don't follow."

"We djinn all have our individual powers," Jasreel explained. "I can call the wind, and Zahrias can make fire do his bidding. But along with those obvious powers, we possess more subtle ones as well. I can hear your thoughts on the wind, and Zahrias can melt metal with the sheer force of his will. And one particular gift earth elementals possess is the ability to shield themselves and those around them from intrusion by other djinn. We could walk right past the place where Qadim has Julia hidden and never know, because he'd be using the very power of the earth itself to block any sign of her presence."

Jessica didn't quite groan, but she looked as if she wanted to. "Well, that's just great."

"It doesn't mean we shouldn't start looking," Zahrias said. "It only means finding her will be more difficult. But we should go now. We've already wasted enough time."

A nod. Her expression was resigned. "I guess I should have brought more coffee."

The bed was comfortable enough, but that didn't mean Julia intended to get a lick of sleep that night. After dinner, she'd been allowed to come up to her designated room on her own. Qadim had stayed in the dining room, finishing the last of the bottle of wine. The satisfied expression he'd worn seemed to indicate that he was confident in the outcome of his battle with Zahrias the next day.

What form that would take, she wasn't sure. She'd witnessed Jasreel's duel with his half-brother Aldair, but they were both air elementals and so had fought on a more or less even playing field. But with Zahrias commanding fire and Qadim controlling earth, she wasn't sure how that would even work.

Well, she supposed she would find out tomorrow.

She was lying flat on her back, eyes fixed on the ceiling. The door was locked, but Julia didn't have much confidence in that flimsy defense. No door locks could keep a djinn out. What unnerved her even more was that she hadn't seen hide nor hair of Margolis since Qadim had sent him packing. He had to be skulking around someplace, but where?

He won't try anything, she told herself. *Qadim would just do that Darth Vader maneuver on him again.*

Maybe. She'd seen the flicker of madness far back in Margolis' eyes, and wondered if that madness would spur him to questionable action, even if doing so meant risking Qadim's wrath. Margolis had never been all that stable, but six months of imprisonment had only served to damage him that much more. It was possible that fear of the djinn who commanded him wasn't strong enough to keep him away from the prize he'd been lusting after for so long.

If only she really was Zahrias' Chosen. She knew that the djinn had a connection with the mortals they'd made their partners, a connection so deep they could reach out to one another across the miles and communicate by thought. But she wasn't anything to Zahrias, only a woman he'd felt some attraction to, but not enough so he would dedicate his life to her.

All right, she could deal with that. The knowledge hurt, but so had a lot of other things in her life. Maybe he'd sensed the flaw within her, had realized that something inside had been fractured early on and could never really be repaired. She could slap a temporary bandage on it and pretend everything was fine, but it wasn't. Because Zahrias was strong and noble, he deserved someone strong as well, not a woman who was so weak that she'd sell the property she'd worked so hard to earn on her own, just because her fiancé told her to, a woman who'd stood there and let him hit her that one time, just because she'd had the temerity to go car shopping without him.

Jessica had tried to reassure Julia, to tell her that she knew Julia would have had the strength to leave eventually if the Heat hadn't intervened, but Julia wasn't so sure. Years of being told you were worthless eventually started to build up. You believed it, even if others tried to step in and tell you it wasn't true.

Restless, she pushed back the covers and got out of bed, then went to the window. She wasn't really sure what she expected to see, because the night was black as pitch beyond the little oasis of light here at the house. But she didn't want to be lying there, consumed by thoughts that chased themselves around and around and never seemed to go anywhere.

But a gibbous moon had risen over the mountains to the east, and its light was enough to illuminate the courtyard, which lay below her balcony. The fountain's water still danced in the moonlight, catching its rays and shimmering like shattered diamonds in the darkness. The water was not the only thing moving out there, however. Julia caught sight of a figure walking in the shadowy courtyard, coming to pause near the edge of the fountain. Margolis?

No, the figure was too tall, and when he moved, she saw the glint of silk along the robes he wore. Qadim. But what was he doing out there?

His arms were extended in front of him, palms flat to the ground. In the next instant, Julia felt the faintest rumble of the earth beneath the house. Not enough to cause any real damage, or even to knock over the bottles of perfume the previous occupant of this room had left sitting on a tray on top of the dresser. But enough to signal that the djinn was exerting his power in some way, even though Julia couldn't begin to guess what that was.

In the next moment, he turned. Even at this distance, Julia could tell he was looking up at her window. Could he see her standing there in her T-shirt and cut-off yoga pants, so very different from the glamorous outfit he'd made her wear at dinner? The moonlight might be reflecting off the glass; surely it was very bright now, and coming in at the wrong angle. But djinn eyes were sharper than mortal eyes....

Rattled, she moved away from the window and got into bed. The covers offered no real security, but it felt better to be burrowed beneath them, just like all the times when she was a little girl and had overheard her parents fighting. Back then, she'd thought if she could only cover her ears, maybe that would make it all stop, even though the bruises on her mother's arms and face after such incidents always gave the lie to Julia's childish hopes.

There was no point in revisiting those memories, however. Both her parents were gone now, and if they'd found some sort of peace in death, she would never know for certain. What she did know was that she needed to be as rested as possible tomorrow—not so she was looking her best, and therefore would make even more alluring bait, but because if she stayed sharp, maybe she could figure out some way for both her and Zahrias to survive.

She shut her eyes and made herself breathe deeply. In...out...in...out. Rest...rest....

Darkness fell.

CHAPTER TEN

Jasreel and Jessica went off in one direction, while Zahrias headed in the other. Perhaps being separated was unwise, but they could cover a great deal more ground this way. He could only hope that if the couple located Julia first, they would come and fetch him before they did anything foolish. Qadim was older and wilier and, Zahrias feared, stronger than Jasreel. Yes, his cousin had shown a good deal of resourcefulness in his duel with Aldair, but Zahrias didn't know if that would be enough.

As Jessica had told him, this was a far more rural area than Santa Fe. The properties were spread far apart, and often set back a good distance from the road. Because Qadim was no doubt doing everything he could to block Julia's presence, Zahrias couldn't rely on the faint but distinctive tingle that told him when a mortal was nearby.

He could only use his eyes, hoping that one of these houses would betray some signs of life. What made it even trickier was that the homes were empty, but quite a few still had some sort of lighting around them because of the human technology that allowed exterior lights to soak up the sun's rays during the daytime and then illuminate a designated area during the nighttime hours. More than once he'd stopped, hope flaring that he'd encountered someplace where people yet lived, only to find nothing there except those deceptive solar lights.

At least he could drift along, using his powers to propel him rather than having to trudge from house to house on foot the way a human would. But as the night wore on, he could feel his sense of unease growing, tension increasing in his neck and shoulders with every house that proved itself empty. Perhaps their speculation that Qadim had remained in the area had been wrong, and this was all just wasted effort. From his studies of the region, Zahrias knew there were other small settlements farther up this road, places tucked away into the folds of the mountains, in hidden box canyons and deep valleys. It would take days to search them all if Pojoaque turned out to be a dead end.

If that proved to be the case, though, he would keep going. He knew he couldn't rest until Julia was found, and safe in his arms. And if he had to go down on his knees and beg her forgiveness for refusing to acknowledge what had been before his eyes all along, he would do that as well. He couldn't change the past, but he could make sure their future was a bright one.

First, though, he had to find her.

No dreams haunted her sleep. Maybe she was so exhausted that she wouldn't allow herself to be tortured by nightmares, although Julia knew she would be haunted for the rest of her life by the sound of those shots fired from Margolis' gun, each sharp *crack* a signal that another good friend had been lost to her forever. Now, though, it was a relief to lose herself in oblivion, to forget all the horrors of the day that had preceded this welcome darkness.

A floorboard creaked, and her eyes flew open. She could see nothing except the bluish glow of moonlight beyond the French doors, not as bright as it had been when she first lay down. Enough time must have elapsed for the moon to have passed overhead, lowering toward the west.

Her ears strained to hear the sound repeated, but only silence rang in her eardrums. She must have imagined that creak. Besides, houses settled and made noises all the time. Startling at every single one of them would only keep her up for the rest of whatever remained of the night.

Julia closed her eyes and attempted to find the still, quiet place that had allowed her to fall asleep the first time. But then the creaking sound came again, and she sat upright in bed—only to feel a rough hand clap against her mouth.

"Quiet," Richard Margolis whispered. "Not a sound."

Something sharp pricked against her ribcage. Heart pounding, eyes adjusting to the darkness, she saw that he held a long knife to her side. God, he really had lost it. He didn't honestly think he could get away with this, did he?

She opened her mouth—to say what, she wasn't sure—and the knife's tip began to dig into her flesh. Even that small contact was enough to make her eyes water. But she kept quiet.

"Good," he said, still in that insinuating whisper. "I know what Qadim's doing. Full of promises, but no payout. So I'll just have you now. I know I can trust you to be quiet...you were quiet the last time, weren't you, Julia?"

Yes, she'd been quiet. Hadn't cried out or protested, only let him do what he wanted, since she'd known no one was around to hear her scream. It had been better to deny him the satisfaction of knowing that he'd hurt her, even though she'd felt another part of her soul begin to crack and break on that black winter night.

Now she gave one tiny nod. A faint gleam of his teeth in the dimness of the room as he smiled, and then his free hand began to crawl up under her T-shirt, moving toward her breast. Despite herself, she could feel the beginnings of a scream building in her throat. This couldn't be happening again. Especially after she and Zahrias—

The door to the room was flung open, slamming against the wall. At the same time, a blinding light filled the chamber. Qadim stood in the doorway, eyes blazing.

"She is not yours!" he thundered.

In the next instant, Margolis was torn away from Julia and flung against the wall. This time, however, unlike the scene earlier in the downstairs hallway, Qadim battered Margolis into the heavy plaster over and over again, until at last there was a final, terrible *crack* and the commander's eyes went glassy, even as his head flopped over at an unnatural angle.

With a sound of disgust, the djinn made a final, dismissive wave of his hand, and Margolis slid to the ground in a heap, his limp form clearly signaling that he was dead, his neck broken.

Julia could only sit there, aghast, not sure how she should react. Yes, she'd prayed that one day Margolis would meet his fate in a manner that he deserved, but now—

Qadim came over and knelt at her bedside, dark eyes flickering over her. "You did not suffer any harm?"

Heat rising to her cheeks, she realized that the commander's manhandling had pushed her T-shirt up far enough that the faint shadow of the lower curve of her breast was visible. Without speaking, she nodded as she tugged her shirt down.

"Fool," Qadim fumed. "Wretched fool. At least he had already served his purpose."

Those words spurred her to ask, "What purpose?"

The scowl that creased his brow only deepened. He didn't reply at once, but reached out and took the edge of her T-shirt between his fingers so he could lift it up. Julia flinched, thinking he must have saved her from Margolis so he could have her for himself. But the djinn only moved the shirt enough out of the way so he could inspect the spot where Margolis had pressed his knife to her side.

"He did hurt you."

"What?" All right, the point of contact there throbbed a little, but she hadn't thought much of it.

Qadim touched his index finger to her skin, then lifted it away. There was a smear of bright blood on his fingertip.

"Oh," she said blankly.

"Do not move."

He went into the bathroom and came back with a moistened washcloth, which he pressed up against her side. She winced, realizing in that moment how much the wound actually did hurt.

"It is not deep," he said. "But you should remain still for a few moments until the bleeding stops."

Which meant she'd have to sit there and allow Qadim to go on touching her. True, she was grateful to him for interceding, for preventing Margolis from carrying out his assault, but that didn't mean she wanted to prolong their contact any more than was necessary.

"Let me," she told him, and placed her own hand on the washcloth. For a few seconds he didn't move, but let her fingers rest against his. At last he took his hand away, and Julia permitted herself a small, barely perceptible sigh of relief. But she wasn't so relieved that she would allow the previous thread of their conversation to be lost. "What was Margolis' purpose? Besides being your lackey, that is."

"Not a very good one." Qadim gestured with one hand, and the chair on the far side of the room, the one next to the highboy, came drifting over. He sat down on it, gaze intent on her. His new position was marginally better than having him stand there and loom over her, but she didn't much care for their proximity. It felt far too intimate.

Julia didn't protest, however. He had just saved her from the proverbial fate worse than death. She could only hope he hadn't done so in order to keep her for himself.

"No, I knew the only thing that would lure you from Los Alamos was some crisis in Santa Fe. Because of your...history...with Margolis, I guessed his escape would bring you out to investigate. And then, once you were out and away from the protection of those infernal devices that keep those of my kind at bay, you could be used to bring Zahrias al-Harith to me."

"Why do you hate him so much?" she whispered. Because while she knew that Zahrias could sometimes appear cold and commanding, she also knew he was certainly not evil, not the sort of man who could have done anything to invoke such hatred. And hatred that had been a long time brewing, if she was any judge of character. In general, people didn't concoct such elaborate schemes on the spur of a moment for a minor slight. Besides, she'd been around the djinn enough to know that, although many of them probably wouldn't appreciate the comparison, they were not so very different from mortals as they would like to believe.

Qadim's jaw clenched. "That is no concern of yours."

"I should think it is," she retorted, "considering you've dragged me into the middle of it."

"Even so, it is not something I wish to discuss with you at the moment." His gaze flickered down to her waist. "Let me see how your wound fares."

With some reluctance, she lifted the washcloth away from her side, trying to ignore the twinge she felt as she did so. Thank God her tetanus booster would protect her for a few more years. After that—well, it was something she'd need to get Miles working on. All right, he was a physicist, not a doctor, but surely he could figure something out.

"The bleeding has stopped," Qadim informed her. "But if you wish a bandage—"

"No," she cut in. The last thing she wanted was to give him another excuse to touch her. "If it's stopped bleeding, then it should be fine."

"As you wish." He rose from his chair, but remained there, gazing down at her.

Her throat tightened. If he intended to try anything....

She forced herself to say, "Thank you, Qadim. Thank you for stopping him."

The djinn nodded. He made a flicking movement with one hand, and Margolis' crumpled corpse disappeared from the room. Then Qadim bent low, his face close enough that Julia feared he intended to try kissing her again. But instead he spoke, saying, "I think there are many things I would like to do for you. All you have to do is ask."

Surprised by her own boldness, she replied, "Then let me go."

A deep rumble of laughter within his chest as he straightened and looked down at her with amusement. "Many things, Julia Innes...but not that."

And then he was gone.

The sun began to inch its way upward above the mountain range to the east. Zahrias leaned up against a split-rail fence that bordered a small ranch and somehow managed to refrain from cursing. His people did not suffer from hunger and weariness and thirst the way mortals did, but he knew he could not go on like this for much longer without allowing himself some sort of refreshment.

He reached out with his mind. *Jasreel.*

Zahrias, came the immediate reply.

I assume you have had no more luck than I.

No, I'm afraid not. We did come across one compound that looked promising at first, but that was only because it had solar power, and the lighting system inside the house was on a timer. But no one was there.

Of course not. It had been an idle question, really; if Jasreel had found anything, he would have contacted Zahrias right away.

What now? the younger djinn asked. *Should we go back to Santa Fe and regroup? I fear that Jessica cannot go on much longer. She needs to eat and drink and rest.*

Something Zahrias should have thought of. If he was feeling wearied, he could only imagine what

Jessica must be experiencing right now, mortal that she was. Her worry for Julia and her attachment to Jasreel would have kept her going through the night, but he could not expect her to continue without any respite.

Take her home, Zahrias told his cousin. *I will continue for as long as I can, but I cannot expect the same of your Chosen.*

But if you should come across Qadim alone—Jasreel began. Apprehension was clear in his words.

Then I will manage him on my own. This was always my fight, Jasreel. I thank you for the assistance you've given so far.

A long pause. *Very well, Zahrias. But reach out to me if you should need help.*

I will try. In his heart, Zahrias knew he would not do such a thing. He had never intended to put Jasreel in harm's way. As he had said, this was his fight, and his alone.

The mental contact ended, and Zahrias pushed himself away from the fence. He had more or less exhausted the area closer to the highway, and so it was time to move deeper along this country road.

With the growing light, he could see that his surroundings really were quite beautiful. Trees bordered the road—which still appeared to have been given the designation of a highway, even though it consisted of only two lanes and was quite narrow—and warm-toned autumn wildflowers grew to either side. But

Zahrias noticed all of this only in passing, because he was too busy pausing at each lane and track that led off from the highway to the individual properties. As had been the case all night long, they were deserted and quiet, their inhabitants dead for the past year. He thought some of his people might have come this way at one point, rescuing farm animals and bringing them back to Santa Fe, but he had not gone on any of those expeditions.

A set of fresh tire tracks made him stop short, however. They cut off from the highway and went down a slender lane. There were even faint black rubber marks on the asphalt right before it turned to gravel, as if the driver had pulled off in a hurry and had been going too fast for the road conditions.

Exactly the sort of thing Richard Margolis might have done.

Pulse quickening, Zahrias turned down the narrow track, which was bordered on either side by long rows of aspen trees, just beginning to turn golden. In a week or so, they would probably be quite spectacular, but right then he paid them little heed. A moment later, he spied a large house, painted a warm dark ochre shade. Parked in front of the three-bay garage was a large black truck. Smoke issued from one of the home's chimneys, sending the fragrant, familiar scent of burning wood on the cool morning air.

She was here. He knew it, for this was the only sign of life he had yet to see in Pojoaque. How best to approach, though? For the moment, he thought the trees shielded him, because the lane curved slightly as it approached the house, and so anyone looking out the front windows wouldn't be able to see someone coming down the lane. However, he was also close enough that Qadim might be able to sense his presence.

Well, that was what they both wanted, wasn't it? To force a confrontation, so this might be over with once and for all?

Zahrias stepped out from the shelter of the trees and strode down the lane. The sun was rising ever higher, casting its golden light on him. It warmed his flesh, reassured him, helped to wash away some of the weariness from his fruitless search of the night before.

Another flash of gold caught his eye. Two figures approached, one tall even for a djinn, in somber earth-shaded robes. The other seemed to be wrought of gleaming metal. No, not metal, but shimmering silk, molding itself to her form, her long, honey-colored hair falling over her shoulders.

Julia.

And next to her Qadim, his expression curiously pleased. "Well met, Zahrias."

"I think not," Zahrias replied. He looked past the earth elemental to Julia. Had she ever been more beautiful than she was in that moment, when she looked like some spirit of air and fire herself, not quite mortal? "Are you well?" he asked.

"Yes, Zahrias. He—he hasn't hurt me." But there was some hesitation in her voice, enough to make him level a glare at Qadim.

The other djinn lifted his shoulders. "She is telling the truth. I have not harmed her. Captain Margolis wished to, but he will bother her no more."

"He is dead?"

"Yes."

Zahrias could not allow himself to feel too much relief at that particular revelation, for his true enemy still stood before him. "Good," he said shortly. "Well, then, Qadim, since that particular matter has been taken care of, let us get down to business."

"'Business'?" Qadim echoed. "Is that how you refer to the woman of your heart?"

"It is business," Zahrias replied, taking care to keep his voice even, "because you know that she has very little to do with any of this. A means to an end, that is all she is to you."

"If you say so." Qadim stepped closer to Julia, then lifted a strand of her hair and let it slip through his fingers. She didn't move, although Zahrias thought he could see a slight shudder go through her. He had to exert all his will to remain standing where he was, to prevent himself from moving closer so he could strike the other djinn for his temerity in touching her in such a way. "I do not think you give her the proper credit. I have not spent very much time in her company, but I am coming to realize that she is far more than a means to an end."

Zahrias ground his teeth. *He is only goading you,* he told himself. *He means nothing of what he says.*

But he had seen the flicker in Qadim's dark eyes, the way his gaze lingered on Julia a little too long before returning his attention to Zahrias. Yes, the earth elemental might have begun this enterprise as a way to get his revenge for the slight on his sister, but it appeared that now he desired a far greater reward than that.

A reward he would never have. Zahrias knew he would die before he allowed Qadim to make her his.

"Yes, a rare jewel," he said. "But a jewel only shines when its beauty is given willingly. And I cannot think you are willing, are you, Julia?"

She shook her head. Then she replied, "He wouldn't tell me what this is all about, Zahrias. I'm only here because he had Margolis bring me to this place." Her eyes met his then, steady enough, but he could see the pleading in that gaze. She wanted him to make this right.

Which he would, no matter the cost. Voice cold, he said, "What is it you want, Qadim? An apology? Some sort of recompense for a slight that was never intended? Name your price."

Qadim smiled. "I could say that my price is Julia Innes, but I know you will never agree to that. But perhaps I am thinking too small. Perhaps I would have her, and control of your little demesne down in Santa Fe as well."

"I will never agree to that." Truly, had some madness seized the other djinn? Zahrias' post had been given to him by the elders of their world, that he might be steward of the community of Chosen there. It was not his to offer up, even if he wished to do such a thing...which he most certainly did not. As for Julia....

"No, I did not think you would." Qadim shrugged. "At any rate, my doing so would certainly not satisfy my sister's need for justice, and since I am her champion...."

"She would have done better to advocate on her own behalf," Zahrias said sharply. "Is she so frail and feeble that she cannot speak for herself?"

A flash of teeth. "You know my sister, delicate, fragile flower that she is."

Hardly, Zahrias thought in some disgust. *More like a Venus flytrap, luring in its prey and then devouring them whole.* But while he guessed that Qadim had a very good idea of his sister's character flaws, Zahrias did not believe now was a good time to mention any of them. "So what will satisfy Lyanna's 'need for justice,' as you put it? The fortune I left behind in our world? I have no need of it here, and so I am happy to give it to her, if it will salve her wounded pride."

During this exchange, Julia had remained silent, eyes flickering back and forth between the two djinn while they traded verbal volleys. Now, however, she crossed her arms and said, "What, were you involved with this woman, Zahrias?"

Voice even, he replied, "It was very long ago." Yes, so long ago that he had lain in Lyanna's arms even before a certain star was seen above Bethlehem....

Julia angled a glance up at Qadim. "Is that true?"

"Yes."

"Then why now?" she asked. "All this maneuvering...all these people dead. *Why?*"

A good question. Zahrias held himself still and waited to hear what Qadim had to say—if he even deigned to answer her at all. He always had excelled at evasion.

But then Qadim turned toward Julia. Once again he reached out to touch a strand of her hair. This time she flinched visibly, but she held her ground, sky-colored eyes fixed on the djinn who stood so uncomfortably close. Looking at her, Zahrias could only admire her spirit, even when facing down one who possessed so much power.

"'Why'?" Qadim repeated. "I should think that would be clear enough. Lyanna has never forgiven him for hurting her so many years ago, but her jealousy was never aroused before now, because he never truly bestowed his heart on another."

"What about the other mortal woman he was with? Evangeline?"

At hearing that name on Julia's lips, Zahrias wanted to flinch himself. That was a chapter in his life which had done so much damage, partly because he had never admitted to himself the real truth of his heart. He had cared for Evangeline, thought her beautiful and high-spirited and witty, but when he first brought her into his life, he had not understood that those high spirits hid an emptiness within, an emptiness that must always be filled by those around her. And when she truly realized that she would not always be surrounded by those who fulfilled her every whim and praised her beauty, that she must constantly be on the move so the secret of her long life would not be discovered, she had decided she did not wish to endure such an existence. *You love me,* she had told him once. *But not enough, I fear.*

And the next day she was dead, overdosed on the laudanum she'd insisted on taking to soothe her nerves.

After she was gone, he mourned her loss, even as he cursed his stupidity for not understanding that she lacked the capacity to cleave to one person and one person only. And ever since then, he had made sure to lock his heart away, to perhaps have an encounter here or there that would slake his physical needs, but nothing more. He had not allowed himself to care for anyone.

Until Julia.

"A sad affair," Qadim said. "But Lyanna knew that Evangeline was not a real threat. Zahrias cared for her, but he did not truly give her his heart. And when the mortal woman took her own life, Lyanna thought he would not risk such an alliance again. However, that changed when he met you, did it not?"

Julia hesitated, glancing over at Zahrias before she looked up again into Qadim's face. "I think you've done a lot of damage based on some very flimsy evidence. Zahrias and I weren't together. We never discussed the possibility of being together. We didn't even—" Her words broke off there, while a flush tinged her cheeks.

No doubt she had been about to say that they hadn't even kissed until a few days ago. True enough. But Zahrias had spent the better part of six months attempting to forget about her. He thought he had done a good enough job of hiding his preoccupation, but apparently not. Jasreel had conjectured that Qadim must have a spy hidden among the djinn in Santa Fe. That seemed to be the case, for anyone observing their leader must have known something was amiss, that he appeared a little too interested in the news coming out of Los Alamos, that he listened intently whenever Jessica commented on her conversations with Julia Innes. Such attention would have seemed strange, since otherwise the two communities had very little to do with one another.

"No, you 'didn't even,'" Qadim said then, an amused glint in his dark eyes. "But it was still enough. And when you did, two nights ago—well, that was all the confirmation we needed."

"How on earth could you know about that?" she demanded, her blush deepening. "It was only the two of us—no one could have seen—"

Hearing her outrage, Zahrias felt himself go cold. Yes, they had been alone, or had thought they were. Perhaps he should have sensed the presence of another of his kind, but he had been focused completely on Julia. The spy—whoever he or she was—could very well have witnessed the impassioned kiss they shared.

But not, apparently, the quarrel that followed. Perhaps the spy had fled once he had the final piece of evidence he needed to pass on to Lyanna.

"Someone could have," Zahrias said evenly. Julia's eyes widened, and he went on, "Very well, Qadim. So my association with Julia Innes roused Lyanna's sleeping jealousy. You still have not told me what she wants, what we must do to bring an end to all this."

"As to that—" Qadim paused then, and gave a negligent lift of his shoulders. "Why, she wants you, of course."

Zahrias felt them before he saw them, at least ten djinn, breaking into this world through the veil that separated it from the elemental plane. They burst into existence all around him, bringing with them their weapons of earth and water, smothering any flame he summoned against them. He knew he was drowning, blackness forcing itself upon his eyes.

The last thing he saw was Qadim's gloating smile, and the last thing he heard was Julia's scream, echoing forever in his ears.

CHAPTER ELEVEN

THIS COULDN'T BE HAPPENING. ONE MOMENT, Zahrias was there, features almost preternaturally calm as he attempted to negotiate with Qadim, and in the next, he was surrounded by djinn she had never seen before, djinn who must have been water and earth elementals, judging by the geyser that erupted out of the ground, drowning the flames he attempted to summon, quenching his fire, even as a tornado of dirt spun around him, blinking him out of existence.

A scream tore itself from Julia's throat, and she flung herself forward, going to the spot where Zahrias had disappeared. But then Qadim's hand clamped down on her arm, and he pulled her back toward him.

"He is gone," the djinn murmured in her ear, breath hot in contrast to the cool morning air.

Julia shuddered. "Let go of me."

To her surprise, he did release her, although he did so while wearing a slow, hateful smile, as if to indicate that he could seize her again whenever he pleased. She stepped away at once, bicep aching where he'd grabbed her. But that was nothing compared to the ache in her heart, the pain of realizing that Zahrias had been stolen from her.

"Where did they take him?"

"Back to our world, of course. To my sister. You will never see him again, I fear."

She didn't want to believe that. Qadim was only telling her what he knew would hurt her the most. But....

Zahrias was powerful, but even he couldn't have prevailed against a dozen djinn, especially those whose powers were so completely opposite his. Which meant he would probably have a difficult time getting away.

Even so, she put aside her doubt and worry, and said, "You're wrong. He'll escape somehow. He'll come back to me."

"You are worth coming back to, that is for certain." Qadim regarded her for a moment, the amused glint in his eyes fading. In fact, he appeared almost regretful. "But I fear I must leave you now as well. I must make sure that all is going as planned, back in that other world."

Despite her anger and her fear, Julia couldn't help experiencing a faint flush of hope, followed by a mixture of worry and curiosity. If Qadim was going to that strange plane where the djinn dwelled, at least it meant he couldn't remain here to torment her. But what would be happening to Zahrias in the meantime?

He must have seen the torment in her expression, because he chuckled and added, "But I will not be gone forever, my lovely. Have no doubt that I will return."

Before she could react, he came to her, pulling her toward him so he could press his mouth against hers. She resisted at once, hands pushing against his chest, twisting her face away to break the contact with his lips.

For some reason, he didn't stop her, although he did not let go of her arms. Face only a scant few inches from hers—breath incongruously scented with coffee—he said, "In time, you will not fight against me. But for now...."

In that instant, he was gone. Julia found herself pushing back against empty air, against the space that only a second ago had been filled with Qadim's all-too-solid form. She whirled, looking around, thinking this must be a new way for him to torment her, but it did seem that he truly had disappeared. Gone back to his own world—to oversee the delivery of Zahrias to his sister, no doubt.

Tears stung Julia's eyes, but she blinked them away. Now was not the time for weakness. She had to get back to Santa Fe and let everyone know what had happened to their leader. Surely they'd be able to come up with some sort of plan to rescue him.

Except...Zahrias had made it sound as if one of them was a spy. Had to be, for how else could Qadim's sister, this Lyanna, have known enough for her to act on?

Think, Julia, she told herself sternly. *What now?*

If nothing else, she had to get out of here.

Her gaze fell on Margolis' black pickup truck. Okay, she had transportation. Or would, once she found the keys. Hot-wiring a car was not included in her repertoire of useful skills.

She went over to the truck, hoping against hope that Margolis had been careless and had left the keys inside, since no one was around to steal the vehicle. But she should have known better. He was far too paranoid to have left them in the ignition, or tucked up into one of the sun visors.

God, she thought then. *What if the keys were in one of his pockets when Qadim blinked his body right out of existence?*

That would truly suck.

No, she wouldn't allow herself to give up so easily. She hadn't seen much of the house besides the bedroom where she'd been sleeping, the dining room, and the kitchen and adjoining family room. Margolis must have had his own space in there somewhere. She just had to figure out which bedroom was his.

It seemed that Qadim must have been here for at least a little while, because the master bedroom had several of his dark silky robes hanging in the closet, and the bed was rumpled, as if he'd slept there. Did djinn sleep, exactly? She had no idea, but this bed definitely looked as if it had been used. Looking at it made her shiver, though. Would she have ended up in there if she hadn't been able to resist Qadim's djinn glamour?

Recalling the sensation of his mouth on hers, she wanted to shudder. But he was gone—at least for now—and the worst hadn't happened. She just had to make damn sure she was nowhere near here whenever he did decide to come back.

A small, square object sitting on the dresser caught her eye. She went closer and realized it was the device Margolis had taken from her wrecked Suburban. Apparently Qadim hadn't trusted him with it. Well, she wouldn't have, either, if she'd been in his position. She wouldn't have put it past Margolis to use the device against the djinn and therefore be allowed free access to her. But Qadim had forestalled that eventuality.

And now neither one of them was around to keep her from using it. The device could come in handy if Qadim decided to return before she was able to vacate the premises. Going to the dresser, she picked up the innocuous-looking box, and then headed out to inspect the rest of the property.

The other bedroom upstairs looked completely unused, as if it had been left vacant even when the previous owners of the house lived here. Maybe it was a guest room. It did have a bed and a dresser, but the closet was empty, as were all the drawers in the night-stands and the one dresser.

So where the hell had Margolis holed up?

Julia descended the stairs and began exploring the ground floor. The only thing past the dining room was the living room, which didn't look as if anyone had been in there lately. Dust covered everything—dust that was conspicuously absent in the other rooms she'd seen so far. Retracing her steps, she headed back to the family room, noting that a hallway led off the opposite side of the chamber.

That corridor led to the laundry room, and from there out to the garage. In the garage was a Porsche Cayenne SUV, covered in dust—and a set of stairs. Frowning, Julia went up those stairs. There must be an apartment over the garage or something.

Which was exactly what she found. It was also clearly where Margolis had been staying; the bed was unmade, and a pair of camo pants identical to the ones he'd been wearing were draped over one arm of the small couch tucked up against the window that faced out over the driveway.

A pair of rifles leaned against one wall. They would probably come in handy on her drive back to Santa Fe, provided she could find the keys to the truck. But there was also the Porsche SUV in the garage below her. Assuming the damn thing would even start, of course. It clearly had been sitting there a long time.

Then she looked over at the little dinette set on the other side of the couch and let out an exhalation of relief. Lying on the table was a set of keys. Those had to be the keys to the truck—or at least she fervently hoped they were.

She scooped them into her hand, then went over and retrieved one of the rifles. Shooting was not something that had ever appealed to her, but she'd learned how to use a rifle and a shotgun and a semi-automatic pistol over the last six months, knowing that she might at some point have to protect Los Alamos by force of arms. After slinging the rifle over her shoulder, she went back down the stairs and into the house.

Her first instinct was to go right out to the truck and drive off, but, looking down at herself in some distaste, she realized that the flimsy golden getup Qadim had made her wear wasn't the most practical thing in the world, especially if she ran into any trouble on the road. So she hurried back to the room that had been briefly hers, and quickly stripped off the silk garments and climbed back into her own jeans and T-shirt and hiking boots. After slipping on her leather jacket, she retrieved the rest of her belongings from the bathroom, picked up the rifle, and headed out to the driveway.

She wanted to sob with relief when she slid the car key she'd found into the ignition and the truck started right up. The driveway was wide enough that she could turn around and point herself toward the main road. Although she wasn't all that familiar with the area, she'd studied the maps at Los Alamos to give herself a general idea of where things were, just because she never knew when she might have to go out on a scavenging operation. Not that she'd actually ever ended up doing such a thing, mostly because everyone in the community seemed to agree that her talents were better put to use elsewhere.

Still, she knew enough to turn left, heading away from the sun so she could get back to the 285. From there it was easy enough to head back down into the heart of Santa Fe.

Only...did she really want to do that? At least one of the djinn there wasn't to be trusted. For a few seconds, she worried about Miles and Lindsay, still working on the "mystery" of how Margolis had managed to escape. But then she realized they should be safe enough. They didn't know anything of what had transpired with her and Zahrias and Qadim over the past day or so, and therefore couldn't possibly be considered a threat by the spy, whoever he or she was.

Maybe she should be putting the pedal to the metal to get back to Los Alamos. That wouldn't work, though. No one there would have the foggiest idea of how to break through to the plane of the djinn and rescue Zahrias. She needed the help of another djinn. But who, if she didn't know who she could trust?

Then it came to her. Of course.

She'd been to their sanctuary once, that perfect refuge outside the djinn community in Santa Fe. True, Zahrias had taken her, in that eye-blink maneuver the djinn seemed so fond of, but Jessica had more or less explained where the house was located. Julia thought she could find it. Down into town, but then heading out on Canyon Road, up into the hills, and then off on a dirt road that wound even further into the wilderness, until you came to a walled house on a hill.

The house that Jace and Jessica now called home.

Zahrias opened his eyes. Every inch of his body ached as if he had been beaten with cudgels, but he supposed that was only to be expected after facing an onslaught such as the one Lyanna's minions had inflicted upon him. He wondered what she was paying them, and then realized that they might not have requested any kind of monetary reward. After all, in the eyes of many of his people, he was a traitor, one of the One Thousand, a lover of mortals. Never mind that the elders had decreed that the Chosen and their partners were to be left alone. Those nominal rulers of the djinn world could not be everywhere at once, and did not see everything...although they tried to give the impression that they did.

He lay on a bed in a room with a marble floor and marble walls. Hanging on those walls were tapestries woven of a dull gray fiber, faintly metallic. Looking at them, Zahrias realized they were *ni-khar*, a substance that repressed the powers of all fire elementals. He would not be able to call his flames to him, or blink himself out of the chamber and thus away from this place.

Clever, Lyanna. But then, stupidity had never been one of her numerous faults.

The light coming in through the tall, narrow windows was constantly shifting, moving from red to green to amber and back again. That was the way of it here; on this plane, there was no sun, no moon, only a light that seemed to come from everywhere and nowhere. After spending so much time in the world of mortals, that light felt wrong to him, unnatural. But then, in many ways, this world was unnatural. It was a construct, a place where the djinn had been sent when they rebelled against God and were denied the Earth because of their defiance.

Fighting back a groan, he sat up and pushed the silken coverlet aside. Everything here—the silk to make the bedding, the marble on the floors and walls—had come from the mortal world. Nothing of any true use could be found here on the djinn plane.

Everything except the *ni-khar*. That accursed element had its origins on this plane. There were four such elements here, each one possessing a particular property that could repress the powers of each kind of djinn. Zahrias had often wondered if that was a cruel joke on God's part, something designed to keep the djinn in check as they played their power games with one another.

In the wardrobe of carved and gilded wood that stood off to one side, he found several sets of fresh garments, all in the shades of gold and crimson and deep wine that he preferred. He pulled them on, knowing he must prepare himself for the confrontation that was soon to come. If he had been bloodied and dirty when brought here, he appeared to have been bathed in the meantime, for there was no sign of sweat or grime or blood on him.

Zahrias found that he didn't want to think too closely about who might have done that bathing.

He had just finished running an ivory comb through his hair when a knock came at the door. Well, that was something. He hadn't been expecting the courtesy of a knock.

Outside waited one of the *jann,* the lowest order of djinn, and as unlike them as apes were from humans. They had been pressed into service on this nether plane, although Zahrias had never employed any in his own house, as something about them always set his teeth on edge.

This one barely came up to Zahrias' waist, and had the features of a wizened monkey. "Your presence is required in the mistress's audience chamber," the *jann* said in its gravelly little voice.

Ah, so now Lyanna had an audience chamber? Well, she always had been one to put on airs.

He followed the *jann* out into a corridor of marble, with more of the *ni-khar* hangings on every side. Clearly, Lyanna was taking no chances.

They descended a wide staircase and went down another corridor, one that ended in an enormous arched doorway. Within was another chamber, this one of pale marble veined with gold, and the ubiquitous ni-khar hangings on every wall. At the far end of the chamber was a dais, and on that dais sat a throne-like chair that appeared to be carved from pure gold. On that chair sat a woman.

She rose when he entered and descended the steps as he approached. Her long black hair lay in perfect waves against her shoulders and fell past her waist, and rings of gold banded her bare arms at regular intervals.

Some might have said she was beautiful. Zahrias had thought so, too, once upon a time. Her nose was long, but not overly so, and, unlike her brother, her mouth was composed of lush curves, promising all sorts of delights. Under the perfect arches of her black brows, her eyes were not dark, like Qadim's, but a clear amber.

Once he had thought to drown in those eyes. Now he stared into them, hatred coiled within his breast.

"Zahrias," she said. Her voice was as warm-tinted as her eyes, but he knew that warmth was a lie. Her heart was as cold as the frozen wastes at the Earth's poles.

"Lyanna," he returned. Off to one side, he saw someone move, and realized it was Qadim. Relief coursed through Zahrias. He might have been torn away from Julia and brought to this accursed place, but if Lyanna's brother was here, it meant he was not back in the mortal world, tormenting the woman Zahrias loved. Julia would have time to get away, to be safe.

If she could be safe anywhere, since it seemed clear that at least one traitor lurked in the heart of his community. The best thing she could do was go back to Los Alamos and forget about him. For some reason, however, he did not think that was her plan. He had seen the look in her eyes just before he was torn away from that plane, heard the despairing cry she gave. That was the sound of a woman who had just lost the thing she cared for the most. He thought she would do a great deal to get him back, even if it meant risking herself.

Lyanna came closer, gaze greedy, and Zahrias' jaw set. The scent of her perfume was cloying, seeming to stick in his throat and make him want to gag. Now that she stood nearer to him, he saw the faint traces of dissipation in her face, the lines that had begun to etch themselves around her large kohl-rimmed eyes and on either side of her ruby-tinted mouth. His people did not age in the same way that mortals did, but even so, the signs of hard living would eventually begin to show in their features.

"You are looking well, Zahrias," Lyanna said once she had finished her inspection of his person.

I fear I cannot say the same for you, he thought, but he kept that opinion to himself. Provoke her at some point he must, but for the moment, he would attempt politeness, if only to gain himself some time to think. "I thank you for that compliment, Lyanna," he replied, "especially considering the manner in which I was brought here. How long was I unconscious, so my wounds might begin to heal?"

Her lips pressed together in what she probably thought was a becoming pout. "As to that, I knew there was no other way to get you here. I told them not to be unnecessarily rough." Reaching out, she laid a hand on his arm. Each finger was adorned with jewels in shades of blue and green, and those same cool shades were echoed in the clothing she wore. Unlike her brother, she was a water elemental, and her moods and tempers were just as unpredictable as the storms and tides of the sea.

Zahrias held himself still under her touch. It wouldn't do for her to see his disgust, even though Lyanna's overly painted appearance only made him think of Julia's clear, unsullied beauty, which shone forth even when her hair was tied back messily and she wore the unattractive, almost androgynous clothing favored by so many mortal women.

"That was very thoughtful of you," he said, and though he thought he had taken care to keep his tone even, there must have been an edge to his voice nonetheless. Lyanna's dark-encircled eyes widened, no doubt in what she hoped was an expression of innocence.

"I only wished you to see reason."

"'Reason'?" he repeated. "What reason was there in bringing me here in such a fashion? Our lives have been separate for many years, Lyanna, so forgive me when I say I cannot understand why you would want to see me now."

As they spoke, Qadim had approached. At those words, he let out a chuckle, eyes glinting with malicious intelligence. "Do not believe him, sister," he said. "He knows all too well from whence this particular jealous rage has sprung."

Her amber eyes glinted, and she glared at her brother. "I am not jealous. I only—"

"You only wished to take back something that was once yours. It had no particular value to you...until you realized that someone else wanted it." Qadim shrugged.

"Not that I mind your intervention, for it has given me the opportunity to take the thing he wants most."

His remark only seemed to anger Lyanna further. Mouth tight, she said, "That insipid mortal? Truly, I cannot understand what either of you see in her."

"So you admit Julia is the reason for all this," Zahrias told her. Yes, Qadim had said as much, back in the driveway of his borrowed house in Pojoaque, but Zahrias wanted to hear it from Lyanna's lips.

"I admit nothing," she retorted. She shot another narrow-eyed look up at her brother. "You disappoint me, Qadim. I thought you had better taste than that."

"Better taste than to want someone who is beautiful and strong and intelligent? Perhaps that is a failing of mine, one you simply will have to learn to live with."

What Qadim hoped to accomplish by goading his sister in such a way, Zahrias couldn't begin to guess. Or perhaps his words had been intended as much for Zahrias' ears as they had been for Lyanna's.

Whatever Qadim's plan, it seemed to be working, for her brows drew together, and she planted her hands on her hips and snapped, "If that is how you feel, I am surprised you have not thrown your lot in with the One Thousand and claimed her as your own." A crafty light entered her eyes, and she added, "Indeed, I think you should, brother. Then Zahrias al-Harith might turn his attentions upon someone more deserving."

"Meaning you, I take it," Qadim replied.

"Who else?"

Not if you should hold me here until the stars fall from the heavens, Zahrias thought, but he only said, "A thousand pardons, Lyanna, if I ever left you with the impression that we might one day rekindle the fires we once shared. Truly, it has been so very long—I had heard that you had found comfort in the arms of others many years ago, had moved on with your life."

She flicked a heavy lock of hair over one shoulder. "Perhaps I thought I had. But a person may move on far enough that she eventually comes back full circle. And truly, I could find no one who could ever match you—just as I thought you had found no one who could erase me from your memory. Why else would you have lived such a solitary existence for all these centuries? This mortal you think you love—she can know nothing of what it means to share these passing years, to come to one another in the fullness of our existence. Her life is but a flyspeck to one of us."

Yes, that was how it would seem to Lyanna, for she thought the same as the majority of their people, that humans were at best something to be used and discarded as it amused them, and now were only an obstacle to be removed so the djinn might enjoy Earth's bounties for their own. But Zahrias knew that although a mortal's life might seem fleeting and finite, it was also a thing composed of its own beauties, its own triumphs and tragedies.

If you had only made Julia your Chosen, her life would not be fleeting at all. It would have been something we could have shared unto eternity.

And she would not have been made a target by Lyanna, for the Chosen were supposed to be untouchable. There were some who had rebelled against those strictures, such as Khalim and his followers, but they had been punished for their transgressions. Zahrias doubted Lyanna would have ever thrown her lot in with them—not because she scrupled at killing Chosen, but because she enjoyed her life of luxury and would not have done anything to jeopardize it. Hunting and murdering Chosen violated the laws laid down by the elders, laws intended to keep those few remaining mortals safe, whereas bringing him here had her standing on much shakier ground. Her behavior might be frowned upon, but it did not violate any specific rules. Kidnapping was a time-honored tradition among his people, one with many uses, although Zahrias had never thought he would be made a victim in such a way.

He shook his head then and opened his mouth to reply, to tell her that she was wrong, but Qadim forestalled him, saying, "Some of what you say is true, sister, but I have come to realize that there are at least a few of them who are worth saving. And since you have Zahrias here now, I think I will take your advice."

Her arched eyebrows lifted that much further. "You will?"

"Yes." Qadim's gaze slid over to Zahrias, both mocking and triumphant. "I will return to the mortal plane, and claim Julia Innes as my Chosen. Then you two will be free to enjoy one another."

Rage flared in Zahrias, and he began to lunge toward the other djinn, forgetting in his fury that the tapestries of *ni-khar* would prevent him from using his powers. Laughing, Qadim disappeared from the audience hall, even as several of the other elementals who had watched from their guard positions along the walls descended upon Zahrias.

Wearing an unpleasant smile, Lyanna backed away. "I fear there is nothing you can do for her, Zahrias. Qadim will take her and make her his...and then you and I will have the leisure to take as long as it requires to become a loving couple once again."

CHAPTER TWELVE

Julia guided the pickup truck southbound on the 285, although she planned to avoid going into downtown by cutting off onto Artist Road and then winding around until she picked up Canyon on the eastern side of the city center. Not too many of the djinn had settled out in that direction, as far as she could recall, and it seemed safer to take that route. Even if the spy—whoever he or she might be—didn't see her, someone might note her passing and wonder why she hadn't come in to town to collect Lindsay and Miles.

The 285 had just turned into St. Francis Road, and she was just beginning to pass the National Cemetery on her left, when a figure appeared in the middle of the street in front of her. She couldn't make out exactly who it was, because the sun was in her eyes, although she knew from the flowing robes that the person must be a djinn. Out of instinct, she slammed her foot down on the brakes, tires squealing and smoking as she came to a stop.

As the smoke began to clear, however, she realized she shouldn't have braked. If anything, she should have sped up.

Because the djinn standing in front of her was Qadim.

He held up a hand, and abruptly the truck's engine died. Frantic, Julia pumped the gas pedal, hoping against hope that she might be able to bring it back to life. But the truck wouldn't respond. Its doors had locked automatically as she pulled away from the house in Pojoaque, but she somehow doubted those locked doors would do much to keep the djinn away from her.

And then she saw Miles's device, sitting next to her duffle bag on the passenger seat. Just as Qadim's fingers were closing on the handle of the driver-side door, she grabbed the device, turned it over, and flicked the "on" switch before dropping it back on the seat.

At once the djinn staggered backward, as if someone had punched him in the gut. His dark eyes fastened on her, wide with surprise. Of course he had known about the devices, but, judging by his expression, this was the first time he'd encountered their effects in person.

Smiling grimly, she pumped the gas pedal again. This time, the engine turned over right away. She was just about to floor it and roar off when she hesitated. Qadim must know something of what had happened to Zahrias. She would never get a better chance to question him, since now he was too weakened by the device to do anything to her.

Still, she hesitated for a second or two before turning the key and shutting off the truck's engine. Then she opened the door and got out.

Qadim stood a yard or so away, panting as if he had just run a marathon. Surprise flickered across his features as he stared at her.

"Where is he?" she demanded.

"Wha—"

"Zahrias, you bastard," she said. "Where is he? How do I get him back?"

The djinn shook his head, although Julia had no idea whether he'd done so because he simply didn't know...or because he refused to tell her.

Mouth set, she went back to the pickup truck and around to the passenger side. After opening the door, she retrieved the rifle and headed back to where Qadim was standing, then held up the gun and pointed it straight at his chest.

"Where is he?" she gritted.

"I—" Qadim paused to gulp in some air, distress showing in every plane of his face. Not that Julia much cared, but she realized then that the device must be broadcasting at its highest setting. It had been calibrated for lower strength and greater range when it had been in her possession, and so she guessed Margolis must have fiddled with it, thinking it would be better to more or less gut-punch Qadim with the thing if he'd decided to use it.

But the djinn had never given him that chance.

Since Qadim didn't seem capable of speech, though, she decided she'd better dial it down a little. Keeping a wary eye on him, she backed away toward the pickup, then reached in with her free hand and ran a finger over the pressure-sensitive electronics on the face of the device, easing it up enough that he should be able to talk but wouldn't have the strength to try anything funny.

She turned back toward him. "Better?"

He nodded. "Yes. Thank you."

The unexpected courtesy threw her off balance a little. Frowning, she set the rifle down, but kept her right hand wrapped around the barrel so she could bring it to bear in a second if she had to. "Where is he?"

"With my sister Lyanna."

Julia had expected as much, but his reply still sent a chill down her spine. What might that unknown woman be doing to Zahrias right at this very moment?

"In the djinn world?"

"Yes."

"And you just left him with her? Aren't you worried about what he might do to a woman who had him kidnapped, especially if her big brother isn't around to protect her?"

At that question, Qadim let out a rusty-sounding laugh. "Lyanna can take care of herself. At any rate, he can do very little. There is an element in our world that blocks the abilities of fire elementals such as Zahrias. Let us just say that it has figured prominently in my sister's decorating scheme."

Great. "So...it works like our little device?"

"No." The djinn gulped in a breath. In the bright late morning sunlight, Julia could see a sheen of sweat on his forehead. "It is not...debilitating. He has his strength, his health, only he cannot use his powers to call the flames, or to carry himself away from that place."

Well, that was a little better, but not much. Zahrias might not be feeling physically ill, but she didn't want to think about the mental torment of being held some-where and knowing that the powers he'd relied on all his life were suddenly inaccessible to him. "So why are *you* here?"

The dark eyes under the heavy brows didn't blink. "I should think that would be obvious."

Julia had to force herself not to look away. She hated him for what he'd done to Zahrias, for what he'd wanted to do to her, but even so, there was something in Qadim's stare that made her wish circumstances had somehow been different. Not that she wanted to be with him, nothing like that...more that she could see he did feel something for her, and she didn't know what she should do about it.

And he had saved her from Margolis. No matter what else, she knew she should be grateful that at least he had removed Richard Margolis from the face of the earth.

"You know nothing could ever happen between us," she said, but she made sure her tone was gentle. From the resigned expression Qadim wore, she could tell he knew that all too well. "I love Zahrias, and I need to find a way to rescue him."

"You can't rescue him," the djinn replied. As she opened her mouth to protest, he raised a weak hand and went on, "Not because I can do anything to stop you, but because you're a mortal. Your kind simply cannot survive in the world of the djinn."

"I refuse to believe that," she said. "There must be something I can do."

He shook his head. "You are an admirable woman, Julia Innes, but I doubt even you can bend time and space to your will."

Those words struck a chord in her, and she went very still. Then she smiled. Of course.

"What is it?"

"Thank you, Qadim."

The look he sent her then was merely puzzled, with nothing of desire in it. "Why are you thanking me?"

In answer, she hefted the rifle over her shoulder and began to move toward the truck. As she laid her hand on the door handle, she said, "I may not be able to bend time and space—but I think I know someone who might."

He hadn't seen luxury like this since he had come to live among the mortals, but Zahrias thought he would gladly give up all the marble walls, the cups of gold, to see Julia smile at him again. After Qadim had disappeared, Lyanna had her captive sent back to his rooms—to give him time to think, she said. A wasted effort, if she'd intended that time of meditation to be spent in considering her charms, because Zahrias' thoughts only strayed to Santa Fe and the woman he'd left behind.

What would Qadim do? He had not, Zahrias recalled with some relief, been one who enjoyed forcing himself on women. During the years that Zahrias had been with Lyanna, Qadim had spent time with a number of partners, all of whom seemed willing enough. His face might not have been particularly handsome, but there were those who seemed entranced enough with his form and didn't mind overmuch that his features were not as pleasing as they might have been.

So, while he wanted Julia, he might not be doing anything more aggressive than attempting to make her see that he was a desirable alternative to Zahrias. That was bad enough, but, he thought, ultimately would lead to nothing. Her heart was given to him. She would not bestow it upon Qadim, no matter how much he importuned her.

But if his pursuit kept the djinn occupied elsewhere, that could make things easier for Zahrias. He would only have to manage Lyanna, and not the both of them...although he did not much look forward to dodging her clumsy attempts at a seduction.

She had sent one of her *jann* servants—not the same one who had brought Zahrias to her audience chamber earlier today, he thought, although it was difficult to tell them apart—to guide him to her private apartments, where a sumptuous feast had been spread out on a low table there.

For Lyanna dined in the old way, reclining on soft pillows on the polished floor. She had changed into a new ensemble, one of shimmering aquamarine woven with gold that left her arms bare and was cut precariously low. Once upon a time, he had thought he could never want anything other than her lush curves. Now, though, he could only think how overdone she looked, how artificial and false.

"Sit, Zahrias," she said, gesturing to the cushion near her.

He lowered himself to the oversized pillow, remembering how he had never cared for this way of sitting down to a meal. It always seemed to give him indigestion.

Or perhaps that was merely Lyanna's effect on him.

He remained silent as one of the *jann* stepped forward and poured a healthy measure of wine into the golden goblet before him. Zahrias wished there was some way to refuse it—after all, he was not entirely certain that Lyanna hadn't stooped to drugging the drink in some way—but to do so would only anger her, and he knew he had to step carefully, at least until he had had adequate time to analyze his situation and decide on his best course of action.

Lyanna lifted her goblet. "Let us drink to renewing old acquaintances."

Ah, if only she were a mere acquaintance. Too much history there, and even though he hated very much what she seemed to have become, he knew he had loved her once, or at least had thought he loved her. It was nothing like the need he felt for Julia, the sense that his world had something essential missing from it when she was not around, but there had been some kind of affection...just not enough.

"To old acquaintances," he said, tone neutral, and took a cautious sip from his goblet. The wine tasted well enough, heavier than the vintages he had been drinking back in the mortal world, but he couldn't sense anything overtly wrong with it.

Lyanna chuckled low in her throat. Perhaps she thought that laugh was an enticing sound, but to Zahrias, she merely sounded as if something had made her cough.

"Look at you," she remarked, mouth pursed. "So dignified. So proper. Has all your time among mortals taken away your sense of fun? I don't remember you being nearly so stiff. At least," she added, a sly light dancing in her eyes, "I don't recall *all* of you being this stiff. Parts of you, perhaps."

He decided to ignore the innuendo. "Lyanna, we both know that there is no point to any of this. Even if I were not interested in Julia Innes, I still have my responsibilities in the mortal world. The elders entrusted the djinn and Chosen of Santa Fe to my care. Do you truly believe they will overlook your actions when they have resulted in my people being left with no one to lead them?"

"As to that," she responded, giving an airy wave of her hand before picking up her goblet once again, "I am sure your brother can manage things well enough. Does it really matter which al-Harith oversees your little group?"

That carelessness about others was one of the traits which had finally made Zahrias break away from her. Dani was a good man, and he did have the knack of making others like him, but a leader he was not, as he was uncomfortable telling others what to do, let alone making the hard decisions required of those in command. Lyanna should have known that—if she had ever bothered to think about anything other than herself.

"I fear that my brother is somewhat occupied at the moment," he said as evenly as he could. "For he and his partner just had their first child. Indeed, my being here means that I cannot be with them to properly celebrate the boy's birth."

Lyanna's amber eyes took on a malicious glint. "I had never imagined you as a doting uncle, Zahrias. Especially when the child is only a half-breed."

His fingers clenched, and then he forced himself to relax and take another sip of his wine. "Children of mixed blood can sometimes be the strongest of all."

"Or they can have so little power that they might as well be all human." She set down her goblet and leaned toward him, breasts swelling precariously against the low-cut bodice of the tunic she wore. "You and I could have had wondrous children, Zahrias."

"I find it better not to dwell on what might have been."

"Why does it have to be 'what might have been'? We could start again now."

The very thought of sharing that kind of intimacy with her made him want to gag. Now that he'd held Julia in his arms, he couldn't imagine being with anyone else, especially Lyanna al-Syan. Sidestepping her suggestion, he said, "Perhaps we should eat. This does seem to be quite the feast you've had prepared."

They'd both been ignoring the food in favor of drinking wine, but Lyanna gave a negligent lift of her shoulders. "Of course, Zahrias. I do want to make sure you keep up your strength."

She snapped her fingers, and the *jann* hurried over so he could heap their golden plates with lamb and rice and fruit swirled with honey. The whole time, Lyanna's amber eyes seemed to laugh at him.

Clearly, she thought it was only a matter of time before his willpower failed him. After all, he couldn't care that much for Julia, when she was only a mortal.

Julia had hoped that no djinn would be loitering around the U.S. Marshals' building—when you got right down to it, there was nothing left for them to guard—but that hope was dashed when she spotted Murrah, the big elemental who was Martine's partner, propped up against one of the pillars in the lobby. Oddly, he seemed to be playing a game on an iPad. That was something she'd thought she'd never see, since most djinn didn't appear all that comfortable around human technology.

Even so, she was less than thrilled to see him. All she could do was hope that he hadn't noticed anything strange about her parking behind the building and coming in through one of the side entrances, instead of walking in through the front like someone who had nothing to hide.

"Hi, Murrah," she said, and summoned what she hoped was a natural-looking smile. "Are Miles and Lindsay still working downstairs?"

"Yes," he replied. At least he didn't appear overly surprised to see her there. Maybe someone had mentioned she might be back eventually to pick up the two remaining members of her team. "Should I get them for you?"

"Oh, no," she said hastily. "I'll go down and talk to them. I've gotten to the point with Miles where he doesn't get too crabby if I interrupt him."

Murrah nodded. "Sure, then." And he returned to the iPad, brow furrowing as he worked away at his game of Candy Crush.

She sent him another smile, then walked over to the elevator as if she didn't have a care in the world. The whole time the car was descending, she kept worrying that Murrah would decide to join her—or worse, that whoever the spy might be had spotted the unfamiliar black truck parked behind the building and would then come in to investigate.

But she reached the sub-basement without incident...and walked into a strangely intimate scene. Miles and Lindsay weren't anywhere near Margolis' former cell. Instead, Miles sat at the guard station, his glasses off and resting on the desk before him. Lindsay was rubbing his shoulders, her lips pressed against the top of his head in a gentle kiss.

It wasn't so much that they were doing anything which couldn't be seen in public, more that the two of them never seemed to share any open displays of affection. Something was going on between them, or they wouldn't have been plowing through those boxes of condoms at a steady pace, but whenever anyone else was around, you'd be hard-pressed to believe they were a couple at all.

As soon as Julia stepped into the room, though, Lindsay lifted her hands from Miles's shoulders, and he immediately picked up his glasses and put them back on. Maybe they were his shield against the world; Julia thought he looked a lot younger, and strangely vulnerable, without them.

"Julia...?" Lindsay said, obviously startled to see her.

"You need to come with me," Julia said, not bothering to mince words. "There's no point in looking for clues here. Margolis was helped out of his cell by a djinn named Qadim, but they had a falling out. Margolis is dead."

"Wait," Miles put in, pushing back the chair where he sat. Lindsay got out of the way just in time. "Why would a djinn help Margolis, of all people? Their goals were diametrically opposed."

Not as much as you might believe, she thought, but she just shook her head. "It's complicated. I'll tell you everything once we get to Jace and Jessica's house."

"Why there?" Lindsay asked. Her tone was puzzled, but not worried.

"Because it's not safe here. The Santa Fe community has some sort of spy hidden among them, only I don't know who it is. So the best place to regroup is with Jace and Jessica, because I'm going to need a djinn's input on this, and he's the only one I can trust." *Well, besides Zahrias,* she added mentally. *But he's a million miles away right now.*

The shifting expressions on both Miles and Lindsay's faces seemed to tell her that they had roughly a hundred questions for every answer she'd given them. Julia tensed, wondering if they were about to start lobbing those questions at her. She really didn't have time for that.

But then they looked at each other, not speaking, and Miles nodded. Lindsay said, "Okay. We have a few things with us here, just because we didn't want to waste time going back and forth to the hotel."

That was something. Julia had no idea how long any of this was going to take, but she knew she didn't dare risk having Miles and Lindsay return to the La Fonda to retrieve their belongings. "Good. Then get them, and we'll head out. Murrah is loitering in the lobby, but we'll just have to hope he isn't the spy." She really couldn't imagine the big, quiet djinn as a spy, since he didn't seem quite as quick-witted as most of his compatriots, but for all she knew, his demeanor could just be an act.

Lindsay went over to a door that proved to be a sort of supply closet, and got out a black backpack and a brown canvas duffle bag. While she was fetching those items, Miles rose from his chair and retrieved a couple of pieces of electronic equipment Julia couldn't identify from where they'd been sitting in Margolis' former cell. He took the backpack from Lindsay and slid the equipment into it.

"All right," he said. "That's everything."

They all headed for the elevator and silently got inside. When they emerged in the lobby, Murrah was nowhere to be seen. Julia wanted to feel relieved, but she didn't know for sure whether or not his absence was a good sign. Either way, the best thing to do was to get out of there as quickly as possible.

She guided Miles and Lindsay out the side entrance and over to the truck. Lindsay raised an eyebrow at the unfamiliar vehicle but didn't say anything.

It was crowded—the truck didn't have an extended cab, just some space behind the seats to stow their duffle and backpack—but no one said anything as they squeezed into their seats and Julia pointed the truck eastward, staying to side streets until she didn't have any choice except to cut over to Canyon Road. As they passed a sprawling adobe-style house, Lindsay and Miles exchanged a glance.

Julia wondered what that was about, and then realized it must have been the home they'd shared before returning to Los Alamos with her. *If only those walls could talk,* she thought, repressing a smile. Lindsay had always sworn up and down that she and Miles hadn't become intimate until after they left Santa Fe, but Julia still couldn't help wondering,

Not that it was really any of her business, but focusing on their unlikely relationship gave her something to think about besides worrying what this Lyanna person might be doing to Zahrias at that very moment. Someone so unscrupulous as to stoop to kidnapping and murder probably wouldn't bat an eye at drugging the man she wanted, if that meant she could be intimate with him.

Torturing herself probably wasn't a very good idea, but Julia's thoughts kept circling that awful possibility. Of course Zahrias would resist...if he was able to. She had no idea what sort of resources Lyanna had at her disposal, but clearly she was able to make her brother jump at her command.

"All right, we're away," Lindsay said at last. Since she was much shorter than Miles, she'd gotten stuck with the uncomfortable middle seat, squeezed in between him and Julia, and she didn't look too happy about it. "So are you going to tell us what's really going on?"

"Yes," Julia replied as she took the cutoff for the dirt road that led out to Jace and Jessica's property. "But I might as well wait until we're at the house. Then I can explain the whole thing to everyone at the same time."

That response didn't seem to please Lindsay all that much, but after a moment she gave a grudging nod. Her practical engineer's brain probably saw the logic in Julia's explanation, even if she didn't particularly enjoy it.

After bumping over the rutted dirt lane for about ten minutes, Julia caught sight of their destination, the shimmering gold of the aspens that surrounded it looking like a beacon. She eased the truck up to the wall that enclosed the property, wondering if she was going to have to stop and get out, but then the gate opened slowly inward.

There weren't any visible signs of a security system, but that probably didn't matter when you had a djinn in residence. She drove up the small hill where the house was built, then parked in the open area to the left of the detached garage. As they got out of the truck, she saw Miles give an oddly grim glance around the property, his mouth set in a flat line.

Julia wondered what that was about, then realized he hadn't been here since he came with Margolis to haul Jace away all those months ago. Was the scientist reflecting on his guilt in that particular scenario? It looked that way, judging by his expression.

Well, Miles definitely wasn't blameless, but the responsibility for that witch hunt mainly rested on Margolis' shoulders. Now that the man in question was dead, maybe it was time for Miles to ease up on himself.

Margolis was dead. She still hadn't quite processed that fact. He'd been such a bogeyman in her imagination that even now she couldn't help thinking he might still appear out of nowhere to torture and hurt her, like an inhuman bad guy from a B-grade slasher flick.

But then Jace and Jessica were coming out of the house, and she deliberately pushed those thoughts away. They had to focus on getting Zahrias back.

"I'd say this was a surprise," Jessica said by way of greeting them. "But Jace detected you coming down the road a few miles out. What's going on? And where's Zahrias?"

So they didn't know what had happened to him. Julia still wasn't sure exactly how in contact the djinn were with each other. She'd gotten the impression that Jace and Zahrias could speak across some distance because of their family connection, but how far that talent extended, she had no idea.

Forcing her words past the sudden constriction in her throat, Julia said, "He's gone. They took him."

"'They'? Jessica repeated, looking confused. "They who?"

Jace stepped forward then. "Please, everyone come inside. I can see that Julia has a story to tell. Better to do so where we can sit down and be comfortable."

She shot him a grateful look, and everyone headed into the house, following Jace to the living room. Although it seemed that in general he didn't tend to use his powers very much, he'd apparently decided it was time to make an exception. A pitcher of iced tea and some glasses appeared with a snap of his fingers, and everyone sat down, Miles and Lindsay on the sofa, Jace and Jessica on the love seat. Julia took one of the chairs that remained and tried not to think about how sitting there only seemed to reinforce her sensation of being utterly alone.

Which was foolish, because she wasn't alone. She was surrounded by friends.

"Zahrias did find me," she said, after she'd picked up one of the glasses of iced tea and taken a long swallow. "I was being held in a house in Pojoaque."

"By Margolis and Qadim al-Syan?" Jace asked.

She startled a little at that question. "You knew who Qadim was?"

Jessica was the one to reply. "Zahrias told us a little bit. He guessed it was Qadim because of some evidence at the scene where your Suburban was attacked." Pausing, she knotted her fingers on her jean-clad knee and let out a little breath, not quite deep enough to be a sigh. "I am so sorry about Brent and Nancy and Eric. I can't imagine—" She broke off, then seemed to gather herself before continuing, "Anyway, Shawn sent out a search party from Los Alamos and found them. They were taken back to the settlement so they can be buried there."

This piece of information did—well, it didn't exactly cheer Julia up, but it made her feel slightly better about the situation. At least they hadn't been left there to rot in the wreckage of the Suburban, would be provided decent burials so their friends in Los Alamos could give them a proper goodbye. "Thank you for letting me know," she said quietly.

"So who is this Qadim?" Lindsay asked, after an awkward pause.

"Someone from Zahrias' past...someone with a taste for revenge," Jace said. "But when you said 'they took him,' which 'they' did you mean?"

"Followers of Qadim and his sister, I guess. Earth and water elementals. They just appeared out of nowhere and snatched him away. It was really chaotic, so I can't say for sure, but I think there were at least ten of them, maybe more." That horrible scene replayed in Julia's mind. If only she could have thought of some way to stop them. But even Zahrias couldn't prevail against that many djinn, so what the hell was she thinking, that she, one mortal woman, could have done any better?

"Yes, that makes sense," Jace said in musing tones. Everyone there, even Miles, shot him glances laced with varying levels of outrage. At once he raised his hands, adding, "I'm certainly not condoning what happened. Only that in situations like this, it is those whose natures are opposite the one being taken who are employed, because they are best suited to defeating their prey."

"So he's been taken to the djinn plane, I assume," Miles said then.

"Yes," Julia said. "To this Lyanna woman—Qadim's sister," she explained in response to Lindsay's confused expression. "And that's what I need you all to help me with. I have to go there, get him back somehow."

Miles's gray eyes took on a glint behind his metal-framed glasses. Julia had seen that glint before. It meant that he'd just encountered an interesting problem, one he'd delight in solving.

Jace, on the other hand, only looked troubled. "I know you want to do this, Julia. But it's impossible.

"There is no way you'll ever be able to rescue Zahrias."

CHAPTER THIRTEEN

THE AIR FELT HEAVY, WEIGHING ON HIS LUNGS. HE tried to breathe in deeply, but the cloying scent of the spices used to perfume the air in the palace caught in his throat, and he coughed. Rolling onto his side, Zahrias placed his hands against the overly soft mattress and began to push himself to a sitting position—only to freeze when he saw Lyanna lying there next to him, her mouth lifting in a malicious smile.

"You do look so handsome when you sleep," she said, then gave a cat-like stretch, one he could tell she'd calculated to show off her curves to their best advantage.

"What did you do?" he demanded, pushing himself up to a sitting position. His head swam. Something in that meal she'd fed him had to have been drugged. Not the wine, he thought. It had tasted safe enough. But there had been enough different dishes created with an almost dizzying variety of spices to almost guarantee that he wouldn't have been able to detect anything amiss with them.

"I?" Her eyes widened, but he saw no innocence in them. Rather, they wore a predatory gleam. "I did nothing. *We* did nothing. You were weary, and slept. I will confess that I found myself missing those times when we slept next to one another, and so I lay down here to be beside you. But nothing happened."

A pitcher of water sat on the table next to the bed. Without responding to her, Zahrias lifted the pitcher and poured some water into one of the engraved silver cups that had been placed there. Perhaps the water had been drugged as well, but he didn't think so. She would not want to risk incapacitating him by giving him too much.

The water was cool going down his throat, and it seemed to help with the churning in his stomach. He drank some more, then set the cup back down on the table. Behind him, he could feel the bed shift as Lyanna got up.

Although he did not wish to look at her, he knew that was a coward's escape. Mouth set, he turned so he could see where she stood a few feet away, arms crossed beneath her breasts.

"Truly, Zahrias, I do not recall you having such a suspicious nature. It must have come from spending so much time among mortals."

He ignored the jab. "Forgive me if I am suspicious. Being kidnapped can have that effect on a man."

Her lips pursed. "Can we not let that go? I wished to have you here with me, and I knew you would not come if I only asked. You are far too bound up in your duty."

One thing certainly hadn't changed about Lyanna. She was still all too eager to tell herself pleasant lies. Far better to think that his reticence stemmed only from his worries about the responsibilities he had left behind in Santa Fe, rather than any kind of disgust at being with her.

"It is my duty," he said. "One I do not take lightly. But even if I did...." He hesitated, for he knew he must walk a fine line here. If he offended her too much, she might take even more drastic action than she had previously. Voice as gentle as he could make it, he said, "We shared a time together once. And it was good... for a while. Is it not better to remember things as they were between us, rather than force ourselves into something that is not natural for either of us at the current stage of our lives?"

As soon as the words left his mouth, he realized he had made a mistake. Her artificially arched brows drew together, and she retorted, her tone crackling with spite, "'Not natural'? Are you saying it is unnatural for me to want to be with you again?"

"No, Lyanna, that is not what I said."

But she would not be mollified. Amber eyes all but shooting sparks, she stalked to the door and laid her hand on the latch. As she lifted it, she spat, "You should guard what you say, Zahrias al-Harith. For I think it is time you learned what 'unnatural' really means!"

After delivering that ominous remark, she stalked out and slammed the door behind her.

For a long moment, Zahrias didn't move. He stared at the door, then went over to it and tested the latch. Locked, of course. Angry she might be, but not so much that she would allow herself to be careless. If only his powers had not been taken from him. He would have blasted that door—and perhaps the wall that surrounded it—into the next dimension.

But it would not be that easy. He could not let himself brood on the threat contained in her last words to him. No, he could only go back to the bed, grateful that at least he would have it to himself this time, and lie down. He knew he must be as rested as possible to face what she had planned for him after this.

"You keep saying it's impossible," Julia said. How could Jace sit there looking so calm and handsome, and yet be doing everything he could to shoot down her hopes? "So please tell me *why* it's impossible."

He flickered a glance at Jessica. They could have been communicating silently; it was difficult to tell for sure. "Because humans can't survive on the djinn plane. The few times they've gone there, they've died within a few hours, gasping and choking."

"Gasping?" Miles asked. "As if they were suffocating?"

"Something like that. I've never seen it for myself, thank God. But that is what I've heard."

"Incompatible atmosphere," the scientist said, tone musing. "Most likely the mix of elements is just enough different from what exists here on earth that any human who goes there slowly dies from a lack of oxygen. Interesting that you djinn can survive here just fine."

"Better than fine, actually," Jace confessed. "We have made our home there on that other plane because we must, but when we're here...we feel better. Not exactly euphoric, and after we've been here for a while, we acclimate, but those first few hours here, we feel almost...."

"High?" Jessica suggested with a grin.

"I suppose so," he said. "I've never used narcotics, so I don't have much basis for comparison."

"What, you've never smoked a little pot?" she asked, still smiling. "Or some opium in a hookah or something?"

"Of course not," he replied, looking offended. "Why would you think that?"

She lifted her shoulders. "I don't know...it just seemed like a 'djinni' sort of thing to do."

Before they could bicker over it any further, Julia interjected, "Okay, so you can't go there without some kind of assistance in breathing. So what if I had something like, I don't know, a spacesuit or something?"

"I think spacesuits are kind of in short supply in Santa Fe," Lindsay said, her tone doubtful.

"Not a spacesuit," Miles said. He was tapping his fingers on his knees, and nodded, as if something had just occurred to him.

"What?" Julia asked. At least he didn't seem determined to shoot her down before she even got started. But then, Miles had always liked a good challenge.

"If the only adverse effects of going to the djinn plane are to the respiratory system, then that should be easy enough to overcome. A spacesuit would be overkill, frankly."

"Not to mention conspicuous," Jessica said dryly.

Even Jace looked halfway amused by that remark.

"So...like scuba gear or something?" Julia wondered how many diving stores might be located in the greater Santa Fe area. The place was hundreds of miles from any coast, but did people dive in lakes? She had absolutely no idea.

"Even that probably is too much," Miles replied. "A simple oxygen tank should do it. There should be some in the hospital."

That did sound a lot simpler. She shifted in her chair, glancing over at Jace. "How much time do you think it would take?"

His expression was troubled. "Honestly? I have no idea. Landmarks on the djinn plane aren't fixed the way they are here. I don't know this Lyanna al-Syan or her brother, but even if I did, there's no guarantee that I could find where they live. Things...drift."

Julia had a hard time wrapping her brain around that concept. Either things were where they were supposed to be, or they weren't. "How in the world do you connect with each other?"

"With our thoughts, our desires. That is to say, I can't find Lyanna because I've never met her. But because I have met Zahrias, and because he's my cousin, I should be able locate him once I'm on the djinn plane."

"I hope you two aren't considering a frontal assault or something," Jessica said, worry clear in her dark eyes. "I mean, it sounds like Lyanna has a bunch of people working for her. One djinn and a mortal woman equipped with an oxygen tank probably won't be enough to do much."

Some men might have argued that they could handle it just fine, but Jace wasn't most men. He knew his own strengths and weaknesses. "True," he said. "Which is why I believe we should seek out the elders and bring this matter to their attention. They will not be happy that Lyanna al-Syan has stolen Zahrias away from here, especially when they appointed him to be the guardian of this community. Lyanna has interfered with their wishes, which will not sit well with them."

Hearing this, Julia could feel herself relax slightly. She recalled how the elders had intervened to get Jessica away from Jace's scheming half-brother Aldair, so she knew they could be sympathetic. Actually, not so much sympathetic as concerned with protocols, with making sure that the unruly djinn population didn't wander too far outside the lines.

Lyanna had definitely wandered outside the lines here, so Julia could only hope the elders would give her the smackdown she so richly deserved.

"So…how do we find them?" she asked. "Wasn't it difficult for the djinn who were trying to track them down last time?"

"Nizar and Alif? Yes, because they'd had no contact with the elders prior to that time. They had to ask for help from others they knew, and trace their way to the elders in that manner. But I've met them, spoken with them. Therefore, we have a connection already."

Hope. It began to flicker to life within Julia. This could all work out in the end. Yes, the thought of going to the djinn plane frightened her, but what frightened her even more was facing a future that did not include Zahrias. Strange how one kiss could tell her so much. She needed him. Craved him, really. Now she wanted to kick herself for giving in to her anger, for not working harder to see his side of things. It couldn't have been easy to reach out and attempt to make a connection with another mortal woman, not when things had gone so terribly wrong between him and Evangeline.

"That sounds great, Jace," Julia said, hands flat on her knees as she regarded the rest of the group. "So let's see about getting those oxygen canisters from St. Vincent's."

No one had come to disturb him for some time. Zahrias paced the confines of the suite where Lyanna had him locked up, restless as a caged lion. Even though he'd known it was no use, he had laid his hands on the door latch, willing it to melt away into nothingness. But the iron had remained stubbornly solid, seeming to mock him. So, too, the latticework that covered the windows. He would not be getting out that way.

Indeed, the whole place seemed so carefully constructed to keep him in that he wondered how long Lyanna had been planning all this. It seemed Julia had been the catalyst that caused his tormentor to finally take action, but perhaps Lyanna had been plotting for some time before Julia even came on the scene.

Thoughts of Qadim also tormented him. Perhaps he had Julia in his power at this very moment, was attempting to seduce her into being with him in exchange for giving Zahrias his freedom. No, that didn't sound right. Not that Qadim wasn't capable of such a thing, but more that the other djinn must know Zahrias would be after his blood the very second he was released.

But maybe she had managed to get away. If she could only reach Santa Fe, then she would be surrounded by other djinn, and Qadim would find it much more difficult to get his hands on her. Except there was the matter of the spy....

He knew if he kept tormenting himself in such a way, he truly would go mad. Very well. He needed to look at the problem logically. He could not get out of here using his powers, for Lyanna had made sure he could not access them. So, then, it seemed he must somehow go through her. He must devise a way to make her think that he was succumbing to her charms. Perhaps then she would let down her guard. All he needed was a chance to escape this palace, because once he was away from the nullifying effects of the *ni-khar*, then he would be able to use his powers to return to the mortal world.

There was always the possibility that she might try to fetch him back, but he could rally his own people to protect him. Assuming that the spy wouldn't attempt to compromise his safety. Once he got away, discovering the identity of the person who had passed his or her information along to Lyanna would be of the utmost importance. In the meantime....

The suite had quite a luxurious bath chamber. Zahrias went in and shut the door, then ran the water to fill the tub. The water came out of the taps already hot; it had always been like that in every place he had ever lived. Djinn magic powered this plane, performing many of the small miracles that mortals had to sweat and strain to accomplish. For all that, he would not willingly live here again. No djinn would, given the chance to live among Earth's beauties. That, of course, was the entire reason for the Heat and all the destruction it had caused.

He lowered himself into the water. A human would have found it too hot, but Zahrias welcomed that heat as it surrounded all his limbs, beginning to soak away some of the tension in his back and neck muscles. Not all, of course; he could only relax so much. But in order to beat Lyanna on her home territory, he knew he had to restore as much of his strength and energy as he could, and that meant taking what refreshment he would allow himself.

But not too much. He did not think even Lyanna was so bold as to intrude on his bath—some things were considered sacrosanct among his people—but he would not allow her that opportunity. Once he knew he was clean, and much of the stiffness from his capture had soaked its way from his weary muscles, he rose and dried himself off.

A mirror framed with ornate inlay work in chips of semiprecious stones and mother-of-pearl hung on one wall. Zahrias gave his reflection a quick inspection, but he didn't see any obvious signs of the strain of the past few days. Perhaps his eyes were a bit more shadowed. Certainly the set of his mouth was more than grim. He would have to work on that if he intended to give Lyanna the impression that he had suffered a change of heart.

No sooner had he drawn on a fresh set of clothing than he heard raised voices from the corridor outside. Lyanna, and the deeper rumble of her brother's responses. The sound of Qadim's voice brought a rush of relief, for if he was here, then he couldn't be with Julia. So she had managed to escape him somehow.

Why they were having an argument right outside his door, Zahrias couldn't be certain, except perhaps that was where Qadim had finally caught up with his sister.

"...just because you were unlucky in your own pursuit doesn't mean that you must take out your frustrations on me!"

"This has nothing to do with Julia Innes," Qadim responded. He sounded angry, but in a tight, controlled way, quite unlike himself. "Or perhaps it does, in a way. Because she did teach me a valuable lesson. Wanting someone isn't enough to make them love you, Lyanna. And you risk yourself—and me as well, for I was foolish enough to assist you in this enterprise—if you do not let Zahrias go."

Lyanna made a scoffing noise. "I had no idea you were such a coward, brother. Please, wash your hands of this if you must, but I will see it through to the end. You know I am not one to abandon a plan, once I have set upon a course of action."

"No, and that is what I fear the most. Things are changing for us—more and more of our people are abandoning this world for the one we fought so hard to acquire. The elders are allowing them a good deal of leeway when it comes to deciding where to settle. Do you want to anger them to the point where our new homes on Earth are in some forsaken location that no one else wants?"

"Why would I want to go at all?" Lyanna flared. "This place suits me very well."

"It may not, if you find yourself alone here once everyone else has removed themselves to the mortal world." A pause then, as if Qadim was searching for words and realizing that anything he said would only anger his sister further. "We are blood, Lyanna, and therefore I went along with your schemes. I did not care at all for how Zahrias al-Harith treated you, and so helping you to get your revenge on him seemed a good idea at the time. Now, however, I realize the stakes are far too high. Whatever you do next, you will do it without my assistance."

Listening to all this, Zahrias burned to know what precisely had passed between Qadim and Julia. It did seem that she had made an impression. Truly, he had not thought Qadim would ever suffer such a change of heart as to turn his back on his sister. But it did appear that he was reevaluating his role in Lyanna's plans.

"Go then!" she cried out. "You are a coward, to think of your own skin rather than remaining committed to the path you chose not so long ago. But I would not wish to have a coward's assistance anyway."

Another silence. In fact, it lasted so long that Zahrias wondered if Qadim had stalked away the moment Lyanna called him a coward. But then he spoke again, his voice heavy.

"If I thought it would do any good, I would beg you to reconsider. Unfortunately, I know you too well to expect such a thing. All I can say is that you should not expect my protection, when all this comes tumbling down on your head."

"I wouldn't expect it, nor would I ask for it," she snapped.

"As I thought. Fare you well, sister."

Quiet descended once again, but this time Zahrias knew Qadim must have finally left. For himself, he hurried back into the bath chamber, then picked up one of the towels he'd discarded. As the door to his suite opened and Lyanna entered, he came back into the main room, blotting his still-damp hair.

Her expression was tight with anger, but it relaxed somewhat when she saw that he must have been in the bath during her quarrel with her brother. "Feeling better?" she asked, tone pleasant, as if she hadn't been threatening him the last time they had seen one another.

"Much," he replied. Recalling his resolution to ingratiate himself with her, he went on, "I fear I must apologize for what I said earlier—"

"Oh, that," she cut in, making a dismissive wave with one hand. "I know you were wearied, and perhaps not thinking clearly. But you look far more refreshed now."

"I am. Thank you." Even that simple courtesy was difficult for him to force past his lips. But he knew he must. Lyanna must think he was softening toward her, or he would remain a prisoner here.

She smiled then. "I am glad to hear it. Perhaps you would like to see more of the house? I cannot imagine that you would wish to remain in this room indefinitely, and there is far more than merely the audience hall and the dining chamber."

No, that was for certain. "I would very much like to see it," he told her. Perhaps by giving him a tour, she would also inadvertently provide him with the information he required to make his escape.

Upon hearing those words, she extended an arm toward him. He forced himself to step toward her and take it, even though he wanted to recoil at the touch of her flesh against his. Luckily, she seemed to notice nothing of his revulsion, and continued to smile as she opened the door and led him out into the corridor.

Good. Her blindness might be the only thing that would aid him in freeing himself from her forever.

Because taking the truck back into town might be too conspicuous, the collective decision was made that Jace would blink Julia into the hospital with him, and then the two of them could select the proper oxygen tank for her journey into the djinn world.

"Obviously, the bigger it is, the longer it will last," Miles had said. "That means it'll be heavier, but you should be able to manage it. You're not dealing with health issues the way someone who used to require one of those tanks would be."

True enough. Right then, she was already feeling tired, but the thought that she'd soon be going to find Zahrias had given her enough energy to know she'd be fine with hauling a tank around.

As to the risk of running into anyone at the hospital, they'd decided that was fairly low. Lauren and the baby—still unnamed, according to Jace—had gone home the day before, so no one should be around. When your community consisted of djinn and the mortals they'd blessed with perfect health and long life, you didn't have much need of a hospital.

Jace popped them into the Pulmonary and Critical Care ward. As they'd predicted, the place was silent and still.

Dark, too. Julia began to wish she'd brought a flashlight, but then Jace waved a hand, and the overhead fluorescent lamps turned on.

"Well, that's handy," she said.

"I suppose so. We'll just have to hope that no one notices."

"Would they? I mean, do people really come by the hospital all that much?"

"Not that I'm aware of," he replied. "But that doesn't mean we should be careless, either." He turned away from her, scanning the signage next to the doors. "Over here."

She headed over to the place he'd indicated, which turned out to be a supply room stocked with what looked like a dizzying variety of cylinders in all sorts of sizes. Jace appeared somewhat surprised by the collection.

"High altitude," she explained. "If you already have health issues, that can make it a lot harder to breathe. So they probably stocked more oxygen here than they would have in hospitals closer to sea level."

He nodded. "What about this one?"

The cylinder in question was about two feet long. "Does it have any kind of rating listed?"

After peering at the label, he said, "Looks like twelve hours under normal circumstances. If you exert yourself a good deal, it won't last quite that long."

Would she be exerting herself? Good question. She really had no idea what travel on the djinn plane even entailed. Maybe they'd just blink in and out until Jace could track down the elders. "Twelve hours is a decent chunk."

"Well, you take that one, and I'll take a second one, just to be safe. We can always pop back here if you start to feel off, but obviously it'll work out better if we can just stay there for as long as possible."

She had to agree with that. If they still hadn't located the elders, even with twenty-four hours' worth of oxygen....

"Sounds good," she told him. "Let's get one of these hooked up."

They dug around and eventually found connector hoses and a couple of cannulas still in their sterile wrappings.

"Have you ever used one of these?" Jace asked as she wrangled the tubing and the cannula and eventually got everything attached. He'd already slung the spare oxygen canister over his left shoulder.

"Of course not," she replied. "I've been in the hospital once in my entire life. Appendectomy. And even that was no big deal, since I caught it early. I barely even have a scar. Anyway," she added as Jace's eyebrows began to lift, "no need for oxygen. But how hard can it be?"

To prove herself right, she fitted the cannula into her nose. It felt strange sitting there, but probably much better than having a full-on mask would have. She turned the valve on the oxygen tank and inhaled through her nose, not too deeply, but enough that she got a decent hit off it. The weight of it hanging from her shoulder would take some getting used to, and it did hamper her mobility somewhat. But it could be the only thing standing between her and slow asphyxiation.

"I think it's working," she said.

"How does it feel?"

"Well, right now it feels like I'm going to get high on this oxygen if I keep breathing it. But I suppose I'll feel different when we get to the djinn world."

At those words, his expression sobered. "Julia, if you start to feel strange at all, *tell me.* It's just Miles's educated guess that the oxygen levels are different on that plane, but it still could be something else entirely. I'll get you back here right away if you think something is off."

"Don't worry—I'll tell you." Since he didn't appear entirely convinced, she went on, "Really, I don't have a death wish. I want to help get Zahrias out of there, but I also want to make sure I'm here to enjoy him when we do get him back. Okay?"

Jace seemed to relax a little after she delivered this speech. "Okay." He shut his eyes and appeared to be concentrating on something. What, Julia wasn't entirely sure, but she figured he was reaching out to that unearthly plane and attempting to determine where the elders might be.

A nod, and then he was pulling her against him, holding her tight. The embrace startled her at first, but she remembered a second later that a djinn had to hold a mortal that close to be able to blink them in and out of reality. She still didn't like it very much, but at least she understood the reason for it.

His arms tightened further, and then the world as she knew it disappeared.

CHAPTER FOURTEEN

COLORS THAT HAD NO NAME SWIRLED BEHIND HER eyelids. She felt alternately blasted by heat, then cold. After a moment that could have lasted forever or taken no time at all, Julia felt solid ground beneath her feet.

Jace's voice came to her ears. "We're here. You can open your eyes."

Cautiously, she cracked her eyelids. She didn't know what she was expecting—some sort of scene out of an otherworldly Arabian Nights, with djinn flying around her on carpets and palaces with fantastic domes and minarets on every side, but what she saw couldn't be further from that mental image.

The sky hurt to look at. It wasn't any one color, but shifted from red to blue to green to a sort of bruised purple with yellowish overtones. The light came from everywhere and nowhere. There wasn't a sun or stars or moon. A brittle wind pulled at her hair, but she had no real sensation of the temperature. It wasn't cold or warm, but somewhere in between.

And the landscape appeared utterly barren, undulating hills of some dark soil from which nothing grew. Off in the distance, she spied a range of jagged shapes that might have been mountains.

Somehow she retained enough of her faculties to breathe in through her nose, to pull some precious oxygen into her system. At last she managed to say, "You— your people *live* here?"

A bitter smile touched Jace's mouth. "It is quite the garden spot, isn't it? Truthfully, we do not venture outside our homes all that often. But you see now why we pull all the raw materials for our food and our houses from your world. Except for a few sheltered gardens, nothing truly grows here." He paused then to glance around, keen dark eyes taking in the empty landscape. "This way."

Julia wondered how he could possibly know which direction to go, but she didn't ask, only followed him as he headed toward that range of distant mountains. They couldn't be his destination, could they? That kind of walk would take hours. She thought of the frighteningly finite supply of oxygen in the tank, and how it was getting lower with every breath she took. No way would she have enough if they really did have to hike all that distance, even counting the backup Jace was carrying.

At least the gravity felt marginally lower here. Not enough to give her any sense of euphoria, though, not when she had to measure her oxygen consumption so carefully. As she walked, she tried to pay attention to her breathing, to see if anything felt off or strange. So far, she wasn't noticing anything. Yes, it felt strange to have that cannula shoved into her nostrils, and the air here had a strange acrid quality to it that burned at the back of her throat, but that was the only real discomfort she was currently experiencing.

Something dark seemed to hover in the air, closer than the mountains, but still far enough away that she couldn't make out any distinct features. Julia frowned at it. The shape was all wrong for any kind of airplane. Then she wanted to laugh at herself. What the hell did the djinn need with any kind of aircraft when they could instantly transport themselves from place to place whenever they wanted?

As they approached, Julia could see that the shape wasn't natural at all, but a construct that looked like the sort of Arabian Nights palace that she'd originally imagined—except that it was floating at least a hundred feet in the air. She sent Jace a questioning glance, and he nodded.

"Yes, that is our destination."

It was beautiful, with its towers of pale stone and banners in blue and purple. From this distance, she couldn't see any sign of life, but then, if she lived here, she probably wouldn't spend much time out of doors, either. If the interior of the palace was anywhere near as striking as its exterior, then you'd get a much better view by staying inside.

They climbed a rocky hill in order to get closer to the floating palace. Julia did her best to avoid breathing hard, but she had to give herself enough air to get up that incline. "If you knew where we were going," she said, trying not to pant, "why didn't you take us there directly?"

"That's not how it works." Unlike her, he didn't seem at all winded. Usually she would have said she was in decent shape, but something about the air here, even with the assist from the oxygen, seemed to suck the strength right out of her body. "All I had was a general idea of where the elders' palace might be. Once we were here, we still had to track it down. Besides," he added, giving her a searching look, as if to confirm for himself that she was managing all right, "it is considered very rude to suddenly appear in another djinn's home, even if you know exactly where you need to go. This way, they'll know we're coming."

"I suppose that's a good thing?"

His expression was calm, betraying nothing of what might be going on behind those dark eyes. "I would think so, yes. They came to our aid last spring."

That was true. The elders definitely didn't seem pleased by anyone who went against their edicts, and so Julia had no reason to believe they would feel any differently now. And even though she hadn't exchanged a single word with the one redheaded elder, Julia thought she might have liked the djinn woman, if they were ever able to deal with one another socially. There had been a decidedly un-djinn-like twinkle in her eyes, one that seemed to indicate she wasn't unsympathetic to the mortals' cause.

When she and Jace came closer to the palace, Jessica wondered how the hell they were supposed to even get in there. Since he'd said it wasn't polite to simply blink into a djinn residence without an invitation, there had to be some other way of getting inside. Or maybe the very fact that the building just kept floating there was a subtle sign that they weren't in fact wanted.

As she watched, however, a gate at the front of the floating structure opened slowly, and from that gate issued a long red streamer. No, not a streamer, but a narrow carpet worked in shades of red and deep blue.

She looked over at Jace. A certain tension around his jaw line seemed to lessen slightly. "That's our invitation," he said. "Let's go."

He headed toward the carpet, while Julia followed, trying not to frown. That long rectangle didn't look very stable. And they were expecting her to walk on it?

But the second her foot touched the intricately woven runner, the carpet stiffened, feeling as solid as if it had been poured out of concrete instead of knotted wool. Eyes wide, she stayed slightly behind Jace while he walked up the carpet as if he did that sort of thing every day. Well, maybe he had, back when this world had been his home.

Even though that magical carpet seemed sturdy enough, she tried not to look down at it as they climbed up to the front entrance of the palace. She'd never been that great at heights, and to be steadily ascending on something less than two feet wide was just a little disconcerting.

After a few minutes, though, they reached the gate and passed through the walls of the palace. Now the ground underfoot was solid marble, a soft rose color shot through with gold. Julia didn't have much time to admire it, however, because a tall, handsome djinn with thick brown hair and blue eyes approached them and said, "They are expecting you. This way, please."

All very polite. Julia couldn't help feeling ill at ease, however. The splendor of her surroundings cowed her, and even though she knew it had been practical to come here in her jeans and hiking boots, she felt small and shabby. Yes, Jace was dressed very much the same, except for motorcycle boots instead of the sturdy lace-ups she had on, but he didn't seem to be aware of any discrepancy between his appearance and the palace around him.

But at least he's a djinn, she thought. *He doesn't care about looking out of place because this is his world, his people.*

Or at least they used to be. He'd been pretty clear about where his loyalties now lay.

The brown-haired djinn who'd been leading them stopped at a high, arched doorway. Spreading a hand toward the arch, he said, "They will see you inside."

Jace murmured a word of thanks, then strode forward, chin high. Julia did the best she could to look similarly confident, although she had a feeling the cannula in her nose somewhat lessened that impression.

The room must have been some sort of audience chamber, but she was relieved to see that there was no audience, only five djinn seated on the dais at the far end of the room. Three men, two women, one of them the redheaded djinn Julia remembered. They didn't stand or make any word of greeting, but only sat there in a set of matching carved chairs, watching as she and Jace approached.

"Elders," he said, stopping a few feet from the dais, and then pressing his hands together and bowing from the waist.

"Jasreel al-Ankara," said the oldest of the group, a djinn who actually had some streaks of silver in his dark hair. His gaze moved to Julia. "Julia Innes."

So at least they knew who she was. She'd wondered if they would pay any attention to her at all, or whether she would have to stand off to the side and let Jace do all the negotiating.

"Elders," she said, imitating Jace as best she could. She had to cut the bow short because the oxygen tank began to slide forward and threatened to smack her in the head if she didn't stand back up immediately. As she straightened, she could have sworn she saw the red-headed djinn woman's mouth twitch with suppressed laughter.

If Jace had noticed her amusement, he didn't give any indication. Since the pleasantries had been dispensed with, he appeared ready to get down to business. "We're here because of a most pressing matter. Zahrias al-Harith has been taken by a woman of the djinn, Lyanna al-Syan, and—"

"We know," said the lead elder. His face was utterly impassive, so Julia couldn't begin to guess what his opinion on the situation might be.

Jace blinked. "You *know?*"

"Yes. There is very little that escapes our attention, Jasreel, especially if it involves one who has been given a position of responsibility. After the incident this past spring with Khalim al-Usar, we knew we must watch all of you in Santa Fe a little more closely."

Stepping forward, Julia said, "But if you knew, why didn't you do anything about it?"

The elder's eyes seemed to linger on the cannula in her nose, the thin tubing attached to the oxygen tank slung over her shoulder. "My congratulations on your resourcefulness. We did not expect one of your kind to come here, not when the risks were so high."

"What else could I do?" she responded. "I wasn't about to sit idly by and let others do the work of getting Zahrias back."

The elders were all silent then, although Julia had a feeling, judging by the way their eyes flickered toward one another, that they were holding one of those disconcerting subvocal conversations. After a long pause, the redheaded djinn got up from her seat and came forward.

"And why is it so important that you be involved in his rescue?"

The question was asked simply, but Julia guessed the djinn woman already knew the answer. As to why she'd asked it...maybe she wanted Julia to make a formal declaration in front of all of them before they'd offer their aid. Which was fine. At this point, she was far beyond pride.

"Because I love him," she said. "I've probably loved him almost since the moment I first met him, but I didn't want to admit it to myself. That's why I've come. We've already lost too much time together."

"And does he love you in return?"

Did he? Zahrias had never spoken the words, but in that moment, Julia realized it didn't matter. The way he had kissed her, held her, looked into her eyes—she knew that he'd fought against the feeling as much as she had, but had finally given up resisting. Sometimes you simply had to accept what the universe decided to send you.

"Yes," she replied.

"And yet you were not his Chosen," said one of the other elders, a man who had not spoken before then.

Hearing that painful detail spoken of so calmly made Julia want to flinch. "No," she said. "But he told me he regretted that he hadn't done so. And I believed him." Of course she had believed him—the truth had been all too clear in every painful syllable he'd uttered. The djinn had many powers, but the ability to turn back time wasn't one of them. All Zahrias could do now was attempt to move forward.

Another one of those thick pauses, one where she could practically feel the mental conversations going back and forth amongst the elders. "Your cause is just," the lead elder said at last. "But I fear we cannot help you."

"What?" Julia burst out. She began to take a step forward, but Jace laid a hand on her arm, restraining her. Belatedly, she realized that making any aggressive movements around such powerful beings probably wasn't the best idea in the world.

"I'm not sure I understand," Jace said, his voice tight. Right then, Julia realized he was doing everything he could to keep himself from lashing out at them as well.

The twinkle had disappeared from the redheaded djinn's eyes. Lovely features so still they might have been a mask, she said, "Zahrias al-Harith has a history with this woman, this Lyanna al-Syan, does he not?"

"Yes," Julia replied, not sure what that had to do with anything. But even as the djinn elder asked the question, Jace had seemed to deflate suddenly, the straight set of his shoulders drooping.

"Oh."

"What is it?" she demanded. "Am I missing something here?"

Deep green fabric woven with copper threads glinted as the djinn woman lifted her shoulders. "We do not interfere in the personal lives of our people. This is something you will have to work out amongst you."

Julia couldn't believe what she was hearing. "But you helped us when Aldair kidnapped Jessica Monroe, Jace's Chosen! How is that not interfering in their personal lives?"

The redheaded djinn ignored Julia's abrupt tone. In fact, her expression softened, and she went so far as to step down from the dais and lay a comforting hand on her shoulder. "It was not the same thing. Aldair and Jessica had never been lovers. In addition, he had allied himself with Khalim al-Usar to violate the compact we had all agreed to, that the Chosen should not be harmed in any way. But Lyanna al-Syan has not broken that compact. Has she hurt anyone?"

"Yes," Julia said at once. "Or at least, a man who was working for Lyanna's brother killed three people, friends of mine. I would say that was hurting someone."

The djinn woman lifted her hand from Julia's shoulder. Her eyes, a deep green flecked with gold, were somber. Tone soft, she asked, "But were they Chosen?"

Of course they weren't. Brent and Nancy and Eric had been among the Immune, but they were under no djinn's protection. The realization only made Julia that much angrier. "So I suppose you're telling me it doesn't matter that they were killed, since they were just ordinary humans."

"I am not saying that," she replied calmly. "But there is no compact protecting the Immune. Any djinn can kill an immune human and not have to worry about the consequences, because there are none."

"That's horrible."

"To you, perhaps. But since Lyanna has broken none of our laws, we cannot prosecute her, or pursue her."

Julia couldn't believe she was hearing any of this. Fury burned in her. To risk so much, and for what? Only to be told that it wasn't their problem, and to run along now? "So you'll just sit back and let her keep Zahrias as her plaything?"

"Regretfully, yes." The djinn woman hesitated, and then she smiled. "But fear not. Even as a captive, I believe Zahrias al-Harith is not entirely without resources."

He had to wonder how much of her family's wealth Lyanna had squandered to build such a place. Dining halls and libraries and galleries and bedrooms and bath chambers—all to support one person? Surely she spent her time in only a tenth of all this space, if even that much.

But of course he did not show his disapproval. No, he smiled at the appropriate intervals, and uttered false words of praise, and made sure she could not detect a note of censure in his voice.

Now she had led him out into a garden of sorts, carefully shielded from the harsh environment outside the palace walls by an enormous pergola covered in thick vines. He did not recognize the plant, but knew it must be something that thrived in hostile conditions, for in general, the flora of Earth did not do well here. Under the protection of that vine, however, more flowers and vines and bushes grew, bringing an incongruous touch of green to a place that did not generally see such abundance.

"It is very beautiful," he told her, the first true word of praise he had spoken all afternoon. Truly, it did refresh his soul somewhat to be in a place that reminded him of the world he'd been taken from.

"I thought you would like it," Lyanna replied. She stepped a few paces away from him to run a fingertip over the velvety petals of a blood-red rose that grew nearby.

"And yet...." he began, then stopped himself.

"And yet what?"

"You could have all this down in the mortal plane as well," he said. "Our people have begun to settle there in earnest, have they not?"

Her scarlet-tinted lips pushed together. "You sound like Qadim."

Zahrias hadn't expected that comment. "I do?"

"Yes. He thinks I am foolish for expending so much energy on this house. In fact, he believes I will be punished for bringing you here in such a fashion. Silly, is it not? The elders do not stoop to involve themselves in lover's quarrels."

No, they did not. Zahrias realized he should have thought of such a thing earlier. They would not intercede in what they viewed as a personal matter. That was something for his and Lyanna's families to take up, if they wished. But his mother had taken the draught of the dark sleep years and years ago, and his father was most likely far too concerned with his latest conquest, whoever she might be, to care overmuch about what happened to his son. Dani would do what he could, given the opportunity, but he had a newborn child to worry about. Zahrias was slightly encouraged that Qadim had washed his hands of his sister and her plots, but that disapproval most likely would not extend to offering any sort of assistance. He feared he was very much alone in this.

"That is true," he said, taking care to keep his tone light. "On the other hand, I have heard that the elders have subtle ways of making their displeasure known, even if they cannot take direct action."

"They do not worry me." Lyanna gave a negligent lift of her shoulders and turned back toward him, eyebrows raised in apparent disdain. "Qadim believes I will get the scraps from the table when it comes time for me to claim my own demesne on Earth, but he doesn't understand one very important fact."

"Which is?"

"I care nothing for living on the mortal plane. What could I have there that I do not already have here? And besides, the face of that world is still covered with the mortals' ugly cities and roads and all manner of things I would prefer not to look at. So I think it is far better to stay here."

"Even if everyone else should leave?"

Her expression turned sly. "Ah, but they won't *all* leave, will they?" She came closer and laid her hand on his forearm. Zahrias made sure he didn't react, but only gazed down into her face with a mildly curious expression. He couldn't allow her to see how violently he wished to tear his arm from her grasp. "You will be here with me, Zahrias. And if I have you, then I certainly have no need of anyone else."

In that moment, he could only wonder what he had done so very wrong, to be tormented by her like this. But he could not waste any of his energies in shouting recriminations at the universe. He must remain focused, no matter what.

Because what he saw now, as he fixed a false smile on his lips, was that the vine-covered pergola did not quite touch the top of the wall which enclosed the garden. A tight fit, for a man of his size, but he thought he might be able to squeeze through, if given the opportunity. That would be the real trick, for he rather doubted Lyanna would allow him to come here alone, and of course he could not slip away from his suite, not when every door was locked against him and ni-khar blocked his powers at every turn.

Still, realizing that her house was not quite the impregnable fortress he'd feared it might be gave him some hope. He would find a way, even if....

Even if he had to do the worst. Never in his life had he raised his hand against a woman, but he doubted anyone would argue that Lyanna had brought that violence upon herself, if matters should come to such a pass.

Only as a last resort, he told himself. *And only if there is truly no other way.*

Tone light, he said, "No one else at all? What about the men who work as your guards, or the *jann* who bring your meals and make sure everything is tidy?"

She wrinkled her nose. "Oh, the *jann*—they cannot really be counted as people. And as for the guards, well, once I am sure of you, I will have no need of them, will I?"

In her mind, perhaps not. Zahrias wondered if he should force himself to do the unthinkable, to lie down with her so she might be gulled into believing he had succumbed to her charms. Perhaps then she would dispense with the *ni-khar* wards, and the djinn who watched the doorways.

But then he saw Julia's face in his mind, those blue-gray eyes of his looking at him with a sort of terrible need, the kind one didn't want to admit even to oneself, and he knew he could never do such a thing. He and Julia had made no true compact, had not spoken any true words of love to one another, and yet being intimate with Lyanna felt like the very worst sort of betrayal. He would have to come up with a different plan.

"No, I suppose you would not need them any longer," he told her, infusing a certain warmth into the words in the hope that she would read into them a kindling desire on his own part. It might not require all that much to push her into relaxing her guard—a smile here, a touch on the hand there. She so believed in the myth of her own desirability that it shouldn't be too much work at all to make her think he had succumbed to her charms and had forgotten all about the mortal woman he once loved.

Or so he hoped. Because he knew he would not be able to endure much more of this.

CHAPTER FIFTEEN

"I'm not going back," Julia told Jace, arms crossed over her chest. "We're here—we might as well see if we can find Lyanna."

He shook his head, strain clear in the taut look of the skin around his eyes. Back in the palace, they had been offered light refreshments by the djinn elders, lemon-infused water and delicate cakes that tasted of honey, but after being shown that perfunctory courtesy, they were told they must leave.

"We can do nothing for you," the redheaded djinn woman said, regret clear in her tone. "And it is not altogether safe for you to be here, even with that apparatus you wear." She'd gestured toward the cannula and oxygen tank Julia was using, and then had one of the guards show them to the front gates of the palace.

Julia had experienced a stirring of fear at the djinn's comment about the oxygen equipment, but brushed it aside. So far, she felt just fine. Well, not exactly fine, not when she was roiling with a particularly uncomfortable combination of anger and frustration and worry. But physically, she thought she was doing all right.

They had walked a good distance from the palace in silence, both of them sharing the unspoken agreement to put the structure that housed the djinn elders a decent way behind them before they would stop to talk. Now, though, she and Jace had paused on a hillside rough with black rocks that appeared volcanic to Julia's untrained eyes. She didn't know for certain, though, and decided it probably didn't matter all that much.

"Look, Julia," Jace said, his voice pleading. "I know it's difficult for you to understand, but I literally have no way of finding this person. I've never met her, don't know her family. Her connection with Zahrias goes back to a time before I was even born. In this world, it's all about our connections to one another, and I don't have one with her. We could wander this place until all your oxygen ran out, and we still wouldn't be any closer to tracking her down."

"I just don't get that," she retorted. In her anger, she sucked in some air through her mouth rather than her nose, and she could feel it burn the sensitive tissues at the back of her throat. Damn it. Voice scratchy, she went on, "Forget about Lyanna. You sure as hell have a connection to Zahrias. So why can't you track him down instead?"

Jace's expression was a study in exasperation, tinged with real worry. "Because he's in her home, her territory. She won't allow anyone to see anything there that she doesn't want them to see. And I know for damn sure that she's not going to broadcast Zahrias' presence to anyone who might be able to do something about it."

This was all going to make her crazy by the time she was done. The djinn plane itself was bad enough, with its shifting light and odd shadows and a sky that didn't really feel like a sky. But the world of the people who lived there was just as bad—rules that didn't make sense, twisted loyalties, powers that worked for one kind of djinn but not another. How they kept track of it all, she had no idea, but she supposed living for an eternity or two might help.

"So what am I supposed to do?" she asked. "Just give up?"

"Of course not. But I think it would be better to go back home and regroup. You still look like you're doing okay, but why push it? I can bring us back here at any time. Staying until you're almost out of oxygen, just to prove a point, isn't going to help Zahrias."

Deep down, she knew he was right. It certainly didn't sound as if she could accomplish much more here. So, back to Santa Fe, and then...

...and then what? Admit defeat and return to Los Alamos with her tail between her legs? No way. There had to be something they could do. If only they could track down someone who did know Lyanna. Well, there was Qadim, but Julia sort of doubted he'd be willing to help them out. And having to skulk around Santa Fe because somewhere in that community of djinn and Chosen there was probably a spy passing on information to Qadim and his sister....

A spy. Julia's brain latched onto that notion. Why the hell hadn't she thought of it sooner? Whoever it was, that person had to know how to find Lyanna.

A smile spread over her face then, and Jace cocked his head at her. "What is it?"

"Yes, we do need to go back. Then we need to root out our spy."

Somewhere off in the house, a baby was crying. Dani had said he didn't want to leave Lauren, and so Jace had brought Julia here to the sprawling pueblo-style home where the new family lived. Jace related that Jessica had seemed a little put out when he informed her she couldn't take part in this convo, but since Jace was the only djinn in town they knew they could trust right then—well, besides Dani—she and Lindsay and Miles all were forced to remain back at Jace and Jessica's home out in the country while he blinked Julia into Lauren and Dani's living room.

"How is he?" Julia asked, glance moving toward the hallway where the crying seemed to be emanating.

"Good," Dani replied. "Strong and healthy and thriving. And Lauren as well." He hesitated then, looking from Julia to Jace and back again. "This business with Zahrias pains me, for I feel I should be able to go to his aid, and yet I cannot."

"I understand why you need to stay with Lauren," Julia began, but Dani only shook his head.

"That is not all of it. I do not wish you to think that I would not offer my assistance, even with my responsibilities here, but the truth of it is, there is very little I can do. I also never met Lyanna—she was a part of my brother's past he did not wish to discuss, and I was born after they had parted." He offered Julia a grim smile. "You see, it is not with us the way it is with mortals. Our lifespans are so long that the time when we are able to have children lasts for centuries. Zahrias is my brother, and we have the same mother and father, but even so, more than a hundred years lies between us, although it may appear to you that we are only a few years apart in age."

Once he had explained it to her, the situation did make some sense. Julia realized she had been too human-centric in her thinking. It was still difficult to wrap her brain around the concept that djinn siblings could have decades or even centuries separating them.

"Okay," she said then. "But you still know the people in the community here much better than I, or even Jace, who hasn't lived among them as much as you have. Someone here has been slipping information to Lyanna and her brother Qadim. I guess I'm just trying to figure out why. Is there anyone in the group who seemed disgruntled with the way Zahrias was running things?"

"Not that I'm aware of." Dani was silent for a moment; his gaze seemed to be fixed on the hallway that led to the bedrooms, where the baby had finally stopped crying. "But then, I've been somewhat preoccupied of late. Still, we djinn are not generally known for holding in our displeasure, so if Zahrias had offended someone, they probably would have let him know about it."

"It's also very possible that Zahrias' actions as leader here had absolutely nothing to do with it," Jace commented. "The more likely scenario—in my mind, anyway—is that the spy is a relation of Qadim and Lyanna, perhaps a cousin, or even another sibling, and has been passing on information out of family loyalty."

Julia had been worried about that. The djinn did seem to take family seriously, for good or ill. Well, except the times when those relationships put them at one another's throats, as had been the case with Jace and his half-brother Aldair. "So," she said, only half joking, "I don't suppose you have a database where you can look all that stuff up."

Dani gave her a weary smile. "I'm afraid not. You know that Zahrias and I are cousins with Jace, of course, but so is Allira, one of the people in our group here, whose mother was my father's younger sister. I can be certain of her, but as for the rest...." The sentence died away, and he shrugged.

"Surely there must be people here you trust who aren't related to you," Julia protested.

"Until this incident with Lyanna and Zahrias, I had thought I could trust all of them," Dani told her, the usual good humor missing from his expression. "And I would have been proven wrong. A few, such as Lilias, I do trust implicitly, because she has never wavered in her commitment to her partner, and to the community here. And perhaps Alshira and Murrah, whom you interviewed after Margolis disappeared. You decided that they could not be involved."

Yes, she had, based on the evidence she'd been given at the time. Now, though, Julia couldn't help wondering if she'd been too hasty in believing their alibis. Qadim had been the one to break Margolis out of his cell, true, but that didn't mean one or both of the djinn guards who'd been assigned to watch over the former commander of Los Alamos wasn't the person who'd slipped information to Lyanna behind their backs.

"Maybe I made the wrong call on that one," Julia said slowly. "I don't know. I hate to think that, but I don't know what else to say. But if you do trust Lilias, then I think we should talk to her. She might have met Lyanna once, or at least have heard of her. Anyway, it's worth a try."

"I'll go fetch her," Jace offered. "Hang on."

He blinked out of the room, leaving Julia to sit there with Dani and try not to feel too awkward. What was she supposed to say to him, after all? *Well, yeah, your brother and I decided we were into each other, but then the ex-girlfriend from hell decided to show up and make our lives miserable?*

Not likely. Anyway, that sort of flip comment was an insult to the people who had lost their lives because of Lyanna's insane pursuit of Zahrias. Still, Dani's dark eyes were curious, but he was too well-behaved to ask any personal probing questions. Thank God.

Lauren came in then, looking frazzled. Not that Julia could really blame her. Actually, she was surprised the other woman was even up and about, considering she'd given birth less than forty-eight hours earlier.

But Lauren was Chosen, which meant she had powers of healing and recuperation that Julia could only begin to guess at. Even with that supernatural advantage, she was far paler than usual, shadows dark under her big blue eyes. Apparently those healing gifts didn't extend to replacing sleep lost due to midnight feedings.

"Wasn't Jace here?" she asked, looking around in some confusion. "I thought I heard his voice."

"He was, but he went to fetch Lilias," Dani told her. "Beloved, please sit down. How is Gabriel?"

"Sleeping," Lauren said with a sigh. She sat down next to her partner and laid her head on his shoulder.

"So you decided to call him Gabriel?" Julia asked.

"It involved a bit of negotiation, but yes," Dani replied. "I fear that my people have not had the most positive encounters with angels, but Lauren pointed out that we are starting a new chapter here. Besides," he added, reaching over to take Lauren's hand in his, "it was her grandfather's name, and I understood her need to honor him."

"That's a wonderful tribute," Julia said. For the moment, she thought it best to ignore his off-hand comment about angels, since her brain was already feeling a bit overloaded. Besides, how awful was it for her to feel a stab of jealousy as she looked at them, saw the easy way they sat next to each other, how Lauren's fingers tightened around Dani's, as if drawing strength from him. She wanted that sort of closeness with Zahrias, wanted to have him hold her hand and brush her hair away from her brow, wanted to wake up next to him every morning. Just what the hell had she been thinking, picking that fight with him? She'd always had a knack for shooting herself in the foot, but she'd really outdone herself with that knee-jerk response.

"We thought it was a good name for our son," Lauren said softly. "We've all lost so much, but if we can honor the ones who are gone by making them live a little through the next generation, then it doesn't hurt quite so much."

Dani didn't speak, but only continued to hold her hand. What thoughts must be passing through his mind? She'd noticed that the djinn here in Santa Fe didn't like to talk about what their brethren were up to in the rest of the world, tried to shy away from the harsh reality that there were those among them who'd coldly plotted to exterminate the human race. True, the Santa Fe djinn had nothing to do with the slaughter, had saved the people they could. But still....

Into that awkward silence, Jace and Lilias appeared in the open space between the two couches where Dani and Lauren and Julia sat. The djinn woman smiled at them, but her expression was troubled nonetheless. Jace must have filled her in on some of the details before bringing her here.

"This is a terrible thing," she said at once, without bothering with any form of greeting. "But I am glad you reached out to me, because I do know something of this Lyanna al-Syan."

"You do?" Julia asked, relief rushing through her. Maybe that reaction was a little premature, but she was damn tired of hearing people tell her that they'd never met the woman.

"Yes," Lilias replied. She went over to the unoccupied armchair that was located between the two couches, then sat down. "I fear my older brother was entangled in her web, many years ago. That relationship did not last, much to my relief, but it still did its damage nonetheless. He became cold, unconcerned with what others thought of him or of his actions." Her lovely features tightened, and she went on, "He is not among us here. He cared nothing for my arguments that what our people planned to do in this world was wrong, and only laughed and said mankind had brought disaster and plague upon itself."

"I am sorry," Jace said. "I didn't know that."

She shrugged, but Julia could tell from her expression that Lilias was not quite as indifferent as she pretended to be. "Ah, well, we all have those in our families who cannot understand this path we have chosen. I suppose I should be glad that at least Baltasar had not thrown in his lot with Khalim and his followers. That was one of my greatest fears, after I saw what they did to my Aidan. For surely I must hate my brother then, if it turned out that he had been involved in the attack."

No one spoke. Jace looked troubled, and Julia guessed he was thinking of his own half-brother, who had pretended to be one of the One Thousand who had selected mortal partners to save. But Aldair had only done so to get close to Jace and take his revenge on the woman Jace loved.

When you got down to it, the djinn did seem to be more than usually vengeful and bloodthirsty. Maybe those traits stemmed from the same pride that had caused them to defy God when he commanded them to bow down before man, his latest creation.

But then, were we really that much better? Julia thought. *We were certainly pretty damn good at manufacturing excuses to kill each other, or lie and cheat and steal. If the djinn hadn't destroyed us, we might have done the job ourselves in a few more generations.*

She didn't really want to believe that. Enough good people had crossed her path even before the Dying that she knew the world wasn't quite so black and white. With some sadness, she remembered Barry Geller, one of the partners at the law firm where she was a paralegal. He'd known her abusive fiancé, had gently tried to persuade her that she deserved better, had quietly left a card for a battered women's shelter tucked into her desk drawer when she'd come to work sporting a bruise that the best pancake makeup couldn't hide. That had been only a week before the Heat struck. During that week, she'd taken the card out of her desk drawer and turned it over and over in her hands, wishing she had the courage to make that phone call.

But she hadn't made the call. She'd endured Ian's verbal abuse, thankful at the time that at least he hadn't hit her again, and then the Dying took away Ian and Barry and everyone else she'd ever known. And she ended up never having to make the decision to leave that relationship. No, the Heat had made that decision for her.

"At any rate," Lilias continued, apparently as uncomfortable with the continuing silence as everyone else, "I know of Lyanna and her relations. Her brother Qadim is her only sibling, but I know that they are connected on their mother's side with Murrah al-Tay-yar. His mother was their mother's younger sister."

"What?" Julia said, not bothering to keep the shock out of her tone. Murrah? Big, calm Murrah, who gave the impression he might not be the sharpest tack in the box? She had a hard time believing he would do anything to betray their community, or even possessed the necessary wit to maintain such a pretense.

"This surprises you," Dani said. "I can understand that, but we must keep our minds open. And remember, he has had a hard time of it with his Chosen, who was taken by Khalim and his followers. Perhaps Murrah blames Zahrias for not doing a better job of protecting her."

"He had nothing to do with that," Jace retorted.

"Yes, we all know that, but we have not had to face Murrah's trial of having a partner brutalized and damaged." Dani's hand tightened on Lauren's, as if to remind himself that she was safe and would never have to suffer that kind of harm. "I am not saying he is right for blaming my brother, only that it is something we must consider."

"And Murrah's first loyalty would be to his family, not to us here," Lilias added. "I know that may be difficult to understand, given that we all chose to be here, often to the disapproval of our relatives. But if, say, Qadim had reached out to Murrah and asked for his assistance in bringing his sister's former lover back to her, Murrah might not have seen anything wrong in such a request. Indeed, there are those who know the tale who still believe that Zahrias wronged Lyanna."

"Wronged her?" Julia couldn't believe what she was hearing. "He's the one who got kidnapped, remember."

Lilias didn't blink. "I am not defending her actions. And as someone who had her own brother damaged by this woman, I certainly don't think she was blameless when it came to her relationship with Zahrias. He was wise to break it off while he could. The problem is that not everyone will see it that way."

The djinn woman's calm, unruffled tone did help to calm Julia down somewhat. She told herself that, no matter what her personal feelings in all this, she needed to keep it together. At least she could be fairly certain that Lyanna didn't mean to physically harm Zahrias. No, she'd want him intact.

Which wasn't exactly reassuring, because the thought of someone else being physically intimate with the man she loved made Julia want to be sick to her stomach. But throwing up wouldn't solve anything. It definitely wouldn't make her feel better.

"So...what now?" she asked. "Do we go to Murrah and confront him?"

"It's not as simple as that," Dani replied. He gently lifted his hand from Lauren's, then stood and went over to one of the windows, as if expecting to find someone eavesdropping outside. Of course, no one was there, but Julia still felt the skin on the back of her neck prickle.

Jace put in, "It's difficult to contain a djinn. Not impossible, because that's how Zahrias was taken. But it took a dozen elementals with powers completely opposite his to take him away. Do we really want to approach Murrah with that kind of force when all we are doing is acting on a suspicion?"

Her first instinct was to reply, "Hell, yes," but Julia realized that Jace had a point. All they had right now were theories. Murrah could be completely innocent. "So what do you suggest?" she asked, fighting to keep from sounding as desperate as she felt right then.

They all exchanged troubled glances. Then Jace seemed to nod to himself. "Julia, you have one of Miles's devices, right?"

She nodded. "It's still on the front seat of the pickup truck I drove to your place."

"Well, then. I'm used to those things." He flashed everyone a quick grin and added, "Not that I enjoy suffering their effects, but I can manage."

"So you'll turn it on to keep Murrah from getting away," Dani said. "It could work. He and Martine live in a house somewhat separated from the others, so as long as you keep the area of effect somewhat controlled, it shouldn't affect any other djinn."

"I can do that," Julia said. Really, she should have thought of using the device. Maybe her brains had gotten a little scrambled, being there on the djinn plane. "Miles trained me how to use it, so getting it dialed in shouldn't be a problem."

Lilias didn't seem to share their enthusiasm. Expression troubled, she asked, "Do you really think that is the best plan of action? I fear that using the device on Murrah will only make him less likely to cooperate. And if he is innocent, he will be wounded that you thought such a thing of him, let alone inflicted that device upon him."

Hers was a valid concern, but Julia didn't think they had much choice. Besides, she was fairly skilled at operating the devices, and knew she should be able to get the one in their possession calibrated to a point where Murrah couldn't use any of his djinn powers but wouldn't be completely debilitated. She thought of Zahrias, being held by a woman who had no true claim on him, and her resolve only strengthened. "That's a risk I'm willing to take."

"We'll go as easy as we can," Jace put in, his tone reassuring. "Believe me, Richard Margolis tortured me with one of those things for weeks. I don't enjoy having to do this. But right now it sounds as if Murrah is our best chance at tracking down Zahrias."

Lilias didn't reply immediately. She glanced from Jace to Dani, still standing tense and silent by the window. Her lips pursed, and Julia wondered if the djinn woman was thinking of how she would feel if it was her brother held captive by Lyanna. It could have been, but somehow Baltasar had been luckier than Zahrias, or at least hadn't made Lyanna quite as obsessed.

"Very well," she said at last. "Our community needs its leader. And even if it did not, what Lyanna has done is wrong. I won't stand in the way of something that might lead to Zahrias being freed."

Thank God. Not that Lilias really had the power to stop them from what they planned to do, but Julia knew they needed as many of the Santa Fe djinn on their side as possible. She sent Lilias a relieved smile, then said, "All right. Time to find out how much Murrah actually knows."

CHAPTER SIXTEEN

A THOUSAND CANDLES FLICKERED IN THE ROOM, sending dancing lights over the walls and floors of polished marble, reflecting in their veins of gold and silver and copper. Zahrias wondered where Lyanna had gotten all those candles, but then realized procuring them would have been easy enough. She might have claimed she wanted nothing from that world, but that was only another of her lies. While she apparently had no desire to live on the mortal plane, she still took anything from there that would make her life more comfortable. There were warehouses full of candles and all manner of other goods back in the mortal world, waiting for trucks to come and fetch them and take them to stores that would never open again.

The thought depressed him. Not so much that the rampant consumer culture which once thrived in a land known as America was now gone, but that his people had been the ones to destroy those who might have once purchased these candles for holiday gatherings and celebrations, or even intimate dinners together.

Like the one he had shared with Julia. How he wished it was she who sat opposite him now, and not Lyanna.

Luckily, his current dinner companion did not seem to notice his abstraction. He thought he had done a fairly good job over the past day of pretending that he was softening toward her—slowly, of course, because a quick about-face would surely raise her suspicions—but still smiling a bit more, asking questions about the house, about the priceless artwork she had collected there.

For she had not been idle, once humanity was gone. How she'd managed to amass so much, when the great collections of the world had become more or less up for grabs after the Heat swept through the population, Zahrias wasn't sure. Despite her contempt for humanity, she did seem to have a great respect for its art. Pieces that had once decorated the walls of the Louvre, of the Museo del Prado, of the National Gallery and museums he couldn't even name, now hung in the corridors and rooms of the grand palace she'd built for herself.

"I thought for sure someone else would want her," Lyanna said, lifting a languid hand in the direction of a small portrait of a faintly smiling woman. "But she was still there when I went to check, so I brought her here to live with me."

"That is surprising," Zahrias replied. He had barely touched his wine, although he was fairly sure it hadn't been doctored. Why would Lyanna bother to breach that trust again, when she thought he was succumbing to her once more? "But truly, she is not all that attractive."

Lyanna laughed, a piercing giggle that hurt his ears. "By our standards, I would suppose not. The mortals seemed to worship her, though, which is why I wanted to have her here."

In that moment, Zahrias wondered if his companion rather regretted all those dead humans. Perhaps in her mind she had thought it would be a fine thing to leave just enough alive that they could worship her as a goddess. Once upon a time, their ancestors had done that very thing.

"She does do very well on that particular wall," he agreed. "Truly, you have created a very harmonious array."

At least that much was the truth, more or less. Lyanna had mainly gathered together what mortals had referred to as "the old masters," and didn't seem to have anything modern hanging on the walls of her palace. The only jarring thing about her collection was how vast it seemed to be.

She preened at his praise, smiling and leaning toward him. He made himself hold still and not back away. Some time earlier, he had made an agreement with himself that he would allow her to kiss him, if by doing so her guard would be relaxed that much more. Nothing else, of course. But surely she would see even that small intimacy as a sign that she had won.

Perhaps she was toying with him, but she stopped herself when she was a hand's breadth or more away. That close, he could still smell the wine on her breath, the musk that clung to her clothing.

He lifted his golden goblet of wine. "To all of your collecting efforts."

She raised her goblet as well, then clinked it against his before taking a sip. "Ah, but you know, Zahrias, you are by far the most magnificent piece I have collected."

"And somewhat livelier than the ones you have hanging on the wall."

"To be sure." Her amber eyes glinted almost gold in the reflected candlelight, and her lips were parted.

He knew that look. Although he had done his best to forget their time together, oblivion did not come easily to his people. So many details of their long lives remained etched in their memories, rather than being smoothed away with the passage of time. And the look Lyanna currently wore told him that she expected more, that the smiles and pleasantries must inevitably move on to something a bit more significant.

In that moment, he wished he had drunk more of his wine. Djinn could not get truly intoxicated, but they could achieve a slightly elevated state if they consumed enough alcohol...and right then he knew he would have been better able to steel himself to do this if the edges had been blurred slightly.

But since he also knew that he must do what he could to buy himself more time, he took in a breath, then leaned forward and placed his lips on hers.

Going back to the house to fetch the device had cost them some time, because of course Jessica and Miles and Lindsay wanted to know what Julia and Jace had learned. Jessica also seemed shocked that Murrah could be complicit in helping Qadim and his scheming sister, while Miles only narrowed his eyes.

"I knew there was something about that one I didn't like."

"Sweetheart, you don't like anybody."

Miles shot Lindsay an irritated glance following that remark, while Julia tried not to grin. It was true; he might care about Lindsay, but Julia had a feeling he only tolerated most other people.

"Anyway, we should be able to catch him off guard using this," she said, hefting the device in her hand. It still shocked her that something so powerful could fit into her palm.

"That's something," Jessica said. Her gaze wasn't on the device, however, but on the djinn she loved. "Are you sure you know what you're doing?"

"Of course not," Jace replied. He'd been standing next to her, and he bent down and kissed her on the cheek while Jessica tried to look annoyed with him and failed miserably. "I'm making this up as I go along. But it's the simple truth that it's very difficult to restrain a djinn unless he's grossly outnumbered. And Murrah is *big*."

That was for sure. Qadim was probably the tallest djinn Julia had ever seen, but Murrah was only an inch or so shorter at the most, and proportionately broad. Jace had some serious muscles from working the farm or whatever else it was he did to keep himself in shape—did djinn even need to exercise?—but Murrah still looked like he could bend the younger man into a pretzel.

Jessica wore a resigned expression. "Well, I know you're going to do what you're going to do, but just be careful. I've kind of gotten used to having you around."

This time the kiss Jace gave her was right on the lips, completely ignoring the fact that they had an audience. Lindsay just grinned, while Miles looked exasperated. And Julia—again, the best she could do was fight back another of those sharp spikes of jealousy.

After all, that could have been Zahrias kissing her, if she hadn't been such a stubborn pain in the ass.

"We should go," she said. "I mean, we don't know for sure that Murrah is home, but Lilias did a quick pop in and out of the downtown area, and she didn't see him lurking around any of his usual haunts, so it's probably safe to assume that he's at his house."

"Yes, ma'am," Jace replied. His dark eyes were twinkling, but then the faint smile he'd been wearing faded. "Let's do this."

He approached so he could wrap his arms around her. That still felt strange, especially with Jessica watching, but it was the only way he could transport someone in the djinns' particular mode of travel.

The next part was the trickiest, simply because Julia had to trigger the device literally the second they appeared at their destination. Any earlier, and Jace's powers would be cut off. She didn't know what would happen if a djinn was yanked back into the real world mid-blink, as it were. But she really didn't want to find out.

Her finger had been resting on the switch, difficult enough because of the way she had to keep her arms wrapped around Jace's midsection. What made it even harder was the mild bump she experienced as her feet touched the tile floor of the house Murrah shared with Martine. Julia's fingertip skated right past the switch, and she frantically grabbed for it again, because standing right there in front of them was Murrah himself.

His mouth opened—whether to ask what the hell they were doing there, or maybe to simply let out a shocked sound, Julia didn't know—because in the next second she did push the switch.

The djinn's reaction wasn't quite as extreme as Qadim's when she'd used the device on him, probably because the power level wasn't jacked up as high. But Murrah still stumbled a bit before steadying himself and fixing them with a shocked glare.

"Why are you using that thing on me?" he gasped.

Julia felt a pang of remorse, followed by worry that Lilias had been right and Murrah had nothing to do with Zahrias' kidnapping. Really, in that moment, the big djinn looked so startled that she had to believe he must be innocent.

Jace didn't seem to be experiencing any such qualms, however. Jaw set, he advanced a few steps toward the other man. "I don't know, Murrah. Why *would* we be using it?"

Almost at once, Murrah's gaze shifted away from them. "I—"

A master spy, he wasn't. What with the way he wouldn't meet their eyes, and only stood there, staring at the polished terra-cotta tile under his feet, he might as well have been holding up a sign that said "I'm guilty."

"We don't want to hurt you," Julia said quickly. "I'm just using the device because it was the only way to guarantee you'd stay put."

"It must affect him, too," Murrah said, with a flash of his dark eyes in Jace's direction.

"It does affect me," Jace said. His tone was so steady that it gave the lie to his words, although Julia could see the tension in the muscles of his neck. He was working hard to make sure he wouldn't shake or lose his balance. "But remember, Margolis used one of these things on me for weeks. I have a lot more experience managing it."

"Oh," the other djinn replied. His expression was so hangdog that Julia almost wanted to reach out and give him a hug, despite everything. "Can I—can I sit down? It's hard to stand."

"Be my guest," Jace told him. "But don't think that means you don't have to tell us what you know."

Murrah gave a sort of grunt, then stumbled over a few feet to a big chair upholstered in dark brown leather. It creaked as he sat down in it, but otherwise it appeared more or less adequate to supporting his weight.

"So, then," Jace went on. "You do admit that you were feeding information to Qadim and his sister?"

"Just to Qadim," Murrah said. "Lyanna would never lower herself to come down here."

Julia didn't know if that particular revelation was good or bad. "Why would you do that, Murrah?"

The djinn looked like a dog that knew it was about to get whacked with a rolled-up newspaper. "They're my cousins. They asked for my help. And in the beginning, I didn't know why they even wanted to hear about what we were doing here in Santa Fe."

"But you figured it out."

A helpless-looking shrug, while once again Murrah stared at the floor. "I began to guess."

"So why didn't you go to Zahrias and warn him?" Jace asked.

"How could I? Zahrias was the leader here, but Qadim and Lyanna are my blood. Besides, I knew Lyanna wouldn't hurt him. She only wanted to be with him again." Expression pleading, Murrah glanced first at Jace, then Julia. "It would have been different if he'd had a Chosen, but he didn't."

The words felt like a knife lodged somewhere in her gut, but Julia forced herself to say calmly, "That may be, but aren't the needs of the people here in Santa Fe more important than Lyanna's needs? I mean, it wasn't as if she needed Zahrias so he could give her a rare blood transfusion or something."

Murrah squirmed in his chair. "Maybe, but—" He broke off and sent another of those pleading looks in Jace's direction. "Tell her, Jace. She's not one of us, so she doesn't understand how family is supposed to come first."

"Family is important to us, too," Julia said, her voice hard. With some effort, she forced aside one of countless memories of her parents arguing. Not all families were like that. "Or rather, it used to be important, until your buddies decided to eradicate the human race. Now we have to make new families, since ours were taken away."

"They were not my friends, the ones who killed the humans," Murrah protested. "And I did not agree with what they did. I have my Chosen, the same as everyone else here in Santa Fe. What I did to help Qadim and Lyanna had nothing to do with that—"

A female voice broke in then. "What's going on here?"

Julia turned to see a young woman standing in the arched opening that led from the living room to a long hallway. Like all the other Chosen, she was very pretty, but there was a strained, haunted look in her dark eyes.

"I'm sorry about this, Martine," Jace said. "But Murrah has all but admitted that he's been passing information along to the people who kidnapped Zahrias."

"Wait." Blinking in confusion, she glanced over at her lover. "Zahrias has been kidnapped? When did that happen?"

"Early this morning," Julia replied. Good lord, had all that happened in the space of one day? It felt like years since Zahrias had disappeared before her eyes, ripped away from this world by a group of Lyanna's thugs.

Maybe she should have been relieved that so little time had actually passed, since it would seem to limit what Lyanna might be doing to Zahrias, but Jace had warned her that time flowed differently on the djinn plane. True, it had felt as if they'd been there for hours, but when they returned from their abortive audience with the elders, only about forty-five minutes seemed to have passed.

"And you had something to do with it, Murrah?" Martine demanded.

He wouldn't meet her gaze. "I had to, Martine. They were family, and they asked."

Her lips pressed together. Some of the vagueness seemed to leave her as she glared at her lover. "I thought we *were* family. All of us here in Santa Fe. Isn't that what this community is supposed to be about? You told me that when you first saved me and took me to Taos. You said it would be all right, because you'd be giving me a new family."

The anguish on Murrah's face made a sudden rush of pity go through Julia. She couldn't forgive him for what he'd done, but it was clear that he hadn't really stopped to consider all the ramifications of assisting Qadim and Lyanna.

"I was," he mumbled. "That is, I did."

"But obviously this family isn't as important as your djinn family, is that right?"

Jace cut in, obviously trying to salvage the situation, "Murrah was probably caught between a rock and a hard place, and I have a feeling he made his choice out of instinct. Isn't that right, Murrah?"

Looking almost absurdly relieved by Jace's intervention, the big djinn nodded. "That is right. And I thought that Zahrias was with Lyanna before, so perhaps he would not mind so much being with her again. We could always have someone else lead us."

Julia couldn't help herself. Tone acid, she inquired, "Someone who would have done a better job than Zahrias?"

Murrah winced, and Martine added, her own voice almost as sharp as Julia's, "That's not the kind of decision you're supposed to make on your own. Losing Zahrias will affect everyone here. And what about Dani? His partner just had their son. Think about that, Murrah. If family is so important, what does it mean that you allowed the baby's uncle to be taken away from here?"

Her words might have been physical blows, raining down on her partner, because with each sentence he flinched, and shrank as far back into his chair as someone of his bulk was able to. "I'm sorry," he said.

Jace looked like he'd had enough, too. He held up a hand, saying, "Okay, Murrah. I know you didn't stop to think about all this. But what we need now is to know how to find Lyanna. I've never met her, but you have. So will you take us there?"

That question made Murrah shake his head. "I cannot do that. If she discovers that I've led you to her—"

"Grow a spine, Murrah," Martine snapped, annoyance ringing through every syllable. Julia didn't really know all the difficulties the two of them had faced since she'd been returned to him after her captivity with Khalim's band of rogue djinn, but it seemed clear their relationship hadn't quite returned to the loving intimacy that most djinn/Chosen partnerships seemed to share.

"You have never met Lyanna," Murrah said. If the look of fear in his eyes hadn't been so genuine, it might have been comical. "I cannot take you to her."

"But I can," came a new voice, one that Julia knew all too well and had hoped she would never hear again.

As one, they all turned toward the front door. Standing just inside, arms crossed, was Qadim.

This is hell, Zahrias thought. *All our lives, we thought that being confined to this plane was punishment enough, but now I know what true torment is.*

Lyanna lay in his arms, eyes hungry. After that first kiss, she had abandoned any notion of continuing with their dinner, and had led him to a softly upholstered divan placed up against one wall. Perhaps he should have been grateful that she had only taken him there, and not to her bedchamber. At least on the divan he could attempt to keep things from progressing much further.

Her mouth had been insistent, demanding. She tasted of the wine they had drunk, but her kiss was not sweet the way Julia's had been. Rather, it was sour, harsh, like the dregs that had collected at the bottom of his goblet. How he had allowed her to kiss him and managed to prevent himself from letting out any betraying shudders, any other signs of revulsion, he didn't know. But for now, it seemed as if Lyanna was still fooled, that his plan to make her think that he was slowly losing himself to her charms was working.

Unfortunately, he knew she was impatient. A few kisses were one thing. But they had shared far deeper intimacies than that in the past, and so she would not be content with these sorts of embraces for very much longer.

He needed to get back to the garden, to the one place where he thought he might have a hope of escaping. A small hope, but better than none. He wouldn't allow himself to think about how she might retaliate if his attempts should come to nothing.

"An idea just came to me, Lyanna."

She gazed up at him, mouth pursed. "Is it the same idea I am having?"

I very much doubt that. "The garden you showed me. It is such a lovely spot. I cannot help but think that it would be a wonderful setting for other...activities."

Her eyes widened a bit, and then she gave him a slow, lascivious smile. "Why, Zahrias, you are getting quite adventurous in your old age, aren't you?"

He lifted his shoulders.

"But I agree," she went on, her tone almost purring. "Let us take this wine with us...and see what happens."

Somehow he managed to smile at her and nod, then waited as she untangled herself from his arms and went back to the table where the wine and the neglected remnants of their dinner sat. She scooped up the decanter, and he got up and retrieved their goblets. The metal was cold against his fingers, chilling him.

If he should fail....

He pushed the thought aside and followed Lyanna through the chambers of the palace, past the sad watching eyes of the portraits she had stolen and the blank-faced marble statues that stood sentinel in the corridors. They haunted him, reminders of all those who had died when the Heat swept over the face of the Earth. Logically, he knew that the artists who had created these paintings and statues were dead long before the djinn had intervened so catastrophically in the history of the human race, but he still wondered how Lyanna could bear to look at them.

Then again, sensitivity had never been her greatest strength.

They emerged into the garden, where the perfume of the flowers growing there hung heavy on the still air. Off to one side was a table and several benches of carved marble. Lyanna went and set down the decanter of wine on the tabletop, and Zahrias came up beside her and put the goblets next to them.

"More wine?" he asked her.

"Of course," she said, eyes gleaming. Clearly, she had already begun to anticipate what was to come next.

He poured a measure of the dark vintage into each of the goblets. Lyanna lifted hers at once and took an over-large swallow, one obviously intended for its effect and not so she might savor the wine.

Only a few minutes ago, he had been hoping for the blurred edges such mild intoxication might bring, but now he knew he must be careful. His wits needed to be sharp, even as hers became dulled.

She took another drink, then waved at the benches. "These look terribly hard, don't they?"

"Perhaps."

A snap of her fingers, and a cushioned divan appeared only a few feet away. "I think that will be far more comfortable, don't you?"

"Yes," he replied, giving her a slow smile. All the better, for she'd conjured the piece of furniture into a spot where the hanging vines that sheltered the garden dropped low. Yes, they might do very well.

He drank some of his wine, so that she might not become suspicious, but a measured sip. Then he set down his glass, plucked hers from her fingers, and pulled her against him. She let out a little gasp, amber eyes warming as she gazed up at him.

"You are becoming forceful, aren't you? Good—I do prefer you that way."

"Then let us see if you prefer this."

Before she could speak again, he slammed his mouth down on hers, kissing her hard, doing his very best to make her think that he wanted nothing more than to possess her body once more. Her tongue touched his, and he had to fight to keep himself from recoiling.

She seemed to notice nothing, however, and did not protest as he moved her toward the divan, then pushed her down into the soft cushions, his body on top of hers. Her eyes closed, although whether her ecstasy was real or feigned, he didn't know, and didn't care. What mattered was that she had lost herself to the spell of his touch, and could not see what he was about to do.

His powers had been denied him, but he still had his physical strength. It was easy enough for him to reach up and grasp one of the vines, then give it a hard yank. The torn piece of plant material fell from the canopy above them, and he took it and wrapped it around Lyanna's wrists.

Her eyes did fly open at that point, but even then he saw no betrayal in them, only a sort of lustful surprise. "Why, Zahrias—I had no idea you enjoyed playing those sorts of games."

"I do not," he told her. "But one must do what one must."

In that instant, he pushed away from her and ran toward the wall. The vines that covered it gave him the handholds he needed, and he grasped them as he desperately hauled himself upward. Shifting light surged through the gap, telling him he was close to freedom. Only that much more—

A hard object hit the center of his back, and he lost his grip, slipping back down nearly a foot before he regained his grip on the vines. Damn. He'd known that the makeshift restraints he'd put on Lyanna wouldn't last very long, but he'd hoped that limited time would still be enough.

Another blow to his back, this time higher up near his shoulder. The pain was sharp enough that he lost his grip for good this time, and fell with a painful thud to the stone pavers below. Lyanna stood over him, eyes blazing.

"You thought to trick me?" she cried. "When all I offered you was love?"

"That was not love," he told her, forcing himself back to his feet. Whatever happened next, he would meet it while standing and facing her, not lying on the ground like a beaten dog. "That was not even a counterfeit of love. Love—*true* love—is not something you can force, Lyanna, no matter what you might think."

Her face twisted with fury, and the fountain off to one side gushed forth a veritable geyser of water. Only a temper tantrum, he knew; he noticed that the water's spray did not touch the walls of the palace. Lyanna would not risk the sort of display that might actually damage the house she prized so much.

Even so, he knew he probably would not enjoy what was to come next. She raised her hands, and he watched her calmly. He could not stop her, but he would not beg.

Forgive me, Julia, he thought. *If only I had been brave enough to declare my love for you, then none of this would have happened.*

And he braced himself for the inevitable.

CHAPTER SEVENTEEN

"WHAT THE HELL ARE YOU DOING HERE?" JULIA burst out, as everyone else only stared at this unexpected apparition. Then she paused, confused. With the device operating, how on earth had Qadim even managed to show up at the house at all?

"I fear that my sister has overstepped herself," he said. "And I have no wish to be dragged down with her. If I lend you my aid, I hope that you will put in a good word for me with the elders."

"'A good word'?" Julia repeated, then shook her head in disbelief. "How are you even here? The device—"

"Yes, it did force me to have to walk that last several hundred feet, rather than dropping in directly. You were all so embroiled in your argument that you didn't even notice when I opened the front door."

Well, all right, that was possible. They had all been facing Murrah, and so had their backs to the door. Julia supposed it wouldn't have been too difficult to open it and slip in. In this community, which was composed solely of djinn and their Chosen, no one seemed to bother with making sure their houses were locked up tight.

"So, let me get this straight," Jace said then. His brows were drawn together, and Julia got the distinct impression that he would have liked to lunge for the other djinn, except that neither one of them was in any shape to fight because of the effects of the device. "You're going to *help* us?"

"That was my idea, yes." Qadim's gaze flickered from Jace to Murrah, then came to rest on Julia. She wanted to look away, but she made herself stare back at him, unflinching.

"And that will magically make it all better?" she said, not bothering to hide the outrage boiling within her. "We're just supposed to forget about the people you killed?"

"*I* killed no one," Qadim replied calmly. "Margolis killed your friends, not I."

"He was working for you," she shot back.

"Perhaps, but I never gave him the order to kill those people. I told him I needed you delivered to me, safe and unharmed. That was all. Whatever else Margolis did, he did of his own volition."

Julia shot Jace a helpless glance. She sure didn't trust Qadim, and yet...

...and yet his words did have a ring of truth to them. Margolis had been growing increasingly volatile. She knew he'd been perfectly capable of killing Eric and Brent and Nancy, just because he could. Maybe he'd seen them as traitors. Especially Brent. It had been Brent who'd urged Julia to come to Los Alamos, who'd said she was the soul of the community. She could only imagine how much hearing that must have enraged the former commander. He'd marinated in that rage for months, and then when Qadim let him out, he'd been only too happy to let it consume him.

"All right," she said then. "Assuming you're telling us the truth, and you do want to help us. Why?"

The djinn gave a short laugh. "It is not because of any love I have for Zahrias, I assure you. While this is a matter the elders could not touch, since it involved a personal issue, that does not mean they have not taken note of what Lyanna has done. The time has come when my people can finally claim their piece of this world. I do not wish to be shut out because of my sister's transgressions."

"The time...what are you talking about?"

Qadim's mouth twisted in an ironic smile. "I suppose it is not something your djinn partners have wished to share with you. But then, you do not even have such a partner, do you, Julia?" He paused significantly while she glared at him, then added, "I would have been happy to cure that particular lack, you know. But enough of that. Save for the communities where my people dwell with their Chosen—and your odd little stronghold in Los Alamos—this world is now empty. It is time for us to begin to settle here."

Although she'd been silent the whole time, watching the exchange among Qadim and Jace and Julia, Martine spoke up then. "What, you mean they're *all* gone?"

"There could be a holdout here and there." He shrugged, a gesture chilling in its indifference. "But, to all intents and purposes, yes, they are gone. Being immune was not enough to save them."

Tears stood out, bright in Martine's eyes. She looked away from Qadim toward Murrah, who had remained hunched in his chair. He did stand up then, laboriously, as if fighting the effects of the device. "My dear—" he said, reaching out to her.

"Don't you touch me," she snapped. "You're all the same!"

And then she fled down the hallway where she'd first emerged. A moment later, Julia heard a door slam.

An awkward silence fell, during which Murrah couldn't seem to meet anyone's gaze. At last Jace said, "You know, Qadim, I do believe you. Because it's clear to me that you never do anything, except out of self-interest, up to and including throwing your sister under the bus."

"Quaint turn of phrase," Qadim replied. "You've mastered the whole 'mortal' thing rather well. No wonder you were able to dupe your own Chosen for so many months."

Jace didn't have the sort of complexion that flushed easily, but his dark eyes took on a dangerous glitter. "I'd watch it if I were you."

"Perhaps." Qadim turned toward Julia. "But since we are all friends here, perhaps you could turn off the device now? It's making my head ache."

With some reluctance, Julia flipped over the device. Her finger hovered directly above the switch that would deactivate it. What if this was all a trick, and Qadim was only trying to get her to turn it off so he could do his worst?

It was a risk she'd have to take. Anyway, she had Jace and Murrah there, and she had to hope they'd step in to save her if something went wrong. Well, Jace would, anyway. Murrah was still kind of a wild card.

Letting out a breath, she ticked the switch over. At once, the three djinn visibly relaxed, while at the same time looking about an inch taller each.

"Much better," Qadim said. He took a step toward Julia, and she backed away at once. An ironic smile touched his mouth. "Have no fear, Julia. I do not have any designs on your person. Even if I did, I doubt Jasreel here would allow me to act on them."

"Damn straight," Jace growled.

Julia was an only child, but right then she wondered if this was what having an older brother would be like—to have someone at your back who made sure you were protected, and safe.

Then again, Qadim didn't seem to care much about protecting his own sister, not once he'd realized that following her whims could harm his own prospects.

"I must be the one to bring you to Lyanna's home, since I am the only one of us who knows where it is." His dark eyes flicked to Murrah, faintly amused. "That is, not including our friend here. But I rather doubt he wishes to accompany us."

Murrah didn't even bother to deny it. "No, I much rather would not."

"Well, then. So I must hold you, Julia, and Jasreel here can take my other hand, so we will all travel together."

That didn't sound appetizing at all, but Julia told herself this was no time to be squeamish. Not when Zahrias' very life might be at stake. "I'll need my oxygen," she said, glancing over at Jace. "It's still sitting back at your house."

"No problem," he replied, then snapped his fingers. The tank—or maybe it was the second, unused one—appeared on the floor immediately in front of her, the cannula resting on top.

Having djinn around could be sort of handy. Well, as long as they were good djinn like Zahrias and Jace.

Flashing him a grateful smile, Julia picked up the tank and swung it over one shoulder, then tried not to make too much of a face as she inserted the cannula in her nose. Qadim watched this entire procedure with a certain amount of curiosity, but he didn't comment.

When she was ready, he said, "Since you've already been to the djinn world, I know I don't have to warn you that this mode of travel can be…unpleasant."

"I know," she replied.

What was even more unpleasant was feeling his arm snake around her waist and pull her close, but she tried to remind herself that Jace had done more or less the same thing when he took her to the djinn plane. There just wasn't any way around that need for physical contact. However, it did reassure her to see Qadim reach out with his free hand and grip Jace's wrist, their hands locking around one another's arms like one of those manly handshakes she'd seen in movies shot in the '70s.

She tried to concentrate on that amusing image, rather than the sensation of Qadim's body pressed up against hers. The heat from him seemed to penetrate the clothing she wore, but there was nothing welcome about it, unlike the warmth she'd experienced when Zahrias held her.

Well, if they somehow managed to succeed in all this, maybe she'd be able to feel him again very soon.

"Ready?" Qadim asked, and she nodded. Actually, she didn't feel at all ready, but she wasn't about to admit that to him.

He didn't ask Jace the same question. A pause while Qadim took in a breath, his arm tightening around her waist, and then again she had that sensation of searing heat, followed by piercing cold. She was falling into a place that didn't have the right gravity to capture her. Surely she would be swallowed by it....

Only she wasn't. Her feet touched the ground, and she blinked furiously against the disorientation that seemed to be the automatic byproduct of that form of travel. She couldn't allow herself to be distracted. Not now.

Good thing, because as the scene before her grew clearer, she realized Qadim had brought them here just in time. Zahrias was pressed against a wall covered in vines, face drawn in pain. In front of him stood a djinn woman with long dark hair and flashing amber-colored eyes. A more impartial observer might have described her as beautiful, but Julia could only see the cruelty in the set of her mouth and the glint in her eyes.

Qadim was the first to act. He stepped forward, saying in coldly casual tones, "Sister."

She whirled at once, painted eyes narrowing as she seemed to realize who had spoken. The look of anger on her face only intensified as she realized her brother was not alone, and had in fact brought her hated rival with him. Although she thought Lyanna wouldn't do anything, not with Jasreel and Qadim there, Julia couldn't help taking a step backward as those strange amber eyes fastened on her.

Lyanna's voice could have cut through stone. "This is none of your concern, brother. And how dare you bring *that* here with you?"

Zahrias took a step forward, but the djinn woman raised a hand. His eyes, filled with despair, met Julia's. In that moment, she wished more than anything that she shared the Chosen bond with him, so they would be able to communicate silently the way all the other djinn and their human partners could. She wanted to tell him that it would be all right, that she didn't blame him for anything Lyanna had done. But since she couldn't, all she was able to do was gaze back at him, willing him to understand that she loved him, that they could move on together once this was all over.

"I dare," Qadim replied, "because I have had enough of your tantrums and foolishness, and I curse myself for letting you talk me into participating in this insane enterprise in the first place. If you let Zahrias go, we may still be able to salvage something from this situation."

A laugh, and Lyanna shook her head. "Are you mad? After all I went through to get him here?"

At those words, Jace let out a low growl of anger, although he didn't say anything. Not that he had to; Julia felt the same outrage pulsing through her. This woman's actions had indirectly caused the deaths of three innocent people. As for what she'd done to Zahrias—he might not be showing any obvious signs of injury, but Julia could tell something had occurred right before she and Jace and Qadim arrived. Zahrias stood straight and tall, but she could tell he was in pain from the way his jaw was set, and from the faint gleam of sweat on his brow.

"You went through nothing," Qadim retorted. "Only had others do your bidding, as has been your wont ever since you were old enough to speak. Your actions have led you to a precipice, but you have not yet gone over the edge. If you let Zahrias go now, it may be enough to prevent the elders from taking action against us."

"What action could they take? This is a personal matter." Lyanna paused then and surveyed her unwanted visitors. The cold gleam in the djinn woman's eyes made a shudder go through Julia. Their unfeeling amber might have belonged to a tiger stalking its prey. "The elders care nothing for those who might have perished because of my actions, as they were neither djinn nor Chosen. In fact," she added, a lazy drawl in her voice that somehow was far more chilling than any outright threat she could have made, "I doubt very much whether they would care if anything happened to this one here. If she is gone, then Zahrias will have no reason to think of her ever again. And then he will truly be mine."

She raised her hand. Qadim and Jace both began to move toward the djinn woman, even as Zahrias shouted, "No, you cannot!"

A crushing force descended on Julia's chest. She couldn't breathe, even with the cannula feeding her the oxygen she needed to survive. The verdant space around her began to blur, and she fell to her knees, gasping.

Darkness began to erode the edges of her vision. Hands reaching out, she gasped, "Zahrias...."

She could not be here. What madness had led Qadim and Jasreel to bring Julia within a hundred leagues of Lyanna? But even as his heart beat with fear at the thought of what his erstwhile lover might do when confronted by the human woman he truly loved, Zahrias couldn't help staring at Julia, drinking in the pure beauty of her face and the low, warm sound of her voice the way a man dying of thirst might soothe his parched mouth at an unexpected oasis in the desert.

Why Qadim was cajoling his sister to release her captive, Zahrias couldn't begin to guess. He and the other djinn had never been friends. Something to serve Qadim's own self-interest must be involved. But perhaps Lyanna would listen to him. Perhaps there was still some way out of this.

Hope died within him, though, as she ignored her brother's pleas, and only looked with hatred on Julia. Raised her hands to blast her with the strength of the energy that pulsed through her, just as she had done to knock him down from his desperate attempt to scale the wall.

And then Julia, falling to her knees, blue-gray eyes wide with fear, pleading with him to do something. Anything.

He stared at her, fury and horror twisting within his gut. She could not be hurt like this. Not at the hands of such a one as Lyanna. She had no right to tell him who he could or couldn't love.

She had no right.

Zahrias realized then what he must do. What he should have done a long time ago.

He held Julia's gaze for a precious second or two, hoping she could still see him beyond the pain Lyanna was inflicting. And then he glanced up at the djinn woman and said loudly, "I claim this human woman as my own. Julia Innes will be forever known as my Chosen, and anyone who lifts a hand against her will answer to me."

A flash of brilliant light, and then the elders were there, gazing at him with some approval. Ashtar, the female elder with the flaming red hair, stepped forward, a smile curving her lips. "And they will answer to us as well." She extended a hand, and Julia, eyes wide with shock, took it and shakily got to her feet. "For you know, Lyanna al-Syan, that to attack one of the Chosen is the same as attacking one of us. In doing so, you break the compact we all agreed upon, and you must suffer the consequences."

Lyanna's face twisted with fury. "He only did that to save her! He does not truly want her—"

"Oh, but I do," Zahrias cut in. "I always did, but did not have the courage to claim her as I should, because I allowed memories of a dark past to stand in my way." He looked over at Julia, who still wore the expression of someone who was attempting to decipher what precisely had just happened. "I can only hope that you will accept my apologies for that, Julia. I swear that I will use every day from here on out to prove to you exactly how much I do want you."

A sunburst of a smile spread over her face, and she came toward him, hands outstretched. He took her and pulled her to him, buried his face in the sweet-smelling fall of her hair. Her arms went around his waist, and she clung to him as if she was afraid he would disappear if she let go.

But he wouldn't. He knew he would be there for her, now and always. He could not change the past, but he could make sure the future held no more hurt for her.

"Well, it seems that is settled," Ashtar said dryly. "As for you, Lyanna...." She let the words trail off, and looked toward Ibram, the eldest of the elders.

He stepped forward, a grim smile on his lips. "I suppose we should thank you, Lyanna, for your own excesses have dictated your punishment."

"Punishment?" she flashed. "I have done nothing wrong. As soon as Zahrias chose this human"—the word dripped with disdain—"I left off. So what is there to punish me for?"

Ibram's smiled faded. "It pains me to realize that you truly believe you have done nothing wrong. Oh, perhaps you followed the letter of our laws, for it is true that we cannot intervene in personal matters, matters of the heart, but by taking Zahrias, you deprived the Santa Fe community of their leader, a leader who watched over his people with our blessing. In doing so, you have shown that you have no regard for anyone but yourself, and therefore I—and the rest of us—are only too happy to make sure that you spend eternity with the only person you do seem to care about."

A brief flash of confusion passed over Lyanna's features, but she still held her ground, chin lifted defiantly.

"Indeed? And who would that be, since you have decided to deprive me of the man I wanted?"

This time, Ashtar stepped forward so she stood next to Ibram. She wasn't precisely smiling, but Zahrias saw a faint lift at the corner of her mouth that seemed to indicate a hidden amusement. "Why, yourself, of course. I would think that was abundantly clear. Your only concern is for yourself, and perhaps for this palace you have taken such care to construct. So you will stay here, Lyanna, alone, while the rest of our kind go to make our homes in the world that is now ours. I hope you can take much joy in your situation, for you will have all eternity to walk these halls and gaze upon your plundered treasures."

At last the enormity of her fate seemed to descend upon his erstwhile kidnapper. Lyanna's eyes widened, and she shook her head. "You cannot mean that—"

"Oh, but we do," Ashtar said. "And we will make sure it is known that this palace is now your prison, and if you are ever seen elsewhere, if even for a moment, then your life will be forfeit, and you can be hunted down with as much impunity as one of the Immune."

Hearing this, Zahrias tightened his arms around Julia. No reason now to worry that Lyanna might ever attempt to come after them. Determined she might be, but she wasn't mad enough to risk her life.

"And I?" Qadim said then. His tone sounded almost careless, as if he had no stake in their reply, but

Zahrias could see the way the other man stood there, the tension in his jaw and shoulders showing all too clearly. "Am I to share her fate?"

This time Ashtar did smile. "No, we shall not inflict that doom upon you, Qadim al-Syan. You must go from this place, and have no further contact with your sister. You have engaged in questionable practices, but you also have had a change of heart, and so we must give you some credit for that."

"And so I will be allowed my place in the world?"

"As to that," Ibram said sternly, "we have not yet decided. Be grateful that you will not share your sister's prison, and go from here. We will determine exactly what to do with you later."

Relief and disappointment mixing in his face, Qadim nevertheless bowed to the two elders before blinking away from the walled garden. In that instant, Zahrias could feel the way Julia sagged against him, as if she had been worried up until the last moment that Qadim might attempt some stratagem to take her away from him, even though he had declared her his Chosen. After all, she had seen for herself that such status had not protected Martine or the other young women taken by Khalim and his band of rogue djinn.

"Zahrias," Ashtar said then, and he nodded. "We think you would prefer to take your Chosen from here by your own powers, would you not?"

"Very much so," he replied. Yes, the elders could have removed him from this garden and brought him back to Santa Fe, but Ashtar was correct—it would feel so much more fitting for him to bring Julia home himself.

"Then lead her from this place," Ibram said. His eyes narrowed as he gazed on Lyanna, who stood with her fists clenched and barely concealed fury furrowing her brow. "You need not fear any pursuit."

Jasreel had been standing a few feet away, watching the exchange. At last he spoke. "Then I will go as well, if there's no more need for me to be here."

"Yes, go home," Ashtar told him, her tone almost indulgent. "You have stood by your friend and cousin, but now I believe your Chosen is anxiously awaiting your return."

He needed no further encouragement than that. After sending a quick smile toward Zahrias and Julia, he, too, disappeared.

Very gently, Zahrias pulled away from the woman who was now his Chosen. "Come, beloved. Let us go from this place."

She gave him a small nod, then cast a look of gratitude toward the elders. Zahrias noticed that she made sure her eyes never met those of Lyanna, which, if she were a fire elemental rather than a being with the power to call the waters, would have been shooting flames by that point.

Taking her hand, he led Julia from the garden, through the corridors of Lyanna's palace. Along the way, he could see his companion start several times, as if she had recognized a piece of artwork but didn't want to slow their progress to inquire about it. Eventually, though, they emerged into a brisk wind that made the confines of the building behind them seem that much more stifling.

As the breeze touched his face, Zahrias could feel his powers return, now that he was no longer within reach of the accursed *ni-khar* tapestries and other items Lyanna had carefully set out around the palace. He and Julia could leave, and never see this place again.

"Let us go home," he murmured.

"Yes," she said, looking up into his face as she grasped his hand. She was so beautiful, even with that device fitted to her nose so she might breathe the alien atmosphere of the djinn world. "Take me home, Zahrias."

CHAPTER EIGHTEEN

By that point, while Julia couldn't claim to be exactly used to the djinn mode of travel, at least it didn't feel quite as jarring as it had the first time she'd experienced it. They came to rest, Zahrias' arms securely around her, in the living room of his home in Santa Fe.

She supposed it would be her home now, too, and she wasn't quite sure how to feel about that.

Very gently, he reached up to remove the cannula from her nose, then allowed her to take it from him. "You won't need that any longer."

"No, thank God." She unslung the oxygen canister from her shoulder and set it on the floor. Doing so helped a little in getting her bearings. It was still hard to believe that they were both safe, and more difficult still to realize that she was now Zahrias' Chosen.

His voice sounded in her mind. *My love.*

Tears sprang to her eyes, and she swallowed. How she'd wished he would call her that, had hoped they would be able to share this kind of communication if he ever claimed her as his. Now, though, it all seemed a little too overwhelming.

This time, that mental communication seemed almost tentative. *Julia, what is the matter?*

"Nothing," she said aloud, then wished she'd tried to answer him in the same manner. Her voice sounded tight with the tears she was trying to hold back, but maybe she wouldn't have betrayed herself if she'd sent the thought to him directly.

He took both her hands in his. God, his fingers were so warm, so strong. Hers must feel like little sticks of ice to him.

"Tell me," he said, abandoning the nonverbal speech of the djinn and their Chosen. "My love, you have no reason to hold anything back from me."

"It's just—" She shook her head, impatient with herself, then tried to start over. "I suppose I'm having a hard time coming to terms with all this. It was so...so sudden."

The warmth in his dark eyes receded, and she saw his jaw clench under the neatly trimmed beard. "This was not something you wished? But I thought—"

Oh, she needed to disabuse him of that notion right away. Going up on her tiptoes, she kissed him on the cheek. Gently, but firmly enough so he would understand she wanted him. "Zahrias, I think you know how I feel. That hasn't changed. And yet—"

"And yet?"

She had to make herself say the words. They'd both danced around each other for too long, and trying to avoid their feelings had only made matters worse. "And yet I can't help thinking that you did what you did only to save me, and maybe you wouldn't have done it otherwise."

For a long moment he didn't reply, only stood there, grave dark eyes searching her face. Then, before she could even blink, he was cupping her cheeks with those warm fingers of hers, bringing her close, mouths coming together. She tasted him, breathed in the rich scent of his skin, and felt a rush of heat pass over her. Heat, and need, and so much more.

Love. Her entire body seemed to thrum with it.

"It was long overdue, nothing more," he said some time later, after lifting his mouth from hers. "I should have said those words to you months ago. Of course I needed to save you from Lyanna, but truly, my love, that was not the only reason. Do you understand?"

"I do," she replied. Her voice sounded husky, although she thought now that throaty quality came from the almost cramping need surging through her, rather than from trying to choke back her tears. "I'm sorry I thought otherwise."

"Do not apologize," he said at once, and brushed a loose strand of hair away from her face. "None of this was any fault of yours, but rather my own cowardice."

"You're not a coward," she told him, shocked that he would even think such a thing of himself. "You're one of the bravest men I've ever met."

Something in the taut set of his mouth relaxed then, although he only shook his head. "Physical bravery is not such a great thing. Courage here"—and he touched his hand to his chest—"that is a much more difficult thing to command. I allowed the hurt I suffered long ago to keep us apart, and I will always regret that."

"You're not the only one." Zahrias was nothing like Ian—*or Richard Margolis,* she thought with a barely repressed shudder—and yet she had also tried to run away from these feelings, sure they wouldn't be reciprocated. Or, if by some miracle they were, that they would only lead her into yet another damaging relationship. It was so much easier to avoid intimacy, rather than allow it to find its way into her heart. "I know I should have—"

Once again he bent to kiss her, stopping the flow of self-recrimination before it could even begin. This time she kissed him back without reservation, reveling in the sensation of the muscular form pressed against her, the strength of his arms as he held her close, the intoxicating brush of his light beard against her skin. All of that was Zahrias...and yet she knew there was so much more to come.

A shiver went through her. She wanted him, so badly, and yet she knew how difficult it would be to give herself over to him completely. Her entire life, she'd always held a piece of herself aside, had always kept a sanctuary within herself that was hers and hers alone. And she didn't want to do that to Zahrias. She wanted to be his in a way that she'd never been with anyone else before.

He paused then, once again running a hand lightly down the side of her face. Maybe he'd sensed her diffidence; she didn't know yet how deep this connection between them ran. Right then, she almost wished she could talk to Jessica, just so she'd have an idea of what to expect.

"This is new for the both of us," he said. "And we have all of eternity together, my love." Another of those pauses as he gazed down at her, as if trying to drink in every detail of her features. "So for now, perhaps we should merely go and tell everyone the good news, that I am safe and we have nothing further to fear from Lyanna or her brother."

Julia nodded, although somewhere deep within she experienced a flicker of disappointment. Which was foolish, she scolded herself, because, as Zahrias had just told her, they would have an eternity together. A few hours wouldn't make much of a difference at all.

His nephew was a beautiful child, with Dani's thick dark hair and Lauren's wide, wondering blue eyes. Strange how the passage of only a few days could make the infant appear so much more *himself*, not just a little mass of waving legs and hands and features that hadn't quite yet resolved themselves into anything distinct.

And to see Julia holding little Gabriel, smiling down into his face—well, that sight awoke emotions Zahrias hadn't even known he possessed. For some reason, he had thought he would never have a family of his own, had never even admitted to himself that he might one day want to be a father. But, watching Julia, he realized then how much he did want such a thing, as long as it was with the woman he loved.

"So the elders have truly confined Lyanna to the djinn plane forever?" Dani was asking, and Zahrias had to drag his thoughts back to the present, rather than to a future that had yet to materialize.

"Yes. She will be able to enjoy eternity in that palace she admires so much. And I know she will be watched at all times, so she dare not attempt to defy the elders' decree."

"Couldn't happen to a nicer person," Lauren remarked with uncharacteristic acid, going to Julia so she could lift the baby, who had begun to fuss a bit, from her arms.

Julia had been smiling, but her expression grew sober. "There isn't anyone who might try to help Lyanna, is there? I mean, she seemed pretty good at coercing her brother into doing her bidding."

"Ah, but Qadim is her brother," Zahrias said. He understood Julia's concerns, but he also knew they were unfounded. "She has no relations closer than that, as both their parents are gone. And I am quite certain that no cousin is going to risk the wrath of the elders on Lyanna's behalf. As they said, this world is now open to the djinn. It is something our people have been anticipating for millennia. To throw that away, out of a sense of obligation to a cousin? I think not. Yes, family is important to us...but some things are even more important. Lyanna will forever stand as an example of how to prevent a djinn from receiving what is thought to be our due."

At his explanation, she nodded, but her expression did not grow noticeably less troubled. Perhaps she was thinking of the reason why this world was now the djinns'. He could do very little to soothe her on that score, unfortunately. He could not change what his people had done. All he could do now was make sure that life here in Santa Fe ran smoothly for everyone in it, djinn and Chosen alike. What happened in the outside world would not affect them...unless they allowed it to.

Lauren had withdrawn to the chair on the other side of the room, the blanket she'd been carrying now discreetly draped over her chest so she could nurse the baby. Zahrias thought nothing of it, since his people recognized such activity as perfectly normal, but he could see the way Julia averted her eyes. Well, perhaps she would feel differently when it was her turn.

"What now?" Dani asked then. "That is, who will take over at Los Alamos now that Julia is to be here with us?"

She sent Zahrias a quick, unreadable glance before replying, "I'm not sure. We hadn't really discussed that...yet."

Which meant she intended to discuss it with him, and soon. That only made sense. Of course she would have to remain here in Santa Fe, for it was impossible for him to live in Los Alamos. The elders expected him to lead this community. Besides, Miles Odekirk's devices ensured that no djinn would ever be able to take up residence in the mountain town the Immune called home, For that to happen, the scientist would need to finally devise a way to alter his fiendish little inventions so they could repel hostile djinn but still allow the friendly elementals within their field of effect to avoid suffering the debilitating weakness caused by the devices.

Dani seemed to realize he had made a misstep, for he said quickly, "Lilias and Aidan came to visit a while ago. She seemed to want to reassure herself that all is well in these human/djinn pairings."

Julia brightened a little at his comment. "Oh, that's right—they're expecting too, aren't they?"

"Yes. Their baby should be here sometime in the late spring, I believe."

The conversation drifted to lighter matters then—how Miguel, their medic, would cope if it turned out they had a real baby boom on their hands, and whether the winter would be a mild one, and if they were going to continue with their small tradition of communal feasts for Thanksgiving and Christmas as they had the year before, in order to let their Chosen feel not quite so abandoned in a strange new world.

Eventually, though, it became clear that Zahrias and Julia should leave Dani and Lauren and the baby so they could be alone. It was something of a walk from the new family's house to the home Zahrias had taken for his own, but he struck out on foot anyway, rather than instantly transporting himself and Julia there the way he'd first thought he might.

Julia was quiet, but he could tell she was enjoying the walk; she had her chin lifted so she might feel the mild afternoon breeze on her face. The wind caught at her long hair, blowing it around her like a rippling curtain of gold. How he loved her hair. The only thing that would make it more beautiful would be to see it spread out on a pillow next to him.

But he pushed that thought away, for he could feel his body begin to respond to the mental image, and he knew he and Julia must talk about all manner of serious subjects. Physical pleasure would have to wait... although not too long, he hoped.

He opened the front door of the house for her, and she went inside. Again, he could have done so by using his powers, but he was trying to put her as much at ease as possible. He knew she was still trying to come to terms with what had happened to her, what her life would be from now on.

"Should we go into the living room?" he asked, then wondered if perhaps he should have suggested another place for them to have their discussion. After all, the last conversation they had shared in that room had not turned out well.

Luckily, he saw no hesitation in Julia's manner as she told him yes, so he led her to that chamber, then asked if she would like some refreshment.

"That's probably a good idea," she said. "I'm trying to remember the last thing I ate and failing miserably."

"Then let me remedy that," he replied, and headed into the kitchen. This was one time when he would summon his djinn powers to do the heavy lifting; all the raw materials were there, but why waste precious time assembling the components when a snap of his fingers could provide them with everything they needed?

A brief look of astonishment crossed Julia's features as she watched him reenter the living room, carrying a tray laden with an assortment of meats and cheeses and fruit, as well as an open bottle of wine and a pair of glasses. He set the tray down on the low table in front of the sofa, then poured some of the wine for her.

"Those are some handy talents of yours," she remarked. "All that probably would have kept me busy in the kitchen for at least a half hour."

"Time which would have been better spent on other things."

"Such as?" Her tone was almost teasing.

"This talk we need to have."

A slight nod, but she didn't reply right away, instead lifting the glass to her lips so she could take a sip. Zahrias tried not to stare. That mouth of hers was far too distracting. After a long pause, she said, "So talk to me, Zahrias."

He raised his own glass of wine but didn't drink. The dark liquid caught sparks of ruby from the lowering sun that came through the living room's windows. "I know we did not have a chance to discuss everything that should be discussed. I know this must be difficult for you, since it feels as if you weren't given a choice."

"I wasn't given a choice," she said distinctly before reaching over with her free hand so she could pick up a slice of pale golden cheese. "Not that I blame you for that," she added quickly as he opened his mouth to speak. "I don't regret what you did. But your actions still will have ramifications for a lot more people than just you and me."

"I understand." Zahrias plucked a grape from the bunch that lay on the tray and set it in his mouth, savoring the sweetness of the fruit, a good contrast to the darkness of the wine he had chosen. "This man you left in charge in Los Alamos. He is a good man?"

"Shawn?" She was silent for a moment, appearing to carefully consider her reply. There was something almost hesitant in her manner, although Zahrias couldn't think why. "He's a very good man. A firefighter...before." A rueful smile touched her lips. "So probably not someone who would be best buddies with a fire elemental."

"My kind do not start fires," Zahrias said stiffly. "We control them."

"Right. Sorry...I didn't mean to offend you. Anyway, yes, Shawn is a good person. I could trust him to keep things running for a few days while I was gone. But for the long term?" She lifted her shoulders, then bent to pick up a piece of smoked sausage and pop it in her mouth. After she had consumed it, she went on, "I honestly don't know. It's not as if he's had any training—" Breaking off, she chuckled, although there was something humorless about the sound. "Listen to me. Like I had any training when it came to running a town. I was sort of forced into it, too."

"By me." In that moment, Zahrias regretted more than ever the remark that had sent Julia back to Los Alamos to be its steward.

To his relief, she laid a hand on his knee. "It's not as if you twisted my arm, Zahrias. Right then, I was willing enough to be a martyr."

Not sure that he understood the remark, he raised an eyebrow.

"I knew I—I knew I was attracted to you. I could have come up with a way to stay around if I'd really wanted to. I know Jessica thought I was crazy for going back to Los Alamos. But I was frightened."

"Of what?" he asked softly, although he thought he knew the answer.

"Of being rejected," she replied. "Or, even worse, *not* being rejected."

On the surface, her response sounded contradictory. But Zahrias thought he knew what she meant. It was a frightening thing, to open yourself to another, and to find them opening themselves to you. Julia had built a shell around herself. He'd recognized that quality in her, for he had constructed a shell of his own, many centuries before she was even born.

"And what do you think now?"

Her eyes met his, wide and clear, the elusive blue-gray of a misty sea. "I think I'm done with being afraid."

The only thing he could do then was take the wine glass from her fingers and set it down on the table, then pull her to him. She tasted of that fruit, dark and heady, and yet there was more, her own flavor, one he savored as their tongues met. He was a being of fire, and yet she somehow managed to ignite an even brighter flame in him, one he knew could only be quenched by burying himself in her.

She was shaking when they drew apart. Concerned, he laid a hand against her cheek. The smooth flesh felt cool to his touch, but he knew that was only because she was human, and did not burn with the same fire as he.

"Are you well, my love?" he asked.

A nod. Her full mouth looked almost bruised by their kiss, rosy and swollen. "I—I think so. I was trying to tell myself that it was all right to take this slowly, but...." She let the words trail off, and then she smiled, a slow curving of her lips that only served to further fan the flames of his desire. "I know there are other things we still need to discuss. I'm just not sure I can concentrate on them with you looking at me like that."

He needed no further urging. His arms went around her once again, only this time to lift her from the sofa. She felt light as a feather to him, despite her delicious curves. The bedchamber he had claimed as his own was down a fairly short hallway, but it felt miles off, so eager he was to take her there. But he forced himself to do this the human way, carrying her in his arms so he might lay her down on the bed. And, like a human, he stopped to tug off her boots and socks, to let her shrug out of her jacket. She was still fully dressed, but there was still something infinitely seductive about the way she lay there in her close-fitting white top, her pretty bare feet showing beneath the hems of the jeans she wore.

His own clothing was less of an impediment; he cast off the long, loose robe he had on, but did not remove the pants. Not yet. He wanted to see more of Julia first.

She did not protest as his fingers pulled her shirt free from the waistband of her pants and lifted it over her head. How beautiful the swell of her breasts, cupped by the lacy bra she wore. The women of his people did not wear such things, and yet he found the sight strangely arousing, the way the flimsy fabric hinted at the beauties of the flesh underneath.

When he unbuckled her belt and pulled down her jeans, he saw that the undergarment she wore was of the same nude-colored lace. His breathing quickened, and he paused with his hands on her hips, feeling the rich curves of her body beneath his fingertips.

"You are so very lovely," he whispered.

She gazed up at him, eyes fixed on his. "I want to be beautiful for you, Zahrias."

"You are."

That was all he could manage, for he knew he needed much more than talk now. He lay beside her and pulled her body against his, while his fingers found the clasp at the back of her bra and worked it free. Then there was nothing separating them, the rich fullness of her breasts pressed to his flesh, causing him to gasp at the wondrous sensation.

Julia wanted more, it seemed, for her hands worked their way down to the drawstring of his pants, pulling it loose, then pushing the fabric out of the way. A small gasp of her own left her lips as she found him and took him between her fingers.

He let out a sound that was half sigh, half moan. Truly, he had not thought she would be quite so forward. But there she was, stroking him, waves of sensation seeming to flow up and down his shaft as she touched him. And more, because she shifted, and then her mouth was on him, and he groaned aloud, hoping he would not spend then and there at the touch of her lips and tongue on the sensitive flesh. No, he would hold on, even though he had dreamed of this moment, dreamed of what it might be like. But no dream could ever hope to compete with the reality of her.

And he knew he wanted all of her. Now.

He pulled away from her mouth, and a flicker of surprise passed over her face. That surprise turned to outright astonishment as he pushed her down on her back and trailed kisses down her stomach, moving lower....

Her voice was strained. "Zahrias, you don't—"

Ah, but he did. He needed to taste her, to bring her pleasure the way she had pleasured him. And after the first several strokes of his tongue, her rich flavor filling his mouth, she abandoned all protest and allowed him to make love to her with his lips and tongue, to breathe in her scent and revel in the way her fingers knotted in his hair, keeping him in position, although of course he had no intention of stopping.

Her climax seemed to roll through her like a breaker falling on a sandy beach. She shuddered on and on, breathing labored. Perhaps it had been a very long while for her. It had been for him.

While she still lay there, breaths coming in short gasps, he moved up to her, his mouth closing on her breast so he could feel the taut warmth of her nipple against his skin. She moaned again, and he began to press into her. At once she went quiet, and he paused.

"My love—do you wish me to stop? If it is too soon—"

"Oh, God no," she responded, halfway between a gasp and a chuckle. "If you stopped now, I think I would die. Please—keep going. I want you there. Please."

He needed no more urging than that. Eyes fixed on her beautiful face, he push in further, feeling her open to him, warm and welcoming and so much more than he could have ever hoped for. Her legs wrapped around him, pulling him in further, and they began to rock together, bodies finding their own rhythm, every breath, every sigh telling him that she was the only woman who would ever be right for him, who could find the broken pieces of his soul and quietly mend them.

Julia, his love, his one.

His Chosen.

She lay there for a long while afterward, saying nothing, only gazing into the depthless darkness of her lover's eyes, memorizing every plane of his face, every angle, the long aristocratic nose and the finely sculpted curves of his lips and the sooty sweep of his lashes.

At last she said softly, "I love you."

Did he know how much it had taken for her to tell him that? Because she'd told Ian she loved him—but had she, really?—and it hadn't mattered. Her love had only been a weapon she'd willingly handed over to him.

But Zahrias was no Ian. She knew that, and yet—

"I love you," Zahrias said. The words were hardly more than a whisper, but they were enough. The truth of his feelings seemed to echo in every syllable. "You are the one I have waited an eternity for, Julia Innes. And I can rejoice in knowing that I will spend the rest of eternity with you."

She reached out for him then, and his arms went around her, drawing their bodies close once more. It seemed the most natural thing in the world for Zahrias to pull her up on top of him so she could feel him buried deep within her once again, filling her, completing her.

That should have sounded so silly, and yet she knew it was only the truth, that her entire life something had been missing, an aching space deep within her soul that she'd never wanted to acknowledge. Being with him now, she knew exactly what she'd lacked. Zahrias al-Harith, a man of a strange and terrible alien race, and the only one who could ever have made her feel this way.

She cried out as the orgasm pulsed through her. In the past she'd always tried to be quiet, hadn't wanted to give this much of herself away, but now that didn't matter. She wanted Zahrias to know what he'd done to her, to know that no one else could make her scream like a banshee.

After, he held her close, lips pressed against her hair. It felt so good to be together like this, to have the heat of his naked body flowing into her own flesh as they lay there next to one another, hip to hip, leg to leg. At last, though, she knew she needed to go get herself cleaned up. So she squeezed his hand before gently slipping off the bed and going to the *en suite* bathroom, where she performed a quick toilette, washing the last traces of their intimacy away, and then splashing some water on her face.

When she returned to the bedroom, Zahrias was sitting with the covers pulled up around his waist. God, what arms and chest that man had. Julia knew she could probably spend hours staring at every muscle, every shadow of the tautly defined six-pack of his abs.

Tempting as that prospect was, however, she knew they still had some unfinished business to take care of. She found her discarded panties on the floor and pulled them on, then shrugged her T-shirt over her head, although she didn't bother with putting on the bra. As she picked up her jeans, Zahrias spoke.

"I have noticed that most of you wear those sorts of trousers. Are they really that comfortable? Perhaps I should try some."

The thought of Zahrias walking around in Santa Fe while wearing a pair of Levi's was so incongruous that Julia wanted to chuckle. Then again, she contemplated what a pair of nicely worn 501s might do for his muscular legs and slim hips, and decided maybe a chuckle wasn't the best response.

"Possibly," she hedged. "What do you think your djinn would do if they saw their leader dressed like one of us mere mortals?"

"Considering that half my people appear to have already adopted your form of dress, perhaps they would only think it was about time."

True enough. Come to think of it, she'd never seen Jace in anything except jeans and work shirts and motorcycle boots. Maybe he thought the djinn clothing was too impractical for milking goats or whatever.

"Well, we can figure that out later," she said. "In the meantime...." After picking up Zahrias' billowy silk trousers, she handed them to him.

With a resigned air, he pushed back the covers and climbed into his pants. Julia thought she did a pretty good job of not staring before he was covered up, but a warm flicker in his eyes told her she wasn't fooling anyone.

Still, he didn't say anything as he also gathered up his discarded robe, then headed back to the living room. Once there, he extended Julia's half-drunk glass of wine to her, and she took it gratefully. He then picked up his own glass and sat down on the couch.

It was hard to concentrate with him so close to her. She wanted to down her wine and go for a three-peat right there on the sofa, but she knew they'd have plenty of time for that later.

All the time in the world, in fact.

A decent-sized swallow of wine helped a little to get her racing thoughts in order. "So...."

One of his eyebrows lifted. "So...."

"I think I'm going to like it here in Santa Fe," she said, and he smiled. "But there's still Los Alamos."

"True," Zahrias agreed. "Do you have a plan?"

Did she? More like an idea. "At first I thought of Miles, since people do sort of look up to him, despite his faults. But then I knew that would never work. He needs to be able to focus on his research. Besides, he has about the worst interpersonal skills of anyone I've ever met."

Zahrias chuckled, and she couldn't help grinning in response.

"And then I realized I shouldn't be appointing anyone. Los Alamos—it's like the last piece of America, you know?"

It seemed he didn't know, because his brows drew together in a faint frown. "Forgive me, but wasn't all of this land part of America?"

"Yes, but the djinn control everything else now, don't they? Los Alamos is the only place where it's just regular people, the last Americans, really. And the American thing for them to do is vote for who they want to lead them. It shouldn't be my decision. It shouldn't be any one person's decision. They can all decide together what's best for them. Does that make any sense?"

For a long moment, Zahrias was silent as he seemed to consider what she had just told him. Then he nodded. "I think this would be a good thing. Margolis wanted to make himself a despot, but that was not how your people did things, and so he doomed himself to failure. I do see how giving them the power to make their own choice will allow the people of Los Alamos to understand that they are also an important part of this new world. Different from us here in Santa Fe, but no less important."

Had she ever loved him more than she did right then? Julia set down her wine glass so she could lean forward and kiss him. His lips warmed against hers, and she knew that the three-peat she'd been fantasizing about probably wasn't too far off.

But then he pulled away slightly, dark eyes scanning her face. "And it is important to you as well. I can see that. I hope our two communities will continue to work together. Perhaps one day...."

He didn't finish the sentence, but Julia thought she knew what he was thinking. Maybe a day would come when the people from the two towns would be able to mingle freely. It wouldn't matter who was mortal or djinn or Chosen, because they were all working together toward the same future, one where their children could safely grow up in this forever changed world of theirs.

"That day will come," she said firmly, then took his hand and held it, felt the encouraging warmth of his fingers.

"And we can begin working on it right now."

THE END

www.ingramcontent.com/pod-product-compliance
Lightning Source LLC
Chambersburg PA
CBHW021522250626
47154CB00006BA/1932